A GOOD DEATH

A GOOD DEATH

A D. I. Tom Mariner Mystery

Chris Collett

This first world edition published 2016
in Great Britain and 2017 in the USA by
SEVERN HOUSE PUBLISHERS LTD of
19 Cedar Road, Sutton, Surrey, England, SM2 5DA.
Trade paperback edition first published
in Great Britain and the USA 2017 by
SEVERN HOUSE PUBLISHERS LTD

Copyright © 2016 by Chris Collett.

British Library Cataloguing in Publication Data
A CIP catalogue record for this title is available from the British Library.

ISBN-13: 978-0-7278-8687-3 (cased)
ISBN-13: 978-1-84751-765-4 (trade paper)
ISBN-13: 978-1-78010-832-2 (e-book)

All Severn House titles are printed on acid-free paper.

Severn House Publishers support the Forest Stewardship Council™ [FSC™],
the leading international forest certification organisation.
All our titles that are printed on FSC certified paper carry the FSC logo.

Typeset by Palimpsest Book Production Ltd.,
Falkirk, Stirlingshire, Scotland.
Printed and bound in Great Britain by
TJ International, Padstow, Cornwall.

A horn blares and Talayeh's heart leaps in her chest as the monstrous vehicle bears down on her, the driver, partly obscured by the windscreen, gesticulating furiously. Scurrying to the safety of the pavement she drags her cumbersome bag up the kerb with a jolt, noting the many pairs of eyes looking her way, their boredom briefly alleviated by a moment of drama, and she glowers back at them. In a few short weeks she has come to hate this place and all its latent aggression. It was not as if life back home wasn't an assault on the senses, but its exuberance seemed somehow more benign. Here everything is so relentlessly bleak and dark, most days quite literally, with an undertow of violence that is never far from the surface.

In the ticket booth the official simply shakes his head from side to side with blank indifference. 'It's gone,' he repeats, slowly and loudly, making a sweeping motion with his hand. 'You missed it.' Showing her his watch, he taps on it a couple of times. 'Next one, tomorrow afternoon, same time.' Talayeh's English isn't great but she gets that message, along with the even more explicit one contained in that flick of the eyes towards the customer behind her in the queue, who is already edging into her space. Their conversation is at an end. Talayeh moves away from the counter as the African woman, a toddler on her hip, pushes past her to the counter.

Now what? She can't go back. For all their earnest civility, it had been made perfectly clear that she wasn't wanted. She was, at best, an inconvenience, and right from the start she'd seen the fear in their eyes that she might do something here to bring even more shame on the family. It had been as much a relief for them to send her on her way, as it had been for her to leave. But now with her journey aborted . . .

Through the big windows at the back of the ticket office she sees people sitting at tables with food and drinks in front of them. In her pocket she has the currency to buy her coach ticket; she *doesn't know exactly how much it's worth but it must be more than enough to buy her a drink and allow her to sit somewhere warm while she thinks about what to do next. In the cafeteria she stands patiently in another line. It had unnerved her at first, this way people had of standing silently waiting, instead of clamouring for attention as they would at home. She hands over the most striking-looking of the notes to pay for her bottled water. The black man behind the counter is unimpressed and responds with a scowl and a handful of heavy coins. Talayeh goes to a seat beside the window overlooking the busy road, watching the line of cars gather and disperse at the traffic signals, like blood pumping around the noisy, dirty veins of the city. As an announcement comes over the loudspeaker, the woman at a neighbouring table gets up to go, leaving behind her a glossy magazine. Talayeh reaches across to pick it up, comforted for a moment by its resemblance to magazines she sometimes buys when she goes into Sana'a. She can't read many of the words in this one, but it is filled with photos of glamorous and successful Western women. They remind her, with a pinch of regret, of what her hopes and expectations were when she came to this country. She had even been foolish enough to boast about it to anyone in the village who would listen; her wealthy husband, her sophisticated life: 'When I get to London . . .' she had bragged. But now she will return home a failure. Suddenly, Talayeh knows she can't do that. She has been too hasty and impatient. Would it have been so bad to go along with what was expected of her? Like the women in the magazine, Talayeh craves the freedom to do what she chooses. But their independence has been forged through their talents; acting or singing or presenting TV; things so far removed from her world that she wouldn't know where to start.*

The cafe is hot and stuffy, and suddenly realising there's no one to stop her, Talayeh takes off her hijab and shakes out her hair, enjoying the feeling of liberation. As she turns her head, her eyes meet those of a man sitting across from her. He is a white man, with dark eyes and a nice face. He smiles, showing good teeth, and there is something in his eyes that Talayeh has seen before. It is the way Ishaq used to look at her. It brings a pleasant warmth to her cheeks, and in that moment, Talayeh realises that there is something that she has a talent for – well, several things. Ishaq taught her some of them, but he also insisted that she had been given a natural gift from Allah; a gift that any man would enjoy and might be prepared to pay for. Sipping her water, Talayeh glances up to see that the man is still watching her. As she shyly returns his smile, he gets up from his seat and comes over.

ONE

Mariner and Suzy drew up outside the row of newly built houses. The small development, of about thirty dwellings, was unfinished. At the moment the gardens were little more than ploughed fields, cut through with open ditches where pipes and utilities were still being laid, and although there were already a number of 'Sold' banners pasted across the windows, the properties looked some way from being inhabited.

'Is this it?' asked Suzy, getting out of the car.

'Think so,' said Mariner. 'It's pretty much where Charlie described it.' Taking out the estate agent's printout of the development, he was struck by the contrast between the artfully composed photograph of a house standing in splendid isolation and the actuality in front of them, surrounded on both sides by a dozen or more identical cloned structures. 'Not exactly ready to move into,' he added, following Suzy up one of the garden paths. Stepping carefully to avoid the wettest of the mud, he peered in through a window. 'Rooms are a bit small,' he said. 'Oh crap.' He turned as a sporty Mercedes zipped purposefully along the newly tarmacked road towards them. 'Try to look inconspicuous.'

The car came to a halt outside the site Portakabin at the end of the cul-de-sac. A young woman got out, unloading a box stuffed with files and papers. Unlocking the door of the cabin, she disappeared inside for several minutes, emerging again minus the papers, and coming across to where they were standing. 'Morning!' she called. 'Anything I can help you with?'

She was in her early thirties at most, a small yet sturdy young woman, 'pear-shaped', Mariner thought was the expression, a feature emphasised by her mud-spattered Lycra leggings and bulky fleece. Her fair hair was tied back from her face, and what with the open, rosy-cheeked face and the impeccable accent, Mariner surmised (a habit that couldn't be shaken, even on his days off) that before coming here she'd been horse riding.

'We were just being nosy.' Suzy made it sound casual. 'We were passing by on the main road and thought we'd take a closer look.' Both of those statements were true. What she left out was that the development had actually been recommended to them by Mariner's colleague, Charlie Glover, and that they had quite deliberately driven out the eleven miles from Birmingham to see it. The hope had been that this early on a Saturday morning, they would avoid the inevitable hard-sell. It seemed that they had failed. The girl had brought a bunch of keys with her. 'Would you like to have a look inside?'

'Well, yes, OK then,' said Suzy, shooting Mariner a look.

'How many bedrooms are you looking for?'

'Two or three,' said Suzy.

'Great, we'll go into number nine.' She gestured towards the house at the end of the terrace and they all traipsed along to it over soiled flagstones and Mariner wondered what the woman made of the formality of his suit, and Suzy's dress, at this time of day.

She unlocked the door and allowed them to step past her into rooms thick with the smell of damp plaster and fresh paint. 'I think it's all pretty self-explanatory,' she said, as her phone buzzed for attention. 'If you have any questions I'll just be along in the office, and perhaps you could pop the keys back to me there when you've finished looking round? No hurry though, take as long as you like.'

'Well, that's a relief,' murmured Mariner, to her retreating back. He'd had his fill of making polite small talk and smiling appreciatively while enthusiastic estate agents detailed, in wildly overstated terms, the merits of a particular property. Being new, this one was modern and clean, with state-of-the-art fitted kitchen and bathrooms, but the rooms were tiny. 'These two should just about do for all your books,' said Mariner to Suzy. 'Where will you sleep?'

Even at a leisurely pace, the grand tour took no more than ten minutes, and they finished it standing in the first-floor back bedroom, looking down into the euphemistically described 'low-maintenance' garden that at the moment was little more than a tiny construction site.

'And not a mature tree in sight,' Mariner remarked. Beyond

the fence was a further row of similarly new properties, then the view extended to flat brown fields that would also no doubt in time be filled by further new housing. In a couple of years Suzy would be living in the middle of a sprawling estate.

'Well, according to these details, it's supposed to be in close proximity to the station, and within walking distance of a very good primary school,' said Suzy.

'That'll be helpful,' said Mariner, 'should you ever decide to go into teaching.'

Suzy sighed hard. 'One for the short list?' she said. It had become their code, normally in the presence of eager estate agents, for *this one's a definite no.*

Mariner walked up to return the keys to the site office. The door was a little ajar and the young woman was on the phone. 'I told you, Sam, he's only trying to help, really.' A long pause. 'Oh, don't be like that—' Mariner cleared his throat. 'Look, we can talk about this later. I've got to go.'

As she switched off her phone, Mariner knocked lightly on the door. 'Thanks,' he said. 'That was really helpful.'

'No problem.' She smiled. Mariner was all prepared with his little speech about 'other properties to view', blah blah, but she was too distracted to even ask.

Mariner's research had thrown up two more developments in the vicinity, this time in a greater state of completion, but equally uninspiring. Then, as luck (or careful good planning) had it, they were left just a couple of short miles from the Cock Inn, only five minutes before lunchtime opening.

'Well, fancy that,' said Suzy, when he broke the good news.

Mariner had wondered about the choice of pub. Ordinarily he could have imagined Suzy making some vaguely smutty allusion to its name – most people did – and he would have responded in kind. But today he guessed that she would feel the same slight inhibition that he did, and it went unremarked. The April afternoon would have made it warm enough for them to take their drinks out into the garden, but Suzy was less keen. 'My heels, on the grass,' she explained, so they took a table inside.

'Why *do* estate agents always bang on about schools?' Mariner wondered, depositing their drinks on the table and sliding on to the bench beside Suzy. 'As if that's the only important factor.'

'You should be flattered that they think we're young enough to have school-aged kids,' said Suzy.

'It would have to be second time around for me,' Mariner pointed out. 'And they certainly always assume that we're both moving in. What did you think?'

Suzy shrugged her indifference. 'They're all starting to look so much the same. I know what I said, but I actually think I'm going off the idea of something new. Sure, it would mean less maintenance and all that, but they're all so . . . sterile.' She trawled a finger through the condensation that had already accumulated on the side of her glass, before looking up at him. 'In fact, that's the last one,' she announced, 'at least for now. I don't think I can bear to look at another "deceptively spacious" residence, however close to "local amenities" it might be, at least, not until after I've settled into the new job. I'll be perfectly OK in postgrad accommodation for the moment. It's convenient, after all. And when I'm a bit more familiar with the surroundings, I can start looking again.'

'You sure?' asked Mariner, trying not to sound too relieved.

'Absolutely.'

He allowed a respectable pause before saying: 'It's just a shame I don't live a bit nearer.'

She shrugged again. 'Not much we can do about that.'

But they both knew that as a rationale, the distance alone was a poor one. In many ways it would have made the most sense for Suzy to move into Mariner's south Birmingham home, if only as a temporary measure. It would only in effect be an extension of the regular weekends she stayed over anyway. True, on a good day the arrangement would mean a ninety-minute round commute to work on a motorway that was subject to regular accidents and other hold-ups, particularly in the winter weather. Nor would that level of fuel consumption sit well with Suzy's environmentalist philosophy. But neither of those factors in themselves were insurmountable. What remained unsaid was what had become obvious to them both: that much as they enjoyed each other's company, after about forty-eight hours together they were both ready to retreat back to their own space. In the interim the university had provided Suzy with a flat in postgrad accommodation, which would tide her over until she found somewhere more permanent.

'What time are we meant to be there this afternoon?' she said idly.

Mariner looked at his watch. 'Shit! We need to get going. I'd forgotten.'

'Really? Dressed like this?' Suzy grabbed her bag as Mariner swallowed the remains of his half-pint. 'Do you know where it is?'

'Roughly,' Mariner hedged.

'So that's a no then,' said Suzy astutely.

Mariner had no idea why Charlie Glover had asked him to be best man at the renewal of his wedding vows to Helen, his wife of thirty years. But as Suzy had pointed out with her usual clarity, it was no great effort to fulfil the responsibility and obviously meant a lot to Charlie. Having agreed therefore to play a key role, it would be polite to at least get there on time.

Mariner did have a vague idea of the church's locality, in the unlikely situation of a late 1980s factory unit development, but the complex was a warren of ultimate dead ends and he had to manoeuvre a number of three-point turns before Suzy finally spotted the angular concrete spire of the Christian Evangelical church. They arrived with minutes to spare.

TWO

The church was modern and new, with multi-coloured light streaming in through abstract stained-glass windows, and the service was a strangely jarring experience; the triumphal punching of the air and random cries in the vernacular, would, Mariner thought, have sat more comfortably on the terraces at Villa Park than addressed to a two-thousand-year-old deity. And while he recognised some of the words to the hymns from school assemblies in the distant past, the music to which they were set was pure Glastonbury, backed as it was by a four-piece rock band in a uniform of torn jeans and T-shirts. He could see that it was a struggle too for Suzy, whose professional life was rooted in the ancient and traditional past.

Mariner did what he was required to do, presenting the rings at the appropriate moment. He played it straight, tempting though it was to go through a charade of having lost or forgotten them, and felt an irrational surge of pride for his sergeant. Charlie was one of the few men Mariner knew who only ever spoke about his wife in affectionate terms, and this was clearly reciprocated by Helen. Mariner's constancy had never been tested over more than a couple of years at a stretch, and he wasn't sure that he would be able to rise to the challenge of more. At present in fact he struggled to rise to anything, but that was a whole other story.

As Charlie and Helen were making their promises, there was a clatter as the door at the back of the church swung open and a young woman hastened in with a smile of apology. Attractive in a figure-hugging dress with her hair loose around her shoulders, she was also strikingly familiar, and as he turned back to the minister, Mariner was still trying to place her. Then it clicked; a couple of hours ago, she'd shown them into a new house.

After the ceremony there was a reception back at Charlie and Helen's link-detached house in Olton. It was a day of scudding clouds and sharp downpours, so the plan was to start off in the garden and hope to avoid the dash inside. Mariner went to the makeshift kitchen bar to get drinks for him and Suzy, then headed towards the garden. Passing a doorway, a snippet of one-way conversation from the next room caught his attention and he found himself pausing to eavesdrop:

'I nearly didn't make it,' he heard the female voice say, into a mobile. 'I was at work longer than planned. Yeah, a middle-aged couple looking at a semi on Oak Coppice. I don't think they were time-wasters but they didn't exactly show much enthusiasm. Anyway, I should go and be sociable. I'll catch up with you soon.' Mariner rounded the corner and, preoccupied with slipping the phone into her bag, she almost walked into him. 'Hello again,' he said.

Her eyes widened as he saw her connect his face, the viewing and the conversation she'd just had. She clearly hadn't recognised him in the church, but then, he'd had his back to the congregation for most of the service. After the slightest hesitation, her upbringing kicked in. 'Gosh, hello. How nice to see you again, and – how peculiar.' The recovery was sealed with a wide smile. About to shake his hand, she realised then that they were both occupied with the drinks, so she settled for a little wave. 'I'm Gaby,' she said. 'You're a friend of Helen and Charles?'

Charles? Mariner had never heard him called that before, even by Helen. 'Charlie and I work together,' he said, gesturing for her to go ahead of him on to the patio.

'Oh, so you're a—?' She stepped outside, Mariner following.

'I am,' he said. 'How about you?'

'Oh, we're friends through church.'

It took Mariner a moment, in the bright sunlight, to see Suzy, standing to one side of the patio. 'You remember Gaby?' he said.

'Of course,' said Suzy. 'What a coincidence.'

'Isn't it?' said Gaby. She wore a sleeveless dress, and out in the cool air goose bumps popped up on her bare arms. Although solid, her limbs were toned and muscular, making Mariner wonder if she was a dancer as well as a horse-rider. 'Helen and Charles are lovely, so it's not surprising that they've got loads of friends. And their marriage is such an inspiration,' she beamed, lifting her left hand to examine the ring on her third finger. 'I'm getting married on St George's Day.'

'Congratulations,' said Suzy. 'Is the lucky man here too?'

She cast about. 'He should be; somewhere.'

'That's what, only a couple of weeks away? How are the preparations going?' asked Suzy.

'Really well, thank you,' said Gaby, warming to the topic. 'Though I'd never have *believed* how much there is to do. The ceremony will be in church, of course, but then we're having the reception at the Botanical Gardens. All the spring flowers will be out, so it will be magical. Then after that, on to our honeymoon in Antigua.'

'That sounds wonderful,' said Suzy.

'I know. I can't wait,' said Gaby. 'How long have you two been . . .?' she wavered, suddenly noticing the absence of rings, '. . . erm, together?'

'Oh, it's early days for us,' Suzy smiled. 'We've only known each other about a year. Long-distance up until now, but I'm about to start a new job locally, which is why I'm house hunting.'

'Oh, I see.' Gaby looked relieved. No co-habitation going on after all then.

'Yes, finding the right place is proving more problematic than I expected,' Suzy said. 'Some people might say I'm too particular.'

'As if,' said Mariner, under his breath.

'The one you showed us this morning is lovely, but I'm really hoping to find something nearer Coventry.'

'Oh, you should have said,' Gaby said immediately. 'Oak Coppice is just one of our developments. There are quite a few we're working on in different parts of Warwickshire. If you tell me exactly what it is you're looking for, I'm sure we'll be able to help you,' Gaby enthused. 'We need to talk to Dad.' She glanced around the garden. 'He's here somewhere – oh, here he comes!'

At that moment the side gate banged as two men walked through it. Neither looked especially happy, and once in the garden they went their separate ways, the older man seeing Gaby and heading straight for her.

'Dad!'

With an exaggerated swagger in his last few steps, the man threw his arms around her and hugged her till she shrieked that she'd spill her drink. When he'd released her, Gaby introduced her father as Clive Boswell. The build was genetic apparently; though of above average height, Boswell was a big man with thick white hair and a pink, clean-shaven face. His candy-striped shirt and off-white chinos made Mariner feel overdressed in his grey lounge suit.

'Is Sam OK?' Gaby asked her father, watching the younger man as he went to join a group of five or six other young people at a table that was being set up with food.

'Course he is,' said Boswell lightly. 'I keep trying to persuade him to come and work for me,' he explained to Mariner and Suzy. 'But he's stubborn and independent.'

'Which is exactly why I love him,' said Gaby. 'Sam already has a good job, so leave him alone. Anyway, Dad, Suzy here is looking for somewhere to live around Coventry. I wondered about the Ridgeway, or Parsons Wood?'

Boswell mulled it over for a moment. 'Hmm, neither of those is going to be ready for another three months at least,' he said. 'But I'm sure we could find you something.'

'Do you have an email address?' asked Gaby. 'It would make sense for us to bypass the estate agents and send you anything new that comes up directly.'

'Oh, I wouldn't want you to go to any trouble,' said Suzy. 'And to be honest, I'm not sure any more that I'm looking for a new property.'

'It would be no trouble at all,' said Boswell. 'And we do renovations too. We've got some lovely old places.' He wasn't a man to be fobbed off.

Suzy had a pen, but they had nothing to write on so Mariner ended up fishing out one of his business cards and jotting Suzy's mobile number on to the back of that before handing it over to Gaby. 'And how about you?' Suzy asked. 'Will you be living in one of your dad's houses when you're married?'

'Oh yes, but we want to be somewhere more local, so we've got a place on Meadow Hall Rise in Kingsmead. I don't want to move too far from church or Dad. It's an older house, but the refurb is nearly finished, and it's looking fabulous.' She slid out from her father's arm. 'I should go and catch up with Sam,' Gaby told him. 'Nice seeing you again and I'll keep in touch,' she said to Suzy. They watched her walk over to the young man, who detached himself from the group and slipped his arm around his fiancée's shoulders, smoothing her dress and tucking in the label at the nape of her neck as he did so. His shoulders dropped an inch or so, as he relaxed, though Mariner didn't miss the uncertain glance towards his future father-in-law.

Boswell didn't appear to notice. He sighed. 'They grow up so fast, don't they?' He sounded wistful. 'I can't believe I'll soon be letting her go. Her mum passed on seven years ago so it's just been Gaby and me since then. I'm going to miss her so much.'

'It sounds as if they won't be too far away, though,' Mariner pointed out.

'Oh, I know, but I don't kid myself. They'll have their own lives to live. And that's how it should be.'

Alongside his other duties this afternoon, it also fell on Mariner to make a speech. It was time. As he cleared his throat, someone clinked a glass and about thirty pairs of expectant eyes turned towards him as a hush descended over the gathering.

Mariner had framed his speech in terms of criminal justice and prison sentences and hoped that he hadn't crossed the line in terms of taste. But judging from the response, he hit the mark, and having raised a few laughs and a couple of heckles, he held up his glass. 'To Helen and Charlie.'

Everyone followed suit, lifting assorted glasses, bottles and cans to join in the toast.

After a couple more hours of small talk Mariner was beginning to approach the limits of his sociability. They found their hosts seeing people out at the front door. Charlie was, as always, conventionally dressed in his sports jacket and tie, his hair neatly combed. Helen, pretty in a floral dress, tucked into his arm as if she'd been specially designed to do so.

'Tom said you're having a second honeymoon too?' said Suzy, after the usual thanks.

'Our trip of a lifetime,' said Helen. 'Thailand and Vietnam. We'll be away a whole month.'

'When are you off?' Mariner asked.

'Taxi's booked for eight o'clock tomorrow morning,' said Charlie.

'Lucky bastard,' said Mariner. 'Just don't get to like it too much out there, eh?'

'No chance of that,' Charlie grinned. 'As soon as we get there Helen will be fretting about the kids.'

'And how will they do while you're away? Lots of wild parties planned?' Suzy asked.

'Oh, they'll be fine,' Helen's smile was less confident than her assertion. 'Church friends will keep an eye on them, and we'll hope to Skype from time to time.'

'Hm,' said Mariner. 'I'll keep that in mind, just in case—'

'Oh no you don't,' warned Helen, seeing where this was going. 'He's having a proper holiday this time.' She turned to Suzy. 'We have been known to get phone calls on the beach in Portugal.'

'That was one time!' Mariner protested. 'But OK. I'll do my best to cope without him.'

'We'll be back before you know it,' said Charlie.

The Boswell clan left the party immediately after Suzy and Mariner, and Clive Boswell gave them a wave as he followed his daughter and prospective son-in-law off in the opposite direction along the line of parked cars, where he climbed into a sparkling white Mercedes parked a little way down the road. Meanwhile Gaby gave her fiancé a long, lingering embrace before he got into a separate vehicle parked behind it.

'Mr Boswell's doing all right if that car's anything to go by,' said Suzy.

'Oh yes,' said Mariner. 'And there's a bit of money about if the newly-weds are moving into Meadow Hall Rise. Not many kids their age would be able to afford an established prime location in Kingsmead.'

'So it wasn't such an ordeal, was it?' she said of the afternoon.

'Not at all,' said Mariner, putting the car in gear. 'And who knows, it might result in you getting somewhere to live.'

'Hm. I'm not sure about that,' said Suzy. 'I know they were only trying to be helpful, but I'd really rather find my own place. I don't want to be pressured into anything.'

As they drove back to Mariner's canal-side home, out of habit, Suzy rested her hand on his thigh. She waited a second before, remembering herself, she removed it again. Just a few weeks ago her next move would have been in the other direction, sliding it down into his groin, causing Mariner to apply a little more pressure to the accelerator. On those occasions they'd often barely made it into the house. But lately something had changed. Mariner tensed, in anticipation of what Suzy might say, but he was glad when she said nothing. By the time they got to his house, the moment had passed. Later they phoned out for a takeaway and watched a DVD; a French subtitled film that had looked promising but then turned out to be too explicitly violent even for Mariner's taste.

Mariner wasn't sure what woke him in the small hours. It might have been the tickle of smoke in his nostrils or the dancing pattern of light on the bedroom wall, but once his senses registered those two things he was out of bed in an instant. 'Suzy, wake up! There's a fire!'

THREE

B ut coming from where? Pulling on clothes Mariner ran around checking the bedrooms and bathroom before racing down the stairs, where he realised that his house was intact; what was burning was on the opposite bank of the canal, just behind the screen of leafless trees. 'What's over there?' Suzy asked.

'Houses,' said Mariner. 'I have to see if I can help.'

'I'll come too.'

By torchlight they crossed the canal a little way up, shuffling along the closed lock gates, then scrambling up the bank, to the rear of the property. The heat struck them immediately, from flames licking out of a downstairs window, and they heard voices and a child crying.

'Up there,' cried Suzy, and, against the glare were three figures in silhouette, inching their way along the flat roof of a ground-floor extension. In the firelight Mariner saw a dustbin. Testing it first, he stepped onto it and at six feet tall, it brought him level with the roof. 'This way!' he shouted, waving his arms. As the children reached the edge of the building, he sat them down, their legs dangling over the edge, and lifted each of them to safety. The woman cried out in pain as he took her hand, his fingers making contact with hot, moist flesh on the palm of her hand.

'My father!' she implored Mariner. 'He's in there.' She pointed to a first-floor bedroom to the right.

Lifting her down, Mariner assessed the situation. The fire was spreading up through the first floor, but if he could get into the building right away, the way they had come, there might be a chance . . . Where the hell was the fire service? He could hear sirens in the distance, but they weren't getting any closer. Making a split-second decision he got a foot on to a window ledge and heaved himself up on to the flat roof. There was a bang as one of the ground-floor windows blew out.

'Don't, Tom!' yelled Suzy. 'It's not safe!'

But he'd already started out. The escape-route window hung open and inside was oppressively hot and dark. Stumbling, Mariner's foot struck something hollow that skidded away. The door to the landing was closed. Bracing himself, Mariner grasped the handle and opened it. There was an ear-popping whoof! as smoke and flames surged at him, like scalding water thrown in his face and he slammed the door shut again. Suzy was right, it was hopeless. Mariner retreated back along the roof, through flakes of ash floating in thick smoke, coughing and gasping for breath, when, mercifully, he saw the blue flicker of the fire engine arriving at the front of the house, and two of the crew appeared around the side of the building. 'There's someone inside!' he shouted, climbing down, his throat raw and stinging. 'An old man. Up there.' But as the firefighters were readying themselves with breathing equipment, there was a thunderous crash as the upper floor of the house caved in, sending an explosion of sparks into the air, and it was too late.

Round at the front of the house, Mariner and Suzy watched as the firemen pumped in gallons of water and finally the inferno began to subside. An ambulance took the mother and children away, the woman still crying for her father, who surely had perished. A small crowd had gathered and a uniformed police officer arrived to keep them back.

Mariner was treated at the scene for smoke inhalation and he and Suzy made their way home as the sky paled into dawn. They went back to bed, but for a long time Mariner lay awake, reliving those moments inside the house, wishing he'd done more to try and get to the old man. But eventually he must have fallen asleep, because he was woken, his eyes gritty and dry, by the ringing of his work mobile.

It was Pete Stone, the duty inspector from Granville Lane. 'Rise and shine,' said Stone. 'Better things for you to be doing on a Sunday morning than shagging the missus. You've got a house fire, and it's a foxtrot.' He said it with relish, and it wasn't easy to fathom whether he was more pleased about the incident fatality or the opportunity to get Mariner out of bed.

It was common knowledge that Stone had been brought into the department six months ago to give it a shake-up. His predecessor had been an original 'plod', who knew his local community from years on the beat, and, based on his wealth of experience, responded to incidents in a considered way. Stone was a targets man, who had taken the inspector's post to pave the way for his rapid promotion, so had no inclination to cultivate relationships. Mariner hadn't decided yet if he liked the man. 'I know,' he said now, not bothering to explain. 'I'll get there as soon as I can.' He was already out of bed.

Suzy had been woken by the phone too. 'Sorry, I've got to go down there,' said Mariner. 'You can stay, though,' he went on as she started to push back the duvet. 'I just need to check in with Fire Investigation to see what's going on. I should be back in a couple of hours.'

'No, it's fine,' said Suzy. 'I'd like to get back to Coventry. I've got some sorting out to do for tomorrow. I'll jump in the shower after you've gone and I can get the train back.'

'That's optimistic,' said Mariner. 'It'll take you all day. Wait for me. I won't be long and I can drop you back afterwards.'

This time, instead of crossing the canal, Mariner walked round on the roads, the half-mile or so to the scene. No point in taking his car and adding to the inevitable vehicle jam. From this side he could see Wellington Road for what it was: one in a whole network of solid, semi- and detached houses built between the wars to accommodate Birmingham's burgeoning middle classes; typical three-bedroom properties with neat front gardens overlooked by bay windows. What remained of number 104 was a square detached that rubbed against its neighbours, and in daylight he could see the adjoining garage which had, at some point after the original construction, been converted into further living accommodation, with another bedroom added on top. It was on this side of the house, to the left of the front door, where most of the damage had been done, and while the rust-bricked walls still looked sound enough, they enclosed a charred shell. Blackened and broken windows were surrounded by a residue of soot, and light shone through the ribs of the roof joists. Wisps of white vapour rose in places and there was enough smoke in the air to catch in Mariner's throat, prompting a fleeting flashback to the events of last night.

The narrow street was blocked by assorted vehicles, including three fire tenders, from which a tangled mass of yellow hoses snaked across the pavement and into the garden. Showing his identification to the uniform standing guard, Mariner crossed the outer cordon of blue police tape and immediately caught sight of a familiar figure standing head and shoulders above everyone around him. Sergeant Ralph Solomon had come a long way since Mariner's first encounter with him as a wet-behind-the-ears constable, when he had stumbled upon a particularly grisly murder. Today it looked as if he was supervising the other uniforms in the preliminary investigations. Seeing Mariner, Solomon broke away from the small group behind one of the squad cars and strode towards him exuding the confidence of an officer who has everything under control. It was essential. Fire investigations were notoriously complicated. Whilst the fire service had responsibility for establishing the cause of the fire, the police were expected to investigate any potential criminal offence; in this case arson, manslaughter or even murder. Both agencies in turn would rely heavily on input from the newly privatised forensic service. Solomon would be overseeing the house-to-house, and interviews with any other witnesses, making sure that his officers were asking the right questions, so ensuring that all possible information was gathered

'Morning, sir,' said Solomon, his gaze lingering on Mariner's face.

'I know,' said Mariner. 'I only live across the canal. I was here last night, but couldn't do anything. I'll need to give you a statement at some point. But broad brushstrokes; what do we know so far?' He framed his question carefully, knowing that he could easily stand here for an hour while the meticulous Solomon recounted every detail at length.

'The emergency call was logged at just after one-twenty in the morning,' said Solomon, without even consulting his notes. He turned towards the street. 'One of the neighbours across there at number 163, a Mrs Putman, called it in when her teenage son saw the flames coming from the ground-floor window.'

'Thank God for nocturnal kids,' said Mariner.

'The fire crew was late getting here because of vehicles

parked on a neighbouring street,' said Solomon. 'They couldn't get through.'

'I thought they were never going to turn up,' said Mariner.

'I understand you got Mrs Shah and her two children out through a first-floor back window?' said Solomon.

'We helped them down, that was all,' said Mariner.

Solomon paused a moment. 'I've currently got a couple of lads interviewing witnesses house-to-house.'

'And the firefighters?' asked Mariner.

'I'll start gathering statements from them when I can.' Their evidence would be vital in determining the origins and progression of the fire. Mariner saw what he saw, but he was no expert. The firefighters' accounts of the colour of the smoke and where it came from, the position of doors and windows, the state of the building, what, if anything, was moved and what – hose reel or main jet – was used to extinguish fire, would all provide valuable clues that would allow them to establish how the fire started and whether it was accidental or deliberate. Solomon would also need to determine the number of personnel going into the building, and what might have been done to isolate electrics and gas.

Solomon pointed to a man who, but for the skin colour and cropped fair hair, could have been his twin, well over six feet tall, with broad shoulders. In full fire kit, he stood in the front garden of the property, his back to them, while he surveyed the building. 'That's Gerry Docherty, the fire investigation lead. He'll tell you more about what's going on inside.'

'What's he like?' asked Mariner.

'Seems like a good bloke,' said Solomon. 'Relaxed, if you know what I mean.'

'Good,' said Mariner. These days, inter-agency working was as much as anything about money. The Fire Investigation team had a service level agreement with the police to provide three hundred man hours per year, over and above which there would be an additional charge. Given the central role of FI in this kind of incident, the last thing they needed was a jobsworth who was going to log every last second.

Mariner had to be signed in to the inner red fire cordon by another uniform before he could approach Docherty to introduce himself. No doubt a former fire fighter, Docherty had an air of competent calm about him. The two-way radio he carried, crackled intermittently as they talked.

'Where are we up to?' Mariner asked, knowing that the fire scene would be treated like a crime scene until proven otherwise.

'I haven't managed to get in yet,' said Docherty. He and Mariner moved a little nearer to the house. 'As you can see we've got a high level of collapse – the roof has caved in to the first floor and the weight of all that has taken it through to the ground floor.' He waved his radio towards the outer wall on the left-hand side of the building. 'That gable end is looking a bit wobbly so I've got a couple of guys in there right now assessing stability. We've got a confirmed fatality in there, but the body is partially buried and precariously placed, so we haven't been able to get near it to begin recovery.'

'Mrs Shah's father,' said Mariner.

Docherty nodded. 'Sixty-six-year-old Soltan Ahmed. Once I've got the all-clear I'll let the forensic team and photographer in to do what they need to whilst the body is *in situ*. Then after it's recovered, we can start the proper analysis. We had a hell of a game getting here,' Docherty went on. 'We couldn't get the tenders past parked vehicles on the access roads.'

'Do you think it was deliberate obstruction?'

Docherty shook his head. 'Just a couple of pillocks who'd parked badly. These narrow streets aren't designed for all the cars we have these days. There'll be an internal investigation into that too.'

'For what it's worth, I don't think it would have made any difference,' said Mariner. 'God knows what there was in that downstairs room, but it went up like a tinder box.'

Docherty nodded agreement. 'There must have been something in there to generate the level of heat. These houses are pretty close together, and that one,' he nodded towards the building a few doors down with a noticeboard in the garden, 'is a nursing home for the elderly, so one of the priorities was to stop it from spreading to the properties on that side. You found Mrs Shah?'

'Just guided her and the kids down over the flat roof and into the back garden. She was dazed and in shock and obviously distraught about her father.'

'How was she dressed?' Docherty asked.

'She was wearing day clothes, so she hadn't been in bed when it started. It might be significant, but at that time of night there might also be a rational explanation.'

Docherty noted it with a nod. 'Was there anyone hanging about who shouldn't have been?' he asked. For some arsonists the thrill they got was from standing back and watching the chaos they caused.

'Not that I noticed. There was a lot going on,' said Mariner, in a study of understatement. 'A couple of our uniformed officers turned up pretty quickly to manage the audience, so they'll know more about that.'

Up until that point the chuntering on Docherty's handset had been indistinct, but suddenly there was an agitated shout: 'Watch it, Dev! That looks a bit—!' A loud reverberation preceded a cloud of billowing ash from the ground-floor window. Anxious eyes turned towards the building until the two fire fighters scrambled outside, pulling off their breathing masks. 'Sorry, boss,' the nearer of the two spoke to Docherty. 'It's too dicey in there. Tech Rescue will need to make it safe before anything else can be done.'

'Shit!' Docherty's frustration was felt by Mariner too. It could take up to a day to clear areas for the technical team to make the building safe, which would mean a considerable delay. But it was unavoidable. The safety of personnel had to come first.

'And if it can't be fully secured?' asked Mariner.

'Then we'll focus on recovery of the body, and any kind of forensic examination will have to be conducted outside using a reconstruction grid,' said Docherty. 'Let's hope it doesn't come to that.'

Docherty explained all of this to the combined police and fire crews, when he called the first of what would be many daily briefing sessions for everyone on-site; this one conducted on the lawn as a light drizzle began to fall. Mariner looked up at the overcast sky; this could be bad news too. Rain could hold things up further and contaminate the crime scene.

FOUR

Mariner could do no more here, so he headed home, leaving everyone else to do their work, his clothes and hair stinking of smoke. Suzy had made herself breakfast and been down to the newsagent's for the Sunday paper. 'How is it?' she asked, getting up to put the kettle on. 'They confirmed on the radio that the man inside died.'

'It's grim,' said Mariner.

'You couldn't have done any more,' Suzy tried to reassure him.

'I know.' But it didn't stop him wishing he had. 'And now we've got to cool our heels for a bit while the Fire Investigation team do their thing, and at the moment the building is unstable, so until that's been addressed it's a waiting game for all of us. But I suppose the good news is that it gives me plenty of time to take you back.'

On a good day the drive back to Coventry took forty-five minutes, and today, apart from a bottleneck around the National Exhibition Centre, the traffic was slow but steady. The postgraduate block where Suzy had a room at the university was a 1990s creation, with flimsy walls that couldn't keep out the murmur of TVs elsewhere in the block, or the ebb and flow of conversation as people walked along the corridor outside.

As student accommodation went, the room was a decent size, with the usual utilitarian furniture, but right now most of the floor space was taken over by boxes and knee-high towers of books. And this was just a fraction of Suzy's library; most of it remained in a nearby self-storage facility until she could find somewhere a bit bigger and more permanent to live. 'Are all these necessary?' said Mariner. 'Most of them must be pretty much obsolete now that we've got the Internet.'

Suzy gave him a look. 'Not at all. There's no substitute for the feel and smell of a proper book. They're having a resurgence.'

'I'll take your word for it.' Mariner himself owned about half a dozen books, and those were mostly made up of photographs.

He'd quite liked English while he was at school but these days the only reading he did was case files and policy documents at work, via a computer screen. Given that books played such an important part in Suzy's life, it was strange that this lack of common ground didn't really seem to matter. 'You need to clear some space,' he said. 'If you're not going anywhere just yet, I might as well have a go at those shelves.' He reached over to one of the cardboard flat packs of bookcases that Suzy had bought a couple of weekends ago and started to pull open the packaging. DIY was hardly ever Mariner's activity of choice, but it would be a solution to the clutter and keep his mind occupied for a while. 'I can do that later,' said Suzy, as he started to pull open the packaging of one of the bookcases.

'I know,' said Mariner. 'But it'll be quicker if we do it together.' He swore as a heavy-duty copper staple pierced his thumb. The units were surprisingly straightforward to assemble and less than twenty minutes later, laying the first particle-board shelf on its frame, he picked up a couple of tomes the size of house bricks, and placed them on top. 'I'm not sure that they're going to be strong enough to take the weight of this lot,' said Mariner. Particularly substantial, he noticed, were those written by Professor Gideon Wiley. 'That doesn't even sound like a real name,' he said.

'What will you do this afternoon?' Suzy asked, passing him another of the books from the pile. 'A walk?'

'Jamie,' said Mariner. Lying awake in the early hours he'd worked out that his last visit to Jamie had been five weeks ago. He thought this might be the longest it had ever been. When he'd first taken on guardianship he'd intended to see Jamie at least fortnightly, recognising the importance of that regular contact. And he'd mostly kept to that. But lately life, and staff shortages, had got in the way and gradually his trips out to Worcestershire had dwindled to three-weekly and then monthly. Now he couldn't think about Jamie without feeling guilty.

It was impossible of course to determine what, if any, difference any of these visits made to Jamie. Mariner had read once that dogs have no sense of time passing, between an owner leaving them in the morning and returning at the end of the day. He kind of hoped it was like that for Jamie too, but accepted that it could well be wishful thinking on his part. What he could be certain of was that Jamie would greet him with the same mild indifference as always, his interest largely governed by any snacks Mariner might have taken with him.

'I do love you,' Suzy said, as she hugged him goodbye a little later.

'Not sure why,' Mariner responded, his tone light. There was something in those words that unsettled him, as if she was actually trying to reassure herself too.

She smiled. 'It'll be all right. It's a phase, that's all.'

They both knew what she was talking about. She was always careful not to put him under pressure, but at the same time Mariner wished he could share her optimism.

Suzy watched the tail lights of Tom's car disappear round the corner and went back to her room. She had meant what she said, but things between them had definitely become less straightforward of late, in a way that she had never encountered in any relationship before. Tom had been candid with her almost from the start of their relationship, about what they euphemistically referred to as his 'bedroom difficulties', but they hadn't surfaced until now, when suddenly, out of the blue, he couldn't stay the course. Now the joke had worn to transparency. And medication hadn't helped; Tom seemed to be one of the few who experienced side effects in the form of blinding and long-lasting headaches. 'Never mind,' she'd said cheerfully, 'other ways to skin a cat.' But it wasn't the same; they both knew that. All this in itself was frustrating enough, but what made it worse was that they seemed to have reached a point where neither of them, intelligent, articulate adults as they were, seemed capable any longer of broaching the subject. So not only were they now avoiding intimacy, they were also avoiding talking about it. In the past, while Suzy had always been sympathetic to friends or work colleagues going through relationship difficulties, she had at the same time invariably thought: *why don't you just talk to each other?* Now she understood that it wasn't always so simple. She was aware that the responsibility probably lay with her, and there had been opportunities on several occasions over the weekend to start the conversation, but each time she had ducked out of it. She didn't know how long they could go on like this.

*   *   *

The drive out to Jamie's residential home was a pleasant one through rural Worcestershire, and as he drove Mariner put his mobile on hands-free to check in with Docherty. 'Any developments?'

'Not for you,' said Docherty. Mariner could hear the disappointment in his voice. 'Tech Rescue have only just got here and now we're trying to make sure they don't plough in and destroy evidence. It's a nightmare; that downstairs room, where we think it started, is crammed with stuff anyway, and the collapse from above has compounded it. They're in there now, trying to shore up the end wall, to stop that from coming down too, but without disturbing anything.' He broke off momentarily, to speak to someone close by. 'Sorry about that,' he said. 'It's a big job, so by the time it's been made safe it's likely that the light will be starting to go. I don't envisage being able to get in until first thing tomorrow morning. If that situation changes, I'll let you know straight away.'

'Thanks.' Mariner too was disappointed. It would mean losing valuable hours. He terminated the call just as he was turning into the driveway of Manor Park. The rural location of the former manor house suited Jamie, and, he supposed, most of the other residents, perfectly. But all the same Mariner couldn't help but view it as a throwback to the times of the big asylums, constructed outside of towns and cities to keep the inmates well away from the general population. It could hardly be helpful at a time when the words 'disabled' and 'benefit-scrounger' had become practically synonymous, stirring up antagonism all over again.

Parking up, Mariner checked in first with a young man called Zac, on duty at reception. 'Sorry, it's been a while,' Mariner said, slightly embarrassed.

'No worries,' Zac was cool. 'You're here. It means that Jamie sees you more often than a lot of our clients see their families.' Mariner hadn't encountered Zac before and for a second he considered explaining the irony of that remark, but decided that it wasn't really important. It had taken other staff at Manor Park a while to get their heads round the fact that Mariner and Jamie were entirely unrelated, and that what had left Mariner with his legal guardianship was simply a series of unfortunate occurrences. The first and most significant of these was the murder of Jamie's older brother, Eddie, which had left Anna, their sister, Jamie's reluctant carer, and brought DI Tom Mariner into their lives. In the course of the homicide investigation Mariner had got to know Anna, and when the perpetrator was caught it was almost inevitable that he would go on seeing her. Their affair had foundered a couple of years down the line, and shortly afterwards life had delivered one of those devastating sideways swipes that defies anticipation, when Anna's life was cut cruelly short. So, by a quirk of timing and legal process, Mariner suddenly found himself responsible for his former (and late) lover's brother. Not an easy arrangement to explain to anyone. To begin with Mariner had been almost pathologically afraid of the responsibility, but as time wore on Jamie had become just another part of his life. 'Besides . . .' Zac tapped his finger on the previous page, 'looks like Jamie had another visitor just a couple of days ago.' Mariner saw the neat handwriting: Mercy. It only made him feel worse. Mercy had helped to care for Jamie for a while, and still visited him often, despite her age and the fact that the journey on public transport must take her all day.

'OK, let's go find him,' said Zac, when Mariner had signed in. This in itself proved no easy task. They found Jamie's room empty and untidy, though stopping off there enabled Mariner to collect Jamie's jacket from behind the door. He and Zac then spent a further fifteen minutes walking the wide, brightly lit corridors looking for him. There seemed to be fewer staff about than usual, and, at one point, Mariner heard raised voices behind closed doors. They finally located Jamie in one of the communal lounges, where he sat in front of a TV that was playing a rugby match. That too was uncharacteristic; Jamie only ever watched TV programmes that interested him, and these were mostly pre-recorded quiz shows.

'Hi, Jamie,' said Mariner, taking in the stubble on his chin and the shapeless tracksuit. He was looking his age, his hair going grey at the same rate as Mariner's, though Jamie was losing his too.

Jamie glanced in his direction for a brief second, enough time for Mariner to see the bruise on his forehead, but he remained seated, tugging at a bandage wound tightly round his forearm. 'What's he done there?' Mariner asked Zac.

'The bandage is covering a bite.'

'An insect bite?'

'A Jamie bite,' said Zac. 'And he banged his head on a door frame, while Nell was trying to get him dressed a couple of days ago. He's become a bit less co-operative just lately, and we're getting some challenging behaviour.'

'Is he being medicated?' Mariner asked.

'Just a small dose of Ritalin,' said Zac. 'There wasn't any choice.'

'How long has this been going on?' asked Mariner, 'and why has nobody told me?'

'I guess we've been waiting to see if things would settle down again,' said Zac. 'Sometimes it's just a blip. I'm sure you'll be contacted if it's deemed necessary.' He sounded casual and Mariner drew breath for a further complaint, but decided against it. All he would be doing was taking out his guilt and frustration on Zac, and it wouldn't help. He wished Nell, Jamie's current key person, was about, but she worked weekdays, so it was unreasonable to expect that she would be here on a Sunday too. He'd contact the management tomorrow and vent his anger.

'Coming for a walk, Jamie?' he said instead, holding Jamie's coat out as a prompt and wondering from the hesitation whether Jamie actually recognised him. Certainly he hadn't addressed Mariner with the customary 'Spectre Man', his best effort at 'Inspector Mariner'. But after a moment, Jamie got to his feet and took his coat.

Jamie was a creature of immovable habit, so, whatever the weather, the two of them always went for a walk around the extensive grounds to burn off some of Jamie's boundless energy. Today, in a strange reversal, Mariner hoped the fresh air might revive him, but it seemed to have the opposite effect, and as they set off on their regular circuit of the grounds, he had to keep stopping to allow Jamie to catch up.

Increasingly Mariner had come to realise how much he appreciated these visits to Jamie, finding that their walks gave him an opportunity to clear his head by voicing whatever might be on his mind, in the secure knowledge that he could do so in complete confidence. Although touching on forty, Jamie's severe autism and learning difficulties meant that his conversational skills were those of a reticent two-year-old. The limited words in his repertoire were the means to the end – a way of getting what he needed – and beyond that, as far as he was concerned, talk was entirely redundant and unworthy of any kind of attention. It placed him in the role of non-judgemental confessor. Today, though, Mariner was much too preoccupied with Jamie's demeanour to do anything other than study him for a clue about what was going on.

Halfway round they stopped beside the tributary of the River Severn that flowed on the other side of the fence and found a patch of grass to sit down. Jamie hovered expectantly, lightly flapping his hands until Mariner produced a packet of Hula Hoops, which he snatched aggressively. Normally Mariner would have made him take them more calmly, but today something told him not to. They sat while Jamie munched his way through them, cramming far too many into his mouth, and when he'd finished, instead of passing the empty packet to Mariner, as he'd learned to do, he let it fall carelessly to the ground. Mariner picked it up and got to his feet to head back. Jamie stood up too, but didn't move. Mariner put an encouraging hand on his arm. 'Come on then, mate,' he said, and to his astonishment, Jamie – who shunned all physical contact – leaned in to him, resting his head on Mariner's shoulder. With caution, Mariner put his arms around Jamie, who relaxed against him in a hug.

This had been a far from routine visit and it made Mariner uneasy. For some time now he had taken Manor Park for granted, having removed Jamie from his previous care home for what looked like neglect. After a stressful few months of trying to care for him at home, the place had come up at Manor Park, which had seemed a much better environment. But Mariner was well aware of recent, highly publicised case reviews into adult care homes, and hoped this wasn't the first indication that all wasn't well at Manor Park.

On their return, approaching an ancient oak tree, Jamie slowed, holding his crotch. This was purely habit; the first time it had happened Mariner hadn't seen the harm in stepping back over the fence and allowing Jamie to pee into the river. This time, standing downstream, Mariner noticed a trail of something in the water. It took a couple of seconds for him to realise what it might be, but when he did, he snatched a tissue from his pocket and tossed it into the water where Jamie's stream of pee hit the surface. It immediately soaked up the water but turned a definite pink colour. As soon as Jamie had finished they went back up to the building and Mariner tracked down Zac. 'I think Jamie's peeing blood,' he said.

When Mariner got home that evening he remembered to text Suzy: 'Good luck tomorrow.'

Her response pinged back immediately: 'Thanks. How's Jamie?'

Mariner hesitated; an economy of truth, or a long and complex text that would only worry her? In the end he had to be honest. 'Not good,' he texted back. His phone rang almost immediately. 'What does that mean?' Suzy asked.

'I don't know,' said Mariner candidly. 'The problem with Jamie is that if he's feeling rough or in pain, he can't tell anyone.' He'd waited around at Manor Park a further hour, plying Jamie with drinks, to confirm that he was right, after which, Zac had undertaken to contact the doctor straight away, to set in motion the relevant tests.

'Trouble is, I don't have much confidence that they will,' Mariner said now, to Suzy. 'Why didn't they pick this up? I've been wondering if I should have Jamie back here to live with me again. At least I'd be able to keep an eye on him.'

There was a pause at the other end of the phone. 'You tried that before,' Suzy reminded him. 'It wasn't all plain sailing then, was it?' She was right. He had just about managed, but only because he had ruthlessly exploited the goodwill of just about everyone he knew.

The following morning the post arrived just as Mariner was leaving for work. Amongst the letters was one from Manor Park. It was from the facility's medical officer, detailing almost everything about Jamie's behaviour that Mariner had seen the previous day. *Referrals have been made for a number of tests,* he wrote. *I will notify you when these are likely to take place.* The letter was dated from the previous Thursday, thus assuaging Mariner's immediate fears. Now they just needed to get Jamie back to his normal self.

FIVE

Detective Sergeant Vicky Jesson was facing her own medical crisis.

'I don't *feel* well,' her younger daughter, Maisie, was whining. Vicky checked her forehead yet again. It wasn't that warm and, apart from the sad face, the eight-year-old looked perfectly fine. But her throat was red and there were those light pink spots. What if—? Any other circumstances and Vicky could have called mum to come over and take Maisie to the doctor's, but today was Doris' morning in the charity shop and dad would be out playing golf, making the most of the sunshine. Vicky knew too that part of her hesitation was simply about bad timing. What she couldn't afford to do just at the moment was to miss any of the morning briefings and task allocations.

Since coming to work at Granville Road station, Vicky had worked hard with Tom Mariner; hard enough to have proved herself capable and reliable. But just lately she seemed to be marking time in terms of responsibility. Charlie Glover had been one of Mariner's sergeants for years, so it was understandable that they often seemed to be boys together. It wasn't that they ever actively excluded her, and she was always invited along if they went for an after work drink, but there were times when they seemed to forget that she had family commitments. She didn't dislike Glover – Charlie was lovely – but easy for him to put the job first when he had his wife at home keeping things going. It was a different story when you were a lone parent to three kids. Thanks to mum and dad, Vicky managed to hold it together most of the time and make sure that family didn't get in the way. The kids pulled their weight too, so she had no complaints there. Although only fourteen, Aaron was pretty good about taking care of his sisters, even though Vicky suspected he took a bit of stick from his mates over it. But Vicky was starting to resent the growing feeling that Charlie Glover's ever-available presence was holding her down in the pecking order at a time when she needed to establish herself. She'd even thought about approaching Superintendent Sharp, but knew deep down that bleating to the management wasn't a solution. It wasn't even as if Sharp would necessarily understand; hers was very much the main breadwinner role in her all-female relationship, so not that different from Charlie in that respect.

Now, though, with Charlie away, Vicky was presented with an opportunity to be indispensable, and she didn't want to screw it up. And she only had a limited window; she felt sure DC Millie Khatoon would be returning from maternity leave very soon, and she and Mariner also had a long-standing partnership. The fire at Wellington Road was bound to be at the top of the agenda this morning. With Charlie away it would make sense for Mariner to appoint Vicky as Senior Investigating Officer; although it would be new to her, she was easily capable of liaising with Fire Investigation. But she couldn't agree to do it if she wasn't there. It wasn't often that Vicky mourned Brian's passing; her late husband had been a bully and not at all the man people thought he was. But just now and again, like this morning, him getting himself shot dead really pissed her off. She reached for the phone and dialled the doctor's surgery.

Vicky had more time than she thought. At the time she was deliberating all this, Mariner was standing outside 104 Wellington Road with Gerry Docherty, as the fire investigator geared up to go into the building. Tech Rescue had finally given the all-clear, having shored up the dodgy walls, and Docherty was all kitted out in his forensic suit and poised to begin his job. But right now he was waiting again, this time because the Forensic Scene Investigator and SOCO, including a photographer, had gone ahead of him into the house to examine the scene and photograph, collect and bag any immediately available evidence. 'Before I plonk my size elevens all over it,' said Docherty cheerfully. Docherty himself might not start work for another hour or two; all this on top of yesterday's delays.

'You need a lot of patience for your job,' Mariner remarked.

'What, more than you?' said Docherty, eyebrows raised.

'I'll leave you to it,' said Mariner, once again superfluous.

'Sure,' said Docherty. 'I'll email through anything we find of interest, and call you if it's urgent.'

Immediately he got into Granville Lane, Mariner went to discuss strategy with Superintendent Sharp, who'd also just arrived from a breakfast meeting at Lloyd House. She looked shattered, even though it was only early morning on the first day of the week. Her normally dark skin was pale and there were shadows under her eyes. She was beginning to look her age, Mariner thought. It was what promotion did to a person. 'Tough one?' he said.

'When is it ever anything else?' Sharp said wearily, sitting back and crossing her long legs. 'Ten years ago we used to think the budget cuts were bad. I sometimes think now the Home Office would just prefer a bunch of unpaid civilian vigilantes.'

'So this is a conversation you won't want to have,' said Mariner.

'The weekend's little pyrotechnic adventure, I take it,' said Sharp. 'I understand you were in the thick of it.'

'You could say that,' said Mariner, and brought her up to date.

'So you'll be putting in a contingency application for over-time?' Sharp surmised.

'Not yet, we don't know what category this will turn out to be, so I'll see how it pans out. But the family is Arabian. I couldn't really tell on Saturday if we'll need to buy in interpreters. And of course it could turn out to be sensitive.'

'And therefore in need of the diplomatic skills of a senior officer, perhaps?' Sharp observed, reading him perfectly.

'Exactly,' said Mariner. 'It's why I thought—'

'Why not Vicky as SIO? She's very competent.'

'I agree,' said Mariner. 'But she's still only a sergeant and hasn't had experience of handling a multifaceted investigation like this one will be. It could potentially mean liaising with fire service, family, community leaders and all that. If Charlie was here I'd have no hesitation, but—'

'—conveniently for you he's not.' Sharp shook her head. 'Sometime, Tom, you are going to have to get used to the idea that DCI and delegation go together, which means occasionally sitting on your arse and doing a bit of paperwork for more than ten minutes at a stretch.'

'What can I say?' Mariner was all innocence. 'I'm a slow

learner. Either way, until we have more of an idea what this might be, I'd like to oversee it.'

'And your involvement on Saturday night?'

'It gives me some useful context, but was superficial. I'm not sure that Mrs Shah would even recognise me again, and there was nothing I could do.'

Sharp regarded him evenly. 'You'd give Ghandi a run for his money in passive resistance,' she said eventually. 'But keep me in the loop, particularly if and when we get to the community liaison stage.' She caught his expression. 'For *information*,' she said. 'Don't be so paranoid.'

Mariner was lucky; he knew that. A lot of other superintendents would have told him to grow up, do the job he was paid to do, and let others do theirs. But Sharp was a pragmatist, plus she liked him. Mariner liked to think it was because, when they'd first met, his bare backside had made a favourable and lasting impression. But he could have been wrong about that.

'Isn't Millie back later this week too?' asked Sharp, as he got up to go.

'She is,' Mariner confirmed. 'But she'll take some time to get back into the swing of things, and she'll only be here three days a week.'

'Just be careful with that "only",' Sharp warned. 'Millie will give it one hundred percent and more while she's here, we both know that.'

'I didn't mean—'

'I know you didn't,' said Sharp mildly. 'But it's what you *said* that matters. Part-time does not mean less commitment, especially where Millie's concerned.'

'Even so, we're going to be stretched.'

'Then ask uniform for another body,' said Sharp. 'Someone to help with the grunt work.'

Mariner had already considered but rejected that idea. 'You think Stone's likely to co-operate?'

Sharp shrugged. 'Like you said, it's a significant case.'

Floaters (an unfortunate term in Mariner's opinion) were uniformed officers who drifted from one department to another picking up the slack with tasks deemed too menial for more

senior ranks, frequently those who, for whatever reason, were
confined to restricted duties. In Mariner's experience they
were often more trouble than they were worth, as it took far
longer explaining what was required of them than it did to
do the work. But his team was now so depleted that they could
no longer run effectively on the staff they'd got.

Before picking up the phone he mentally composed his
argument for securing one of Inspector Pete Stone's officers;
Stone would naturally fight losing one of his team at a time
when they were all hard pressed, and he could be an awkward
bugger. But when it came to it, very little persuasion was needed.
'Just let me check the roster,' said Stone. He was back in less
than a minute. 'That's fine,' he said. 'I've got the just the bloke
for you. You can have Brown.'

'Thanks.' Mariner replaced the receiver thinking that had just
been too easy. Ten minutes later, as he was beginning the briefing,
his colleague's generosity became clear, when Brown appeared,
making the kind of entrance that put Laurel and Hardy in the
shade. 'Hello,' he said to no one in particular. 'I've been sent
up from uniform, I was told to—' He faltered, realising then
that he was interrupting a meeting in progress. Heading for the
nearest vacant office chair, which happened to be Vicky Jesson's,
he stumbled, sending it skating away from him, and grabbing
on to the adjacent desk to steady himself, knocked a pot of pens
and paperclips flying through the air to scatter all over the floor.
'Sorry.' He scrambled to pick them up. Having retrieved them,
with the help of a couple of the admin staff nearby, he finally
managed to sit down and, having retained one of the pens, sat
clicking the mechanism on and off, until Mariner stopped him
with a glare.

'Well, I would say welcome, PC Brown,' said Mariner, beginning to understand Stone's easy compliance. 'But you've already
made yourself at home.'

'Yes, sir.'

'Do you have a first name?'

'Kevin.'

'OK.' Mariner began the briefing, with his team of what
seemed mostly to be support staff, by going over the events of
Saturday night and the background information they had garnered

so far. First he invited Ralph Solomon to go through the main points of what had been learned from the house-to-house. 'We have a witness who saw someone walking along the street and past the Shahs' soon after midnight,' he said. 'But we have to keep in mind that this is a through route to get to the Nansen estate. And the witness is keen to make it clear that this person was walking quickly, not running, as in running away. Several vehicles were also seen coming and going through the evening, until quite late, but nothing unusual has so far been recorded at around the time when the fire started.'

The office door opened again and Mariner glanced round as Vicky Jesson hurried in. There was a Three Bears moment as she registered, with noticeable disapproval, that Brown was sitting on her chair at her desk, but then she walked over to the only other available seat, kicking over a waste bin along the way. It began to feel to Mariner as if he was managing a class of eight-year-olds. 'Might be what a smart person would do,' he answered Solomon, while watching Jesson cross the room. 'Running tends to draw attention.'

'He was also wearing hoodie, with the hood pulled up, even though it was a dry, mild night,' said Solomon.

'Mild?' said Vicky, tuning in. 'Where are you living?'

'Obviously it's not in itself incriminating, but it would be helpful to track this individual down and talk to them,' Solomon went on. 'I've asked the press office to revise the appeal for witnesses to include a specific reference to this individual.'

'Good,' said Mariner. 'Anything else?'

'One of the neighbours mentioned a bit of trouble between the Shahs and another family in the street. She didn't know exactly who, but Mrs Shah complained to her about it.'

'OK,' said Mariner. 'Brown?' Brown looked up, pushed his wire-framed glasses up his nose and blinked hard. 'You're on restricted duties, is that right?' said Mariner.

'Yes, sir, I've got a metal plate up here,' he said, tapping the back of his skull.

Hint of an accent there, though Mariner couldn't quite place it. 'You've been a nominal before?' he asked. Brown looked blank. Christ, did he even know what that was? 'Have you ever run a policy book?' Mariner added, to help him out.

'Oh right,' said Brown. 'Gotcha.'

That was something then. 'I want you to start collating and indexing the intel as it comes in,' Mariner told him. 'Witness statements – civilian and fire crew – officers' pocketbook notes, all of that. It needs to be done carefully and methodically, cross-referencing where necessary, so that we don't miss anything. Think you can do that?'

'I'll give it a go,' said Brown brightly.

It wasn't a response that immediately instilled confidence, but Mariner wasn't in a position to be choosy. 'You can use Charlie Glover's desk for now, over there in the corner.'

This was Vicky's big moment. 'Do you want me to—?' she began to volunteer, but Mariner cut her off with a raised hand. 'While Charlie's away I'll be taking the lead on this, at least until we have more information from Fire Investigation and know exactly what we're dealing with.'

Vicky hadn't meant to tut and she certainly hadn't intended it to be loud enough for everyone around her to hear. A couple of people turned her way. She couldn't help it; it was a reflex reaction to her disappointment, both in her failure to secure the fire investigation, but also in the boss. Never meet your idols, they always say, but she really hadn't expected this of Tom Mariner.

Her feelings about him had always been complicated. Before the service reorganisation had brought her to Granville Lane she'd known him by reputation, and he was pretty much the personification of everything she aspired to be. She admired and respected him, and if she was honest with herself, she'd have admitted that she'd fancied him a bit too, until ambition and professionalism had eclipsed any other feelings she might have had. Besides which, she'd quickly come to realise that there were certain aspects of Mariner's personality that would drive her to distraction if she had to live with him. She had no idea how his other half, Suzy, put up with it. But then maybe she didn't, because lately Vicky thought she had detected definite signs of tension there.

In the past Vicky had been in plenty of situations where she'd been overlooked in favour of male colleagues; she'd come here to get away from some of the gits who allowed that to happen. But the last few minutes seemed to confirm her growing belief that Mariner might be one of those gits too. As the group broke up, so deep was Vicky in these thoughts that at first she didn't hear her name being called. When it did seep through to her consciousness, she realised it was Mariner who was addressing her. He flicked his head towards his office. 'Can I have a word?'

Oh hell. Was this because she'd been late, or was the chippiness starting to show? She followed Mariner along the corridor. 'Everything all right?' she asked, hurrying to keep up, and aware as she said it that she was sounding aggressively defensive. Mariner turned, slightly startled by her tone, but said nothing. Having arrived in his office, he didn't sit down so neither did she, leaving them standing on either side of his desk as if they were about to start a game of ping-pong.

'You OK?' Mariner asked, picking up his phone and pocketing it.

'Yes, thanks,' said Jesson tightly. 'Something I had to take care of at home.'

Mariner nodded, going for his coat. 'I know you're keen to get your teeth into this fire, but I don't think now is quite the right time. However, it may be one for you to take over, further down the line. According to Solomon we don't need an interpreter, so are you all right to take the lead as family liaison, and start with leading the questioning with Mrs Shah?'

'Yes, of course.'

'I'll meet you out front in five minutes then, after I've checked that PC Brown actually knows how to switch on a computer.'

Walking back to the main office Vicky Jesson's feelings were in turmoil; glad that she hadn't blown it, but now annoyed with herself for having been so distrustful. It was just the kind of feminist crap the blokes resented and succumbing to that wouldn't do her any favours. And Mariner? Well, at some point she may allow him to climb back up on his pedestal.

Having checked on Brown, as he descended the stairs to follow Vicky out to the car park, Mariner remembered to text Suzy good luck on her first day too.

SIX

Salwa Shah and her children were still at the Queen Elizabeth hospital, being treated for minor injuries and the effects of smoke inhalation, though when Mariner and Jesson tracked them down to a sunny playroom off the children's ward, there didn't seem any doubt that they would all make a full physical recovery. Psychologically it might take a little longer to deal with the trauma, and Salwa Shah was evidence of this, leaning forward in her seat and rocking gently, a handkerchief clutched tightly in one fist. Bandaging on the other hand went halfway to her elbow. The room was stuffy, and she must be hot in her black *abaya* and *hijab*, but it didn't show. Her children seemed oblivious, the little girl sitting beside her, quietly drawing, whilst her son lay on his stomach on the floor, constructing some elaborate imaginary game with a range of emergency and other miniature vehicles. He had a dressing wrapped around his left knee. Salwa turned anxious eyes on Mariner and Jesson as they went in.

Showing Salwa her warrant card, Vicky made the introductions and sat down across from her.

Salwa studied Mariner for a moment. 'You're the man who helped us from the roof,' she said.

'Yes,' Mariner showed her his warrant card. 'I'm also the police officer who will be leading the investigation. But right now, my colleague would like to ask you some questions.' Taking out his notebook, he took the seat next to Jesson.

'Do you know who it was?' Salwa asked straight away.

This was an interesting start, and caught Jesson off guard. 'Who what was?'

To Salwa Shah it was obvious. 'The people who did this to us.'

'You think the fire was started deliberately?'

'It has happened before.'

Mariner and Jesson exchanged a look. Had it? That wasn't quite what they'd been told. Mariner made a note.

'We're working very closely with the Fire Investigation team,' Jesson said, smoothing things over. 'And until their findings are conclusive, we have to keep an open mind. Now, I appreciate that this is difficult,' she went on, 'but we just need to hear your version of the events on Saturday night.'

Carefully cradling her injured hand, Salwa closed her eyes for an instant, as if the act of remembering was almost too much. 'It was an ordinary evening,' she began. 'My husband is away, so we were on our own for dinner then the children watched TV while I tidied the kitchen. My father went to bed early; he likes to go up and read, where it's quiet, away from the television. I have to help him up the stairs.' Her English was faultless and clearly articulated.

'What time was that?' asked Jesson.

'I'm not sure, perhaps a little after seven.' As she relaxed she became more fluent. 'I watched a couple of programmes with the children – they like the talent shows – and then at about nine o'clock I took them up to bed. When I went up later, at about ten-thirty perhaps, I could hear Yousef, muttering in his sleep. He seems to so often have nightmares at the moment.' Her son looked up at her and said something in Arabic that Mariner didn't catch, but it made Salwa smile. She reached down to touch his head. '*Ana aasif*, I know, you can't help it,' she said. She turned back to Jesson. 'I didn't want him to wake his sister, so I went to sit with him for a while, to comfort him. I must have fallen asleep, because the next thing I remember was waking up very suddenly. I don't know why. I think I was disturbed by something, a loud noise.'

'What kind of noise?' Mariner asked.

'I don't know.' She frowned. 'Like a crashing sound.'

Mariner signalled for Jesson to go on. 'And what time was that?' she asked Salwa.

'I'm not sure. It felt like the middle of the night. I knew straight away that something was very wrong. It seemed darker than normal and then I smelled the smoke, it was so strong, so I knew there must be a fire, and my father . . .' She tailed off. 'I opened the children's bedroom door a little and squeezed on to the landing, but the smoke gushed at me like a solid wall. It was so thick that it felt like . . . like I was breathing wool. I tried the light switch but nothing happened, so I wrapped my scarf around my face and keeping low, as I know you should, I felt my way across the floor to my father's door. But when I grabbed the handle it was so hot my skin stuck to it.' She winced at the memory. 'I couldn't turn it. I shouted to him as loudly as I could, but the smoke alarms were going and I couldn't hear him.' There was desperation in her eyes, and the fingers of her bandaged hand curled involuntarily. 'The smoke was making my head feel strange. I was afraid I might pass out, and then what would happen to my children?' She sniffed, and Mariner glanced up from his notebook to see tears running, untended, down her cheeks. 'I found my way back to their bedroom and shut the door behind me.' Sniffing again, she wiped her face with the handkerchief, taking in the enormity of that decision.

'You did the right thing,' Jesson soothed. She waited a moment. 'What happened next?'

'By now Yousef was becoming hysterical and Athmar had woken too,' said Salwa. 'I had to get them out. That part was easy. I climbed out of the window first and lifted them on to the roof below. I didn't know if it would hold our weight. I couldn't see much in the dark, except the flames coming out of the downstairs windows, but I knew if we could go to the edge, we could get down from there.' She looked across at Mariner. 'That is when we saw you in the garden and you helped us down. You know what happened after that.'

'We need to hear your version,' said Jesson gently. 'You may have seen or heard something that will help.'

'We were waiting for the ambulance,' Salwa went on. 'I kept hoping that I would see my father, that he had somehow— I think the firemen tried to get to him too, but the fire was too much. And then the roof fell in,' her voice caught, 'and there was nothing we could do.' She stared out of the window, lost in her thoughts.

'We're very sorry for your loss,' said Jesson. After a moment she said: 'You seemed to suggest that the fire was started deliberately. Do you know someone who would want to harm your family?'

'There have been incidents since we came to the house,' said Salwa. 'Some people didn't exactly make us welcome in the neighbourhood. We moved out from Sparkhill three years ago. We wanted our children to go to schools with children from lots of different backgrounds. My sister-in-law said it was a mistake,' she added, 'and that we should have stayed nearer to our community. She was right.'

'Where is your husband now?' Jesson asked.

'He is in Sana'a on business,' said Salwa. 'He was on his way home, but now— He will travel first to my father's village to pay his respects and to make the arrangements for him to be returned. Then he will come home.' She looked up at Jesson. 'When will we be able to have my father's body? We have to perform the *ghusl mayyit*, and say prayers at the mosque, before he can be flown home for burial.'

'We understand that,' Mariner said. The body would be washed and wrapped in white cloth, before burial in an L-shaped grave. 'But I'm sure you also realise that in the event of sudden and unexpected deaths such as this one, we also have procedures to follow.'

Salwa nodded assent. 'Yes, of course.'

'What kind of man was your father?' Mariner asked Salwa, as they prepared to leave.

'He was kind and clever. Like many of the older men at the mosque, he was respected for his wisdom. He urged moderation at a time when many of the young men feel they should take action. His views weren't always popular. But one of the reasons he brought his family to this country is because it is possible to express views freely, without persecution.'

'He was in good health?'

She looked away, tears threatening once more. 'He was recovering from a virus that had laid him low, but that is all. Do you know when we will be able to go home?'

'Sorry,' said Jesson. 'That's something the doctors will decide. And it will be some time before you'll be able to return to the house. Is there somewhere you can stay?'

'We will go to my sister-in-law's. It will be crowded, but we'll manage.'

They stood up to go. 'It would be helpful if we can also talk to the children,' said Mariner. 'Perhaps in a day or two?'

'Yes, of course.'

Before they left Mariner wrote down the address of the sister-in-law's house in Sparkhill and Jesson gave Salwa her card. 'In case you have anything you would like to ask, or if you remember anything more about Saturday night.'

They also sought out the nurse who treated the Shahs on arrival. 'We'll be allowing them home later today,' she told them.

'And Mrs Shah's hand?' asked Mariner.

'She has severe burns and blistering to the palm, consistent with what she told us – that she tried to open a red-hot door handle. She must have held on for several seconds,' said the nurse. 'But sometimes there's a delay before the body reacts to the pain of the damage being done.'

On their way back to Granville Lane, Mariner and Jesson stopped by at Wellington Road to catch the midday briefing with the Fire Investigation team. It had been raining on and off all day and now a tent had been erected in the front garden to protect any retrieved evidence from the elements. When he'd finished updating the crew, Mariner introduced Vicky Jesson to Docherty.

'The good news is that the body has been recovered and we can finally get going,' said Docherty.

Jesson surveyed the devastation. 'God, where do you even start on something like this?' she asked.

Docherty was philosophical. 'This is nothing, compared with some of the incidents we get called to. Factory fires can cover acres. But whatever the size of the fire, rigour is the key. It's counter-intuitive, I know, but I'll actually start from the point that's furthest from where we believe the seat of the fire to be, and excavate it meticulously, bit by tiny bit.' He held up a hand-trowel, no more than six inches long.

'With that?' said Jesson.

Docherty feigned hurt. 'Size isn't everything. Sure, it'll be a long job, but it will be thorough.'

'And what are you looking for?' asked Jesson.

'Every fire creates a pattern based on the structure and avail-ability of fuel. My job is to reconstruct the sequence backwards from when the fire started, to establish how exactly it started. We take a scientific approach, setting out to prove that the fire was started deliberately and testing the evidence within a radius of error. That way if there is a criminal offence that goes to court, I know I'll have addressed any factors the defence could throw at us. It's a bit like archaeology in that sense.' Docherty was in his element, Jesson gazing at him with something close to admiration, and Mariner wasn't sure who was enjoying this conversation more.

'You've talked to Mrs Shah?' Docherty asked Mariner, who deferred to Jesson.

'Yes, and her initial reaction is that the fire was a deliberate attack,' she said.

'She may be right,' said Docherty. 'But it's too soon for me to confirm that.'

'She reports hearing a crashing noise that might have woken her,' Jesson said. 'Someone breaking a window maybe?'

'It's possible,' said Docherty. He walked them over to the ground-floor windows, blackened and broken, the UPVC frames almost buckled beyond recognition. 'Some of these have shattered in the fire.' He ran his finger along one, close to what remained of one of the window panes. 'These wavy lines suggest thermal cracking, caused by the heat. What Mrs Shah might have heard was them being blown out. We'll keep it in mind, though, and see what else we come up with. All I can say for certain at this stage is that the seat of the fire was somewhere in that downstairs room.' He indicated the converted garage. 'But it's going to take time to wade through all the debris in there.'

'We should leave you to get on then,' said Mariner.

Docherty nodded. 'I'll let you know when I can walk you round the least damaged areas.'

'He seems to know what he's talking about,' said Jesson, as she and Mariner walked back to their car.

'Yes,' Mariner agreed. 'We may not get answers very quickly, but I think we'll be able to rely on their accuracy. Nice-looking bloke too, isn't he?' he added, watching Jesson turn an interesting shade of pink.

'I didn't really notice,' she lied.

By the time Mariner got home that evening it was late, but before doing anything else, he called Suzy. 'How was the first day?'

'Good.' She sounded upbeat. 'Except that I already feel so

old. Most of the other researchers are in their mid-twenties and straight out of university.'

'Well, they're probably there because they can't get proper jobs,' said Mariner.

'Charming,' said Suzy, affronted.

'You know what I mean.'

'Yes, I suppose I do,' she conceded.

'So are you managing to cope with all these bright young things?'

'Actually, most of them are frighteningly capable,' said Suzy. 'And certainly full of self-confidence. I don't think I was so sure of myself at that age. But some of them are quite sweet. And thank God for Rosalind.'

'Rosalind?'

'The only member of the team who's anywhere near my age, who I have something in common with, and who isn't surgically attached to a smart phone. She's lovely, though unfortunately only part-time – she cares for her husband who has some kind of illness – but on the days she is around she will be a breath of fresh air. How did you get on with Manor Park?'

Mariner told her about the letter that had arrived that morning.

'So your fears about Manor Park were unfounded,' she said.

'Yes, now we just need to find out what's wrong with Jamie,' said Mariner. 'It's funny. Jamie's never ill and it's never really occurred to me that he would be.'

SEVEN

On Tuesday morning Mariner and Jesson returned to the Queen Elizabeth hospital, this time to the basement, for the post-mortem on what remained of Soltan Ahmed. It seemed to Mariner that he spent an inordinate amount of time in this mortuary, and by now he had his own routine for getting ready. Stuart Croghan was there waiting for them. The body on the gurney was not a pretty sight, as there was not much of the old man left, and though the overwhelming smell of the examining room was chemical, Mariner thought he could also detect another more human odour, real or imagined, through his surgical mask. 'So what's the story?' he asked.

'Very little that you hadn't already worked out for yourself,' said Croghan. 'Mr Ahmed died of smoke inhalation and suffered multiple burns; in that order, which may be some small consolation for the family. The old man's dental records check out – he is who we think he is, which always helps.' Croghan picked up a clipboard. 'Toxicology is likely to be inconclusive, but we might get some trace elements. I'll do what I can. I understand he'd been unwell and was taking over-the-counter medication to help him sleep.'

Jesson confirmed that, and when he'd shown them what he could from the body, Croghan took them over to the scene photographs, so that they could see how the body was found; Ahmed appeared to still be lying in his bed, which had half fallen between the two floors, coming to rest on the huge pile of material below. 'That he was still in bed might not mean anything,' said Croghan. 'If the smoke got to him first he wouldn't have had the chance to move.'

'The family are pressurising us to release the body,' said Mariner. 'They want him taken back to the Yemen for the proper funeral service as soon as possible.'

'Of course,' said Croghan. 'As far as I'm concerned there's no reason why we shouldn't let him go. We're unlikely to find

anything in the examination of Soltan Ahmed that's going to tell
you who or what started that fire. I'm afraid you're going to have
to find the answer to that at Wellington Road.'

And now they could start; when they got outside into the fresh
air Mariner found a couple of missed calls from Gerry Docherty
to say that they could make their initial tour of the house. Thanks
to this small step forward, Docherty was in good humour today
as he equipped them with gloves, overshoes and safety helmets,
taking extra care in checking Vicky's, before they went in to the
blackened shell that had once been a family home. Mariner had
been inside many of these houses before; there were whole streets
of them across the city and their porches often featured stained
glass and ornate tiles, but here any kind of decorative extravagance had been obliterated by the flames. It may just have
been his imagination, but Mariner even thought he could still
feel a slight heat coming off the walls.

'The crew had to force entry,' Docherty told them, pausing
at what was left of the solid wood door, which now hung limply
from its hinges. 'It was locked from the inside as you'd expect.'
As they stepped into the hall everywhere was charred black,
reminding Mariner of a badly painted fairground ride, and what
remained of the carpets squelched underfoot, sodden by the
thousands of gallons of water pumped in via high-pressure hoses.
White artificial light was cast by arc lights and they bypassed
a couple of forensic technicians, white-suited and almost
entirely hidden behind their masks and goggles, going about
their work.

Part way into the hall, Docherty opened the door to an under-
stairs cupboard: 'And here we start with something interesting
already,' he said. The beam of his torch picked up the electricity
mains fuse box and meter. 'One of the first priorities when we
get in is to isolate the electrics, but this is a real Heath Robinson
set-up. The place should have been rewired years ago and there's
no evidence of any certification for the additional wiring that
was done to the garage conversion, or new bedroom, from this
junction here. I doubt that whoever did it had anything in the
way of formal qualifications, and it could even be that Mustafa
Shah did it himself. It's one of the first things you'll want to ask
him about when he gets back.'

'So it's possible that we could be looking at an accident?' said Mariner.

'Thanks to this little lot, I wouldn't want to rule it out,' said Docherty. 'The downstairs room seems to have been crammed with papers, and if there was a source of ventilation, however small, an electrical overload could easily have smouldered then caught.' Ignoring the door to the garage conversion, he walked them further into the hallway, where they came to a remarkable delineation. The rooms at the back of the house, and to the right, seemed to have been barely touched by the fire. Jesson commented on it.

'It's not uncommon,' said Docherty. 'A fire's always going to burn upwards, unless there's something in the way to block or divert its path.' From there, he led the way up the smoke-stained stairs, the walls slick with foam residue, to the first floor and a fire door that opened on to the bedroom. It had a brass handle; the one that had seared into Salwa Shah's palm. With a gloved hand, Docherty pushed it open and they over-looked the devastation that was what remained of the bedroom immediately over the garage. The floor had gone, but such was the density of material in the room underneath, the collapsed debris had not travelled far. They could have stepped out and walked across the sooty roof tiles that littered the surface, finding their way by the eerie daylight breaking through the gaping holes in the roof. To one side, the melted edge of a synthetic carpet hung over charcoal stumps of floorboards and the smell up here was the bitter stench of melted plastic. 'The old man was sleeping up here, but we recovered his body from over there, where those markers have been placed,' Docherty told them. 'We can only hope that he didn't know much about it.'

'According to the pathologist the smoke got to him first,' said Mariner.

'Well that's something,' said Docherty.

'Mrs Shah tried to open the bedroom door to get to her father,' Jesson told him.

'Even if she'd got to him, I doubt she'd have stood a chance,' said Docherty. 'Apart from the fire itself, it would have been pitch black and thick with smoke.'

Jesson nodded. 'So she did the only sensible thing and got her children out.'

'They escaped through the back bedroom window along here,' said Docherty. Closing the door on the ruin, he took them along to a soot-smeared door, which opened on to the back bedroom, the room that Mariner had entered on Saturday night. Apart from the smell, which was already in their nostrils, and partial muddy footprints, the room had hardly been touched by the fire, the carpet still cluttered by kids' toys, one of which Mariner remembered kicking across the floor. 'Mrs Shah was in here with Yousef and Athmar, safely behind this, when the fire started.' Docherty knocked hard on the fire door, his knuckles leaving a row of smudged prints.

'The boy had been having nightmares,' said Jesson. 'So his mum was in the habit of sitting with him while he went off to sleep and she'd fallen asleep beside him.'

'Lucky for her that she did,' said Docherty. 'It meant they could quite easily get to safety.'

While they were there, Docherty took them on a brief tour of the rest of the house. The parents' room, like the children's bedroom and the bathroom, was relatively untouched by the fire, and the bathroom was disconcertingly clean. Docherty had nothing more for them at this stage. He would carry on with his painstaking work. Meanwhile the witness statements and fire-fighter statements would help start to build the narrative of what had gone on here on the night of the fire.

Restricted duties often meant a late start in the mornings, but Mariner was reassured to see Brown already at his desk, working, when he and Jesson arrived. The next thing he observed was that the constable was not in uniform, but wearing just a white T-shirt. He wondered if one of Brown's health issues included a clothing allergy. It wasn't entirely unheard of. He'd once come across an officer confined to desk duties because he couldn't wear a hat. He was about to open his mouth to ask about this, when he noticed the regulation shirt lightly steaming on the nearby radiator.

Brown blinked. 'Bit of an accident with a coffee mug,' he explained.

'Jesus wept,' said Mariner, hastily retrieving his own freshly brewed tea from the edge of Brown's desk and placing it out of harm's way on the window sill. 'What have you got for us?' he asked, as Vicky rolled up her office chair to join them. Brown turned back to his screen. 'The fire was called in at one twenty-two a.m. by Mrs Putnam at 163 Wellington Road. Do you want to hear the 999? It's pretty standard stuff.'

'Not right now then,' said Mariner.

'When the fire service got there they found the fire had taken hold and acted straight away to extinguish it. Salwa Shah and the kids were found in the back garden, with a DCI Tom Mariner, who had helped them to safety.'

Mariner tried to discern any mockery in Brown's voice, but couldn't.

'Mrs Shah was in a state about her father, still inside the building, and had serious burns to her right hand, from where she had attempted to reach him. An attempt by DCI Mariner had also been unsuccessful. The fire crew now deemed the building unsafe, and no more rescue attempts could be made. Although after one in the morning, Mrs Shah was wearing everyday clothes.'

'Which she explained by saying she had fallen asleep in the children's room earlier that evening,' said Mariner. 'It's in my notes from the interview yesterday.'

'Firefighters had things under control by two-forty a.m.,' Brown continued. 'Apart from our man in the hoodie, yet to be identified, no one else has been reported as behaving suspiciously in the area before or during the fire. And all the onlookers our guys spoke to appear to have been neighbours, coming to be nosy. According to everyone along the street we've spoken to so far, the Shahs are a "nice family".'

'Mrs Shah told us they'd previously been the target—' Jesson began.

'Yes, previous incidents, I was coming to that,' said Brown, pushing up his glasses. 'I had a few spare minutes, so I trawled back through incident reports for anything linked with Wellington Road. Soon after the Shahs moved in, there were a couple of what were logged as racist incidents. But the trouble seems to have died down since a particular family moved out of the neighbourhood.'

'What exactly are we talking about?' asked Mariner.

'There were complaints of verbal abuse made by the Shahs in July and September last year, but by far the most serious is what looked like a thwarted arson attack in October. The Shahs heard noises at around midnight on the twenty-seventh, and it seemed that an attempt had been made to start a fire in their porch. Because the floor is tiled and there was nothing in there to ignite, it fizzled out before any damage was done. A couple of suspects were brought in for questioning, and the main person under suspicion was Jordan Wright, a nineteen-year-old who lived a little further along the street, due to a dispute between him and Mr Ahmed, though it wasn't clear what this had been about. Wright had an alibi for the night in question, and as there was no other evidence, like the fire, it didn't go anywhere.' Despite initial impressions, the constable seemed to have achieved a lot in a relatively short time.

'That's a good start, well done,' said Mariner.

Brown blinked at him. He looked as if no one had ever said that to him before and he didn't quite know what to do with it. 'It might just be worth seeing what the Wrights were up to last Saturday night,' he said. 'I'm trying to find out about insurance policies. And—' He hesitated.

'Yes?'

'I'm guessing that you'll want confirmation that Mustafa Shah was out of the country?' said Brown. 'If we can get the dates, I can request the flight manifests.'

'Shit, yes, I should have asked Salwa about that,' said Jesson. 'I'll give her a call.'

It had been a long day. Mariner's head was pounding and even after an afternoon in the office, catching up with paperwork, the residue of smoke damage still lingered in his throat and nostrils and clung to his clothes when he got home. He needed something to eat and then an early night, but first a shower. As he stepped under the jet of water he was vaguely aware of chiming in the background and he emerged some time later to hear his mobile going again. By the time he located it, the ringing had stopped, but he saw that there were four missed calls all from the same unfamiliar number. He returned it, hoping somebody wasn't about to try selling him solar panels.

'Hello,' he said cautiously. 'I believe you've tried to call me?'

'Is that Tom?' It was a woman's voice, relieved.

'Yes . . .'

'This is Gaby Boswell. We met at Charles and Helen's party on Saturday, and at the site—'

'I remember,' said Mariner. 'How did you get this number?' he asked, more irritably than he'd intended.

'You gave it to me,' she reminded him. 'It was on the card with your girlfriend's email address?'

Of course it was. 'So what can I do for you?' Mariner asked, towelling his hair.

'I'm sure it's nothing,' she said. 'It's just that Sam's sister Fiona suggested we ought to do something. If Charles wasn't away I would have talked to him.'

'Why is that?'

'It's Sam, my fiancé. He seems to have disappeared.'

'OK.' Mariner stopped towelling. 'When did you last see him?'

'Same as you. On Saturday afternoon when we were leaving Charles and Helen's celebration. We said goodbye and I went home with Dad. I haven't seen him since.'

'Where did Sam go from Charlie's house?' asked Mariner, remembering how he'd been that afternoon and the apparent tension between future father- and son-in-law.

'He was going to our house; the one we're moving into after we're married. The bedrooms are almost finished so he went to start sorting out the furniture. We bought some flat-pack stuff and he was going to assemble it. Dad's men would have done it as part of the refurb, but Sam insisted on doing it himself. Some man thing about getting more involved, I think. So he went off there and I went home with Dad.' She was talking fast, not pausing to draw breath.

'And how did Sam seem?' asked Mariner, keeping it light.

'Fine,' Gaby told him. 'I think he was quite looking forward to it. I mean, it gets a bit frustrating at times; you know what that stuff can be like to put together—'

'I do,' said Mariner with feeling, unconsciously rubbing a finger over the puncture wound in his right thumb. 'And that's the last time you saw Sam?'

'Yes,' she said. 'He was going to do the shelves and then go back to his place.'

'You didn't think of going with him, staying the night?' Mariner asked, thinking that's surely what most young couples would be tempted to do.

'No.' A hint of defensiveness crept into her voice. 'I know it's not fashionable, but we're waiting until after we're married.'

'And you're both happy with that arrangement?' Mariner asked.

'Of course.' So firm was her conviction, the question seemed to surprise her. 'It's the right thing to do. Anyway, I wasn't feeling too well.'

'And that's the last contact you had with Sam, when you both left Charlie's?'

'No, he texted me at about eleven, to say goodnight, like he always does,' she said.

'And where was he then?' asked Mariner.

'He was just leaving the house to go back to his flat. I reminded him to set the burglar alarm.'

So they couldn't be sure that he'd got home. 'Have you checked with anyone else who might have seen Sam after that?' Mariner asked.

'Everyone I can think of,' said Gaby. 'And nobody has. That's why I'm worried. I've been to his place and he isn't there and nor is his car. He has to park on the street, but there are several regular spots where he would normally leave it, and it's not in any of them. And he hasn't turned up to work, which is really unlike him.'

'What sort of car does he drive?' Mariner asked. While they were talking he'd had found a pen, retrieved an old envelope out of the bin and had begun to jot things down.

'It's a dark grey Vauxhall Astra Sport. And the number plates are distinctive: SAM 51. I gave them to him for his birthday.' Mariner wrote it down. 'And it has a bike rack on top, for when he's doing competitions.'

'Competitions?'

'He does triathlons.'

If Sam was missing, from the last time she'd had contact it was less than seventy-two hours; way too soon to take any kind of official action for a mature, responsible adult. But Mariner had a gut feeling that this one wasn't about to go away, especially given the link with Charlie. 'When is it that you're getting married?' he asked.

'The weekend after next.'

Mariner tried to be tactful. 'Is it possible that Sam might just want some time to himself before the big event?'

'What do you mean?' asked Gaby.

'Well, marriage is a big life change,' Mariner said, thinking that Vicky Jesson would have handled this so much better.

'Are you suggesting he's having second thoughts?' She sounded prickly. Point proven.

'Not at all,' Mariner hedged. 'I was just wondering if perhaps he needed a bit of space.'

'We don't live in each other's pockets,' Gaby retorted. 'He goes out with his own friends and so do I. And he has his space, on the weekends when he works away.' It sounded rehearsed, like ground that had been covered before and Mariner wondered if it was a contentious area. He was about to point out that working away is not quite the same thing, when she continued: 'Anyway, if there was any problem, he would have talked to his Guiding Light about it, and he hasn't.'

'His Guiding Light?'

'All the young people in church, when they embark on long-term relationships, have a nominated Guiding Light,' said Gaby. 'Sam's is Laurie, one of the elders of the church. If there was anything wrong, he'd be the first person Sam would talk to, but I've checked and Laurie hasn't seen him either.'

Mariner couldn't help thinking that having all these people watching over him might be the very reason Sam had felt the need to get away. But Gaby was clearly anxious and he felt some responsibility towards her, or at least to Charlie. 'All right,' he said. 'I'm going to text you my office email address. Send me the contact details of Sam's workplace, his family and any other friends you think he could get in touch with, and I'll make a few enquiries. A recent photo would help too. But I'd try not to worry. Getting married is a big thing. It really just may just be that Sam needs a bit of time to himself. You said that your sister-in-law suggested you contact us?'

'Yes, that's right.'

'Could you give me a contact number for her now?'

'Of course.'

It was just before seven, so it didn't seem unreasonable for Mariner to ring and speak to Fiona Fleetwood straight away. There was a lot to do tomorrow and he wouldn't have much spare time. Given that Fiona had prompted the call to him, he wanted to check if she knew anything Gaby wasn't telling him. He preferred to identify himself face-to-face and she agreed immediately that he could come out and talk to her. 'I just want to know where Sam is, and that he's safe,' she said, giving him her address.

Fiona Fleetwood lived in a modest two-up-two-down terraced house in what used to be a fashionable part of Moseley. The interior had a 'new age' feel to it, Indian print throws brightening up shabby furniture, and Mariner had to duck his head to avoid the numerous wind chimes and dream catchers dangling from door frames. The underlying hint of sandalwood evoked a powerful memory of his grandparents' house, where he'd grown up.

In terms of physical attributes there were certain similarities between Fiona and her future sister-in-law: she was well built, with fair hair, but she was taller and less well groomed, her complexion suggesting a harder life. She looked to be in her early forties, so she was older than Sam.

'Would you like a drink?' She made tea and Mariner sat on a sofa next to bookshelves to rival Suzy's, though the titles here all appeared to feature 'mindfulness' or 'karma'.

Fiona dropped on to a giant bean bag and lit up a herbal cigarette. 'You're not asthmatic or anything, are you?'

'No. You suggested Gaby should get in touch with us?' Mariner said.

'Yes.' She plucked a stray tobacco strand from her lip. 'I had an important meeting with social care this morning, about our mum. I knew that Sam wouldn't be able to come along, he rarely can because of work, but I was surprised that he didn't at least call me afterwards to find out how it went. He's always utterly reliable at remembering stuff like that, and it has implications for both of us too, in terms of how much we're going to have to pay towards Mum's care. At the moment she's in sheltered housing, but she can no longer move around independently and needs more support, so she'll have to move to a nursing home. I've been trying Sam on his mobile all day, but there's no reply. When I called his office they said he hadn't turned up for work, yesterday or today. They didn't seem that worried, but it's so unlike Sam and I can't understand where he would be. That's when I called Gaby.'

'Sam is a grown man,' Mariner pointed out.

'I know, but he's my baby brother so I have to look out for him, and this is so completely out of character. It's just— it doesn't feel right,' she concluded.

People were reported missing all the time, often too soon, and often by relatives overreacting to a falling out of some kind. But with Fiona Fleetwood, Mariner didn't get the impression of a hysterical woman. Quite the opposite, in fact. 'How has Sam seemed lately?' he asked.

'I hardly ever see him,' she said. 'Not properly, anyway. He's too busy planning the wedding and his future life; he has to dance to someone else's tune now.' Although pointed, the remark appeared to be without rancour. 'Any conversations we have these days tend to be on the phone, and then it's only really to discuss Mum. We've never been massively close, mainly because of the age gap, but now I don't really fit in with his new spiritual life and friends either.'

'So the church hasn't always been important to Sam?' said Mariner.

'God, no,' said Fiona. 'That all started when he met Gaby. But I can't deny that it's helped him. Sam has always had a restless streak. Our dad walked out when he was only seven. It was hard for him; old enough to know what was going on, but too young to manage the emotions, so I think Sam suppressed them. He's got more introspective as he's got older.'

'Is he prone to depression at all?'

'No.' She was unequivocal. 'I know what you're thinking, but Sam's not like that. It's more as if he's been searching for something.'

'And Christianity fits the bill?' said Mariner.

'Seems to – especially when it comes with an attractive and wealthy girlfriend attached.' Her smile was wry. 'But Sam wouldn't be going into marriage lightly. I'm glad for him.'

'How long have he and Gaby been together?'

'I suppose it must be about eighteen months or so.'

It didn't seem that long to Mariner. 'Do you know how they met?' he asked.

'At a club, I think.'

'So not at the church?'

Fiona laughed. 'Oh no, that came later.'

'And you don't have any idea where Sam might have gone?' Mariner asked her. 'Friends he might be staying with, anything like that?'

'No, and nor did Little Miss Perfect have any ideas.'

Mariner raised an eyebrow.

'I know. She's really quite sweet, but you must have seen how much her dad dotes on her. Anything Gaby wants, Gaby gets. Anyway, we both think it's just odd for Sam to go so completely off the radar, which is why I thought we should do something. When Gaby said she knew a policeman, it seemed the ideal solution.' She frowned, trying to work it out. 'How is it you know her?'

'Oh, I don't,' explained Mariner. 'We just happened to meet at the weekend. The friend she was talking about goes to her church, but he's away on leave, so I've stepped in. Am I to take it that you don't get on with Gaby?'

'Let's just say we don't have much in common,' she said. 'But I'm sure you had already worked that out for yourself. Apart from anything else, I'm an abomination in the eyes of the Lord.' She caught Mariner's blank look and said it as the penny dropped. 'I'm a lesbian.'

'I've asked Gaby to send me contact details for anyone she can think of who might know where Sam is. Perhaps you could do the same? I know there will be some overlap, but hopefully between the two of you I'll have a comprehensive list.'

On his way out Mariner passed a number of old framed photos displayed on the wall, their colours faded. They featured two children, one pre-adolescent, the other about five or six. In all of them the younger child had a teddy tucked under his arm, including one in which he was comically dressed in an oversized jacket and an old lady's felt hat, with what looked like a feather boa draped around his neck.

Fiona smiled. 'Yes, that's Sam,' she confirmed, amused by the captured memory. 'From before Dad left. He was such a little character back then.'

By the time Mariner had driven home again he saw that two lists of names and phone numbers had already appeared in his email inbox.

EIGHT

Vicky Jesson made it in early on Wednesday morning and was feeling virtuous until she got to CID and saw Brown already at his work station, glued to his computer screen. 'God, you're keen, aren't you?' she said, dumping her bag beside her desk.

'Nothing wrong with that, is there?' he said, without looking up.

Jesson walked over. 'I didn't mean anything by it,' she said.

'Sorry, it's just . . .' He shrugged, but kept his eyes fixed on the screen.

'Pete Stone's an arse,' Jesson told him. 'We're not like that up here. Anything new come up?'

'Not much,' said Brown. 'Nothing more from the Fire Investigation team, and I'm still trying to track down any insurance policies the Shahs had. Something interesting with Mustafa Shah's bank account, though,' he added. 'He drew out ten thousand quid in cash, about a—'

He was interrupted by a knock on the door. 'Anyone home?' They looked up to see a young Asian woman, walking hesitantly towards them.

'Millie! Thank God!' said Jesson. 'How are you?' She jumped up and went to meet her returning colleague. 'How's Haroon?'

'He's great,' said Millie with a sigh. 'Outgrowing everything. It's been tough leaving him, though.' She forced a smile.

Vicky pulled a sympathetic face. 'I know, but it will get easier, I promise. I remember it well. But we're *so* glad to see you. It's about time for a cuppa, do you want one?'

'I'll get them,' said Brown, getting up from his desk.

'Oh, this is our newest recruit,' said Vicky, making the introductions.

'And this is it?' said Millie, looking around the office, where there were just a couple of other support staff and Max, the IT specialist.

'While Charlie's away, yes,' said Vicky.

'And is the boss about?' Millie asked. But the noisy welcome must have found its way to Mariner's office because there he was, coming in to give Millie a hug. A HUG. Vicky had to stop herself from staring. Word had it that back in the day Mariner and Millie had a thing going, and this seemed to add a bit more fuel to the rumour.

'What about this fire?' said Millie, keen to get started. 'You want me to cover family liaison?' Brown had returned with tea, and she took the mug from him with a nod of thanks.

'No, there's something else I need you to look into,' Mariner said. 'Come with me.' And he headed back towards his office, Millie following on. Jesson watched them go.

'New kid on the block,' observed Brown.

'And you can shut up,' said Jesson.

'We're a bit thin on the ground, as you'll have noticed,' Mariner said to Millie, when they were seated in his office. 'And PC Brown, as you'll soon find out, seems to have relocated from the Keystone Cops, although I have to admit he seems to be doing all right with the collation so far. But something else has come up, as of yesterday evening, that no one else knows about yet; a possible MisPer.'

'Sounds intriguing,' said Millie.

He explained Gaby and Fiona's concerns to her. 'There may be nothing in it,' he said. 'The poor bloke's probably taking some time out. But given the connection with Charlie, I feel obliged to at least make some initial enquiries, and I know I can rely on you to do a thorough and discreet job on his behalf. I've scribbled down some stuff from the conversations I've already had with Sam Fleetwood's sister and fiancée. Between them, they've raised the alarm.' He gathered together the various scraps of paper that littered his desk; printed lists of the contact details and some handwritten notes.

'Scribbled being the operative,' Millie said, already casting an eye over the hieroglyphics on the back of what looked like an old utilities envelope. She came to the photo of Sam that Gaby had emailed through. 'Hm, attractive bloke,' she said. 'The original tall, dark and handsome. He could be a model.' She looked up at Mariner. 'So this isn't official,' she said, understanding at once.

'It's informal and low key,' said Mariner, 'until we've established – if we do – that Sam Fleetwood has gone missing unwillingly. The impressions I had, in the short time I saw them, were that his future wife, Gaby, and her father, are used to getting what they want. His father-in-law is putting pressure on for him to join the family business. What with that and the church, which clearly has a big influence, I could imagine it all getting a bit claustrophobic for Sam. It would also be helpful to find out from friends and acquaintances if there's any chance that he could have been having second thoughts about this wedding altogether. It seems to me that there are one or two reasons why he might.'

'And if I manage to find him?' Millie asked.

'Make cautious contact and let him know that family and friends are concerned,' said Mariner. 'They just want to know that he is safe and well. And let me know too. If you need someone else on the legwork, you can try twisting Inspector Stone's arm, but don't hold your breath.'

Millie got up to go. 'This fire's a nasty thing,' she said. 'Any idea what caused it?'

Mariner shook his head. 'Still waiting for Fire Investigation to do their bit. We've had some delays, but it's probably time to check in with them again.' He lifted his coat from the hook on the wall and they walked out of the office together. 'Keep me informed, eh?'

It seemed to Mariner that Vicky Jesson was looking forward to the morning briefing at Wellington Road, and he was pretty sure it had nothing to do with him or the fire. The scene had changed subtly since the last time they were here, as Gerry Docherty and his team started to get to grips with the job. Chunks of blackened timber and upholstery, with a hint here and there of the colours they had once been, were starting to appear on the front lawn, seemingly in random fashion, but Mariner knew that each would have been examined, catalogued and carefully placed. This morning he and Jesson were to be allowed in to the exact location for the first time. 'We've a long way to go,' said Docherty cheerfully. 'But come and see what progress we're making.'

Putting on forensic suits this time, along with their hard hats, Mariner and Jesson followed Docherty into the house. This time he stopped at the doorway to their left; the front ground-floor room that looked out on to the street and ran the depth of the house, front to back. They couldn't go in very far, the pile of charcoaled debris so high that it obscured the windows front and back. Sheets of tarpaulin had been laid across the exposed roof as protection against the weather, so arc lamps provided the only light. 'The room was chock full of stuff anyway, and then we've got to try and differentiate the material that has come in from above,' said Docherty. From this angle it was impossible to see that there had once been a bedroom up there. The only remnant visible, now that some of the surface debris had been shifted, was the flimsy metal bed frame, tipping over the edge, with the molten lump of mattress stuck to it. The place where Soltan Ahmed had died.

'I haven't changed my opinion that this room is where it all kicked off,' Docherty continued. He pointed to black conical patterning on the wall, the apexes at floor level, which confirmed the supposition. 'I understand the family used it as a kind of office-cum-store room, so it was piled up with stacks of documents, some of them loose, the rest in cardboard boxes. It would have formed a massive fuel-load, so once the fire took hold, the intensity would have been immense. The old man wouldn't have stood a chance.'

'This room is easily accessible, front and back, from the road,' Mariner observed.

'Which opens the way for a possible arson attack,' said Docherty. 'But until we've gone through this little lot,' he indicated the debris, 'I don't want to rule anything out just yet. Come and take a look at this.'

He led them through to the kitchen, which seemed to have become a temporary evidence collection point, where various artefacts were being bagged for further examination. 'Underneath the crap in this corner we found this.' He picked up a plastic forensic bag, inside which was what looked like a molten plastic spider, with spikes sprouting from it at all angles.

'What is it?' asked Jesson.

'It was,' said Docherty, 'a multi-socket extension. They seem to have been running a number of appliances off it, though we haven't identified exactly what yet. Again, it could have easily set things off.'

'So we're back to accident again?'

'Right now, your guess is as good as mine,' said Docherty.

Emerging from the house, Mariner found a couple of missed calls on his mobile. Leaving Vicky talking to Docherty, while she peeled off her forensic gear, he walked a little way down the street to return them. It was Nell at Manor Park. 'Jamie's got appointments for tests at the QE tomorrow, first thing,' she said.

Mariner suppressed a ripple of anxiety. That was quick, so someone was taking it seriously. 'How will it work?' he asked Nell.

'They'll have him in for most of the day, I think, while the tests are being done,' said Nell. 'One of us will go with him – hopefully me – but of course it would be great if you could come along too.'

Tomorrow morning. It was sudden, and not at all the best time for Mariner to absent himself from the fire investigation, but did at least give him the rest of today to put things in place. 'Thanks,' he said. 'I'll see you there.'

DC Millie Khatoon was in pursuit of Sam Fleetwood and his car. As Mariner had suggested, she phoned down to uniform to ask about getting some help, but got short shrift from Pete Stone. 'We don't run a staffing agency down here,' he said. 'Tom Mariner's already got one of my officers, I can't spare any more.'

'Charming,' said Millie, replacing the phone.

'It's what he does best,' said Brown, from behind her. 'Anything I can do?'

'Haven't you got enough on your plate?' said Millie.

'I'm pretty much up to speed.'

'Well, if you're sure then. Can you ring round the local hospitals, see if they've admitted a Sam Fleetwood in the last few days?' She gave Brown the description. 'Let me know straight away if you get anything, will you? Wild goose chases are not really my thing.'

Mariner had asked Gaby to drop in the keys for the marital home and her key to Sam's flat first thing that morning at Granville Lane, and by nine thirty Millie had received a call to say they were there. So, after familiarising herself with Mariner's background notes – in itself quite a task thanks to his appalling handwriting; he'd clearly missed his vocation as a doctor – she decided the best place to start was Fleetwood's flat.

Alone in the car, without Haroon, Millie felt horribly empty, and the sluggish traffic gave her more than enough time to think about what her baby son might be doing right now. Napping? Playing with his Amma? Picturing his chubby little face, a surge of panic threatened to surface. What if he did something new today, while she was away from him? He'd been edging towards crawling for a while now. Stop it! she told herself. If he did, then it would be lovely for his grandparents to have that experience, and it was a small price to pay for them taking on most of the childcare while she and Suli were at work.

It was only natural that she would have doubts about coming back. Millie was well aware of how lucky she was. She had choices. Suli had fully supported her return to work, but he'd also be delighted if she said it had been a mistake, and she wanted to stay at home to care for Haroon. Finances would be a bit tight, but they'd managed so far and Suli's recent promotion had helped. Much of this insecurity, Millie knew, was the strangeness of being back here again. In some ways it felt as if she had never been away, but much had changed while she'd been off, and she missed having Tony Knox and Charlie around. She was apprehensive too about this first assignment. Would she still be up to it? Would she remember to cover all the bases? Most of all, she had to keep reminding herself that at this stage Sam Fleetwood was only a *potential* MisPer. All she needed to do was try to establish if he had got himself into any kind of trouble.

Sam's flat took up the attic space in a converted Victorian house in the less fashionable part of Edgbaston, close to its boundary with Ladywood, one of the most deprived localities in the country. Since the redevelopment of the city centre this was no longer a popular area for young professionals, so prices would be low. There was no off-road parking, so Fleetwood would have to compete with the dozens of other local residents for a kerbside spot. Before going into the building, Millie walked the length of the street in both directions, then took a series of left turns that took her in a circuit around the block, including a couple of plots of off-road parking. But there was no sign of the grey Astra, at least not with the plates Mariner had described. It wasn't entirely conclusive; Fleetwood might have just parked further away, and if he wanted to hide his car it would be simple enough, but there was no way that Millie could carry out an exhaustive search on her own.

Frustrated already, she used Gaby's keys to let herself into the building and climbed up the three narrow flights of stairs to the flat. Unlocking the door, she tentatively called out before going in, but could tell right away that it was empty. It was small and compact; living room, bedroom, bathroom and tiny kitchen, all visible from the doorway. Although the furniture was dated, it was all very squeaky clean for a bachelor pad. Millie glanced around her at rooms that were scrupulously tidy. In the kitchen the bins had been emptied and the washing up done. 'It's not completely unheard of for a bloke to be tidy, is it?' she remembered Mariner saying to her once. His tendency to orderliness was legendary. It didn't on the other hand look as if Sam Fleetwood had gone anywhere unexpectedly or in a hurry. There were two possibilities: either Sam always left the flat like this when he went out, or this indicated preparation for not coming back. She'd be able to make a better assessment of that when she knew more about what his habits were.

The bed was made, in that the duvet had been thrown back across it, and the cupboard doors and drawers were closed. There were clothes in the wardrobe, but not many, which may simply indicate that Sam Fleetwood wasn't into fashion. She'd need to find that out from Gaby. More significantly, there was no PC or laptop and no phone, though to make sure she tried the mobile number Mariner had given her. It rang out, but went unanswered.

There were few other personal belongings; the bathroom yielded an electric toothbrush and a couple of disposable razors, both of which would be cheap and easy enough to pick up elsewhere. But, if he had gone AWOL, there was nothing Millie could find here that gave any clue about where Sam Fleetwood might be. She sifted through a collection of personal papers and bills in a drawer. None of them was particularly recent, and they were interspersed with old postcards, a handful of birthday cards and two Valentine cards. Anonymous, of course, but while

one was tasteful and romantic, the other was much more senti-
mental, and the style of handwriting in each was quite different.
Millie took out the envelope that had contained the keys, on
which Gaby Boswell had written: *FAO Detective Inspector
Mariner*. Hers was the romantic card, without a doubt, so who
had sent the other one? Millie photographed them both, along
with the inscriptions. She found no passport. Sam would need
one of those for the honeymoon in Antigua, but perhaps it
hadn't come through yet. The passport office would be able to
tell her that.

What struck Millie as most interesting about Fleetwood's flat,
was the absence of anything to do with his fiancée. Perhaps it
just meant that they always went to Gaby's place. Millie had
seen something in Mariner's notes: *no vet before mortgage*. Of
course; that might explain it. But then, closing what she thought
was an empty drawer, she felt something shift. Opening it again,
she ran a hand around the back, where she found two items. One
was an unopened pack of three pairs of tights, in a neutral beige,
size medium. The other was a zipped make-up pouch, which
contained lipstick, mascara, a powder compact, a small perfume
spritz and a pack of plasters. Taken altogether, it was the kind
of emergency kit that a woman might keep somewhere that she
spent the weekends. Since this wasn't official, Millie wasn't
authorised to remove anything from the flat – Sam Fleetwood
could walk in at this precise moment and rightly complain if
anything was missing. So, she made a note of the details and
placed the items back where she had found them.

Millie descended the stairs just as an Asian man emerged from
the flat on the floor below. She showed him her warrant card.
'Do you know a man called Sam Fleetwood?' she asked. 'He
lives in the flat above yours.'

'Oh, is that his name?' The man turned the deadlock on his
own door. 'I know him to say hello, but that's about it. I've only
been here about a month.'

'When was the last time you saw him?' Millie asked.

'I'm not sure; a week, ten days ago maybe?'

'Do you remember seeing him at all last weekend, on Saturday
or Sunday?'

'I don't think so, but actually—' The man pocketed his keys

and checked his phone. 'I'm pretty sure I heard someone moving around up there on Sunday morning, early.'

'How early?' asked Millie.

'Maybe about eight o'clock? I was cursing him because I'm pretty sure he woke me up and it's the only day I get to lie in. Sounded like something heavy was being shifted around. But I could have been wrong about that. Noise carries in this building.' He studied her. 'Is everything all right?'

Millie smiled reassuringly. 'I was just hoping to speak to him,' she said. 'It'll keep.'

A smaller key on the fob Gaby had given her opened a mail box in the hall. Millie followed the man down the stairs, stopping off to open it up. All it contained was a number of junk flyers for pizza delivery and gardening services. If Sam Fleetwood had decided to disappear, he'd left everything in good order.

NINE

The work address that Gaby Boswell had given Mariner was an office block at Five Ways, and it made sense for Millie to go there next, as it was so near. Mariner had noted down that Sam worked as what looked to Millie like a *wanker margarine infector*; presumably not a real job. Whatever it was, it was a function of the Environment Agency, whose offices took up several floors of the rust-brown building. As his sister had said, his work colleagues had been surprised when Sam didn't turn up to work on Monday or Tuesday – it was unlike him – but they weren't unduly worried, assuming that he was ill, and it had slipped his mind, or he was too rough to phone it in.

'Not unheard of,' said his boss, Mike Figgis. 'Must happen in your line of work too, sometimes.' A man in late middle age, Figgis was tall and gangling, with a thin, rodent-like face that carried a slight sheen of perspiration. Stress-related, perhaps, as all the time they talked Figgis' eyes were scanning the room, keeping watch on what was happening. Twice he had to break off their conversation to respond to queries. The offices were almost exclusively open plan, so the conversation was conducted at one untidy end of an expanse containing about thirty work stations and the same number of staff, male and female, though no one seemed remotely interested in Millie. Picture windows overlooked the Hagley Road, their brownish tint giving it the tinge of an old sepia photograph.

Sam Fleetwood, it transpired, was a waste management inspector. 'What does his job involve?' asked Millie.

'What it says on the tin,' said Figgis. 'Conducting inspections of environmental waste facilities and monitoring them to make sure they're adhering to regulations. It wouldn't be on your radar,' he added. 'But there's such a thing as "waste crime". In 1997 a landfill tax was introduced that has to be paid at the point of disposal of any large quantities of waste. It meant that straight away some firms saw a way of making money by setting themselves up as brokers, if you like, taking and disposing of other people's rubbish, mostly from the construction or demolition industries, but for a price. They set up what we call "waste transfer stations". A lot of them are legitimate, but for the greedy ones, the way of increasing profits even further is to avoid paying the landfill tax, by simply accumulating the waste, covering it up with sand or gravel to hide it, or getting rid of it by illegal means.'

'How do they do that?' asked Millie.

'Oh, you'd be amazed the number of unexplained fires that just happen to "start up" around sites,' said Figgis. 'There are other violations too that can compromise on health and safety. They store potentially harmful stuff like asbestos incorrectly. The list goes on. Historically the whole industry has been run by people on the fringes, who don't necessarily recognise the boundaries of the law. Cowboys.'

A sudden image flashed into Millie's head, of Clint Eastwood, on horseback riding across the fields of north Worcestershire. 'Sam's fiancée hinted that he'd been a bit stressed out by work just lately,' she said, from Mariner's notes. 'Any thoughts on why that might be?'

'We're an inspectorate,' said Figgis. 'We're quite new, and not universally welcomed by the people whose businesses we regulate. We've been brought in to impose structure on a service sector that has always been a complete law unto itself. As you can imagine, we're not popular. Sam knows the rules inside out and he's thorough. Good for us, but he can sometimes be perceived as being a bit pedantic, which doesn't endear him to people.'

Here was a man who relished his job, thought Millie. 'I can't imagine they're too delighted with that,' she agreed. 'What's Sam like?'

'Solid as a rock,' said Figgis without hesitation. 'One of the most conscientious workers I've known.'

'And apart from the unexpected time off, has there been anything different about him in the last week or so?' Millie asked.

Figgis shook his head. 'Not that I noticed. He's quiet, doesn't mix much, but he turns up and does his job, and that's what counts. He's like the proverbial paperclip.'

Millie looked blank.

'Only time we notice him is when he's not here.' It sounded like a well-worn line.

'When was the last time you spoke to Sam?' she asked.

'Friday, I think it was. He's getting married soon and trying to get his new house sorted out. We talked a bit about that.'

'Anything bothering him?'

'Not that he told me,' said Figgis.

They started towards the door. 'I understand Sam's job involves him travelling widely?' said Millie.

'I wouldn't say widely,' replied Figgis. 'He's based here in the West Midlands, so most of it is local. He might occasionally have to go out as far as Shropshire or Staffordshire.'

'So how often is he required to be away at the weekend?'

Figgis frowned. 'There's no need for anyone in this department to work away for the weekend. Apart from anything else, the government wouldn't fund the expense accounts. So why are you lot involved?' he asked. 'Something going on with him that we don't know about?'

'We might not need to be involved,' said Millie. 'Sam hasn't been seen for a couple of days, so his family are concerned about where he might be. It's probably nothing. Most times people turn up again. If Sam does make it in to work, would you get him to give me a call straight away?' She gave Figgis her card.

Millie travelled down in the lift with one of the young women who had approached Figgis with a query; Zara, he had called her. 'Do you know Sam Fleetwood?' Millie asked.

Zara shook her head. 'Not really,' she said. 'It's quite a big department.'

'And what's Mike Figgis like as a boss?' She was really just making polite conversation.

'Hm,' said the girl. 'I wouldn't trust him as far as I can throw him.' She opened her mouth as if she was about to say something else.

'And . . .?' Millie said encouragingly.

But Zara shook her head. 'Nothing,' she said. 'Really. Nothing at all.' The lift came to a halt, and with a brief smile she stepped out into the foyer.

On her way back to the car Millie tried Sam's number again, but once more, no one picked up.

*   *   *

Salwa Shah and the children had been released from hospital and the family were staying at her sister-in-law's house in Sparkhill. When Mariner and Jesson located the address Salwa had given them, the house turned out to be uncannily similar to the one that had been destroyed by the fire, but lacking the garage conversion. The front door was open and a group of people had gathered on the pavement: mourners waiting their turn to say prayers with the family, as a mark of respect, something which would last for three days. It took Mariner and Jesson several minutes to work their way politely through and ascertain who was the owner of the house, and then to establish the whereabouts of Salwa Shah and convey that they needed to speak to her. Eventually, having made their presence known, they were shown into an empty front sitting room that was cool and dim, and asked to wait.

After a few minutes, Salwa and a woman she introduced as her sister-in-law, Ettra, appeared. The delay was explained by the tray Ettra carried, bearing cups of mint tea and a plate of unleavened bread, which were passed to Mariner and Jesson as if they'd been requested. Mariner was neither hungry nor thirsty, and guessed that Jesson felt the same, but refusing hospitality would have unsettled their hosts, so he smiled thanks and took a sip of the tea and bit into the dense, dry flatbread, which he had to chase around his mouth for a couple of minutes before he was in a position to speak. He was grateful to Jesson for exchanging a few pleasantries while this was going on.

'We need to talk to the children,' he said eventually, 'perhaps with their aunt here?'

'Yes, of course,' Salwa went to fetch them and they came in; Athmar shyly, sitting close to her aunt on the opposite side of the room, while Yousef bounced down on to the sofa and didn't look as if he would stay in one place for long.

'Hello again,' said Jesson, smiling warmly. 'This must be nice, staying at your auntie's house.'

'Too many people,' said Yousef, with a slight frown, already sliding off the sofa, impatient to get this over with.

'Well, we won't keep you long, we just need to ask you about the fire at your house,' Jesson went on. 'We're trying to find out how it started and there might be something important you remember that can help us with that. Is that OK?'

There wasn't much indication that Yousef had even heard her, but Athmar nodded silently, obediently.

'Are the fireman there?' asked Yousef.

'Yes, they're having a good look too, to see if they can find any clues,' Vicky told him. 'Tell me about what you did on Saturday.'

'We went to play with our cousins,' said Athmar, her voice so small at first that they had to lean in to catch everything she said. 'Then we came home, and it was just Mama and Grandpa. We had our tea and watched TV.'

'What did you watch?' asked Jesson.

'*Doctor Who* was awesome!' Yousef announced. 'He was getting attacked by the Zygons.' He was off the sofa now and acting out the drama, swiping at the air with an imaginary weapon.

'And what about later, when you went to bed?' asked Jesson. 'Did you see anything or hear anything different?'

Athmar shook her head again, and Yousef didn't appear to have even heard Jesson's question, but then he said suddenly: 'Mama woke me up and there was a funny smell. She said we had to get out of the house, so we climbed out of the window!' He gave Mariner a 'how cool was that' look.

'What kind of smell was it? You mean the smoke?' Jesson asked carefully.

'No, not like that.' Yousef wrinkled his nose. 'Like the car.'

As he spoke they all became aware of a commotion that seemed to begin outside on the street, before spreading into the house. There was a loud and prolonged, and what seemed at times heated, conversation in Arabic that Mariner and Jesson didn't understand, though Mariner thought he caught the odd English word, including the name 'Radford'. The two children were instantly alert to the disturbance, and consequently distracted from any further questions. Their aunt's reaction was more guarded.

'What's—?' Mariner was about to go and investigate, when another small child burst into the room and jabbered something in Arabic. Ettra immediately stood up, wringing her hands, her face an unreadable mixture of surprise and relief. 'It's my brother,' she said. 'He is back.'

'Good timing,' murmured Mariner, catching Jesson's eye.

Seconds later Mustafa Shah walked in, hand in hand with his wife. The two children rushed at him and he scooped them up, Yousef climbing all over him. Shah nodded an acknowledgement to Mariner and Jesson over his son's head before returning his attention to his children. After several minutes of responding to their chatter, he sent them off to play. Ettra went after them, and they didn't stop her. All the time Salwa Shah held on to her husband. She looked as if she had been crying. As the children scampered off, Mustafa Shah fully took in the presence of the two strangers. In his mid-forties, he was tall and good-looking behind rimless glasses and he wore collarless *kameez* with a cream linen suit that was creased from travelling.

'That's a great welcome,' Mariner smiled. 'How long have you been away?'

'Just a few days,' said Shah. His tone was relaxed but he was studying them carefully.

'These are police officers,' said Salwa. 'They've come to ask some questions about the fire.'

'We could come back later,' Mariner offered, being deliberately tentative; there were lots of reasons why he would prefer to proceed now.

'You should eat and get some rest,' Salwa interjected, putting her hand on her husband's arm. 'You've had such a long journey.'

'No, it's fine,' said Shah, sitting down. 'I want to know what happened; why your father died. And if there's anything I can do to help—'

'We're very sorry for your loss,' said Mariner.

'Thank you. I feel bad that I wasn't here. I keep thinking that if I had been, perhaps it wouldn't have ended this way.'

'The fire took hold very quickly and was fierce,' said Mariner. 'Even if you had been in the house it's unlikely that you would have been able to do anything more.' He didn't know if that was strictly true, but there seemed little sense in Shah berating himself for something that could not be rectified.

'I thank God that you and the children are safe,' Mustafa Shah turned to his wife. 'But I'm so sorry about your father.' He lifted his wife's bandaged hand to his lips, and her eyes filled with tears. He slipped an arm around her, hugging her close. 'Hush, I know,' he soothed.

Mariner and Jesson sat still and quiet, observing the scene, trying to remain unobtrusive. Only when he had comforted his wife did Mustafa Shah address himself to them.

Without the need for communication, there was a tacit understanding that Mariner would now take the lead in questioning. It was an assumption, but based on many years of experience, that Mustafa Shah would respond better to a male. Mariner began with more formal introductions, and he and Jesson showed their identification once again. 'We need to ask you some questions about the house,' he began. 'Did you make the alterations to the building?'

'Yes,' Shah sat back a little. 'We built the bedroom on top of the garage first of all, so that my father-in-law could come to live with us. Salwa is an only child. A little later, when we needed more space, we made the garage into an office.'

'And that was what it was used as; an office?' Mariner checked.

Shah cast a look at his wife. 'That was the idea, but it didn't quite work out like that. You know how things accumulate. We began to put more and more things in there, and so it has become a store room, and the chances of being able to work in there . . .' He let them draw their own conclusions.

'The fire investigator has said that there seemed to be mostly paper?'

'That's right,' said Shah. 'There are boxes of documents and papers, from my and my father-in-law's businesses. The premises are small, so there is nowhere to keep anything.'

'Was there anything of value?' He seemed to be taking it very calmly. 'Most people these days would have a computer—'

'We hadn't got that far,' said Shah. 'It never became a proper working space. Most of the documents brought here were no longer needed. The plan was to sort through them and destroy most of them and create an archive for any that might be important. You know how it is, I hadn't started to do that yet.'

'What kind of business are you in?' Mariner asked.

'Soon after they first came to England, Soltan and some of his friends founded the Yemeni Advice Centre in Sparkhill. Perhaps you know it? It's a kind of drop-in place for people from the Yemeni community. I qualified as an accountant so mostly I act as a financial advisor, but the nature of people's problems is very varied, so I help people with all kinds of things; often people who are newly arrived here.'

'And when you did the conversion on Wellington Road, who did the building work for you?' Mariner asked.

'My friend Adil Tariq. He is a builder by trade. In our community that is often how it works. You help a friend and he will also help you.'

'Did Mr Tariq do the wiring too?'

Shah thought for a moment. 'I think he had someone, a specialist, come in to do that.'

'Yes, you remember,' said Salwa. 'The young man.'

'The fire service found some irregularities,' said Mariner. 'The work doesn't conform to safety standards.'

Perhaps because he was tired and jet-lagged, Salwa Shah understood before her husband did. 'So the fire might have been an accident?' she said hesitantly. 'There was a problem with the electricity?'

'It's possible,' Mariner said.

Salwa said something sharply in Arabic to her husband, to which he responded equally curtly. Mariner didn't understand the words but he felt sure it was along the lines of: *I told you we should have got a proper builder.* 'We won't know for sure until the fire investigators have finished their work,' he said. 'There would have been a need for ventilation. Did you ever leave windows open in that room?'

'Not open,' said Salwa. 'But one of the windows at the back of the house, it doesn't fit properly. There is always a draught. We were going to get it fixed.'

'The more positive news,' said Mariner, 'is that we should be able to release Mr Ahmed's body quite soon.'

'Thank you.' It was Mustafa Shah who spoke but they both looked glad of that. It seemed a reasonable point at which to end the interview.

'Will you be staying here for the moment?' Mariner asked as he and Jesson stood up to leave.

'We don't have anywhere else to go,' said Mustafa Shah.

'When will we be able to go back into the house?' his wife asked. 'We need more clothes, and the children would like to have some of their toys.'

'I'm sorry,' said Mariner. 'Until we know exactly how the fire started, and can be sure about how your father died, it has to remain a crime scene. But if you can put together a list of the things you need, DS Jesson can go and get them for you.'

'I'll do it now,' said Salwa. 'You can wait a few minutes?'

'Of course,' said Mariner.

Mustafa Shah got up to go and shook hands with them before leaving the room. 'And when was it that you flew out to Sana'a?' Mariner asked, before he went.

'It was the weekend before last,' said Shah. 'The third.'

Salwa returned in just a few minutes with a list of about twenty items for Jesson to collect. 'I think that is all,' she said.

'You can always let me know if there's anything else,' said Jesson.

'But we will be able to go back eventually?' Salwa wanted to know.

'As long as the structure is safe,' said Mariner. 'But it will need a lot of work before you can use that part of the house. We need to have details of insurance policies for the property too. Can you pass them on to my officers as soon as possible?'

'That might be difficult,' said Salwa. 'The papers and the details were in the room, I think. But now he is home, my husband will be able to help. We have a good policy.'

'And is that why you had installed the new fire doors?' Mariner asked. 'Sometimes it's a requirement.'

She gave a wan smile. 'The doors in the house were in poor condition and needed to be replaced. We thought fire doors would be the best.'

'Not many people would want to go back and live in a house where a close relative has died,' said Jesson, as she and Mariner drove away a little later.

'Except the Yemen is a poor country,' said Mariner. 'I imagine the Shahs came over here with very little. They have to be pragmatic. But the installation of fire doors might also mean a recently taken out insurance policy, and that might be significant.'

TEN

Returning to her car in the Tesco car park, Millie felt the buzz of satisfaction that accompanies a restored identity, any doubts she may have had about coming back to work, all but dissipated. She was beginning to feel normal again. From Five Ways she headed back to the south of the city feeling more confident of what she had to do.

Mariner had intimated to her that the Boswells were wealthy, and nothing said it more than the house that Sam Fleetwood and his fiancée were moving into. It was an imposing detached, built of pale Peterborough brick, and in another league to Sam's tiny bachelor flat. As Mariner had warned her, it was in the process of being renovated, and still very much a work in progress judging from the three different sizes of workman's van on the drive. On this warm spring day both front door and double garage were wide open, with the sounds of construction emanating from within.

'Hello?' Millie called out as she walked into the hall, breathing in the dusty, paint-infused air. The interior had been completely gutted and replaced with all mod cons, including a sleek glass-and-oak staircase that rose up from the centre of wide hallway to a galleried landing.

A young man in overalls stomped out of one of the rooms in paint-spattered overalls and a woolly hat pulled down over wires trailing each side of his chin. 'Who's 'ad my fuckin' lighter?' he yelled at no one in particular. Seeing Millie, he stopped short.

'Hi,' she said. 'I'm looking for Sam Fleetwood?'

'Huh.' He snorted. 'Ted! When's the last time we saw the tosspot?' Without waiting for the answer, and still muttering under his breath, he clumped past her and out into the front garden, pulling a tobacco tin from his pocket as he went.

An older man popped his head out of a nearby doorway, plasterer's trowel in hand. 'All right, bab?' he said. Millie repeated the question and Ted's mouth turned down as he thought. 'Mr

Fleetwood hasn't been here for a few days. Last week sometime – Thursday, I think it was. He turned up just as we were leaving.' He ducked back behind the wall.

'Your friend doesn't seem to think much of him,' Millie observed, following him back into what turned out to be an enormous living room.

'Yeah, well, he caught Robbie smoking in here, didn't he? I told him not to, but he thought he knew better. They haven't really hit it off since then. It doesn't help that Mr Fleetwood takes it upon himself to drop by unannounced sometimes, like he's trying to catch us out.'

'This is going to be quite something,' Millie said, stepping back to admire the room. It must have been more than thirty feet deep, running from the front to the back of the house, with floor-to-ceiling windows looking out over decking and the back garden.

Ted had got back to his plastering. 'You can say that again,' he said, smoothing over a patch. 'No expense spared for the gaffer.'

'You work for Mr Boswell?' asked Millie.

'Have done for twenty-five years or more.'

'What's he like as a boss?'

'He's all right,' said Ted. 'Likes things done properly.'

'Like this?'

'Oh, especially this. She's his ray of sunshine all right. Nothing's too good for her.'

Millie walked the length of the room towards the back of the house, her shoes crackling as they stuck to the heavy-duty plastic that covered newly sanded floorboards. More polythene was wrapped around a couple of large, bulky objects; brand-new items of furniture, she deduced from the attached department store labels. The windows at the far end of the room turned out to be patio doors, partly open to let in the air, so Millie stepped outside and was startled to see what at first glance looked like a strip of snow at the bottom of the garden, before realising that it was actually the afternoon light reflecting off an expanse of water. The long lawn ran down to what was a small private lake, about the size of a couple of football pitches.

Ted must have sensed her reaction. 'Comes as a surprise, that, doesn't it?' he said.

'I had no idea it was here,' said Millie.

'Me neither, until we came to do this job,' said Ted. 'And I only live over Primrose Hill. That's a nature reserve on the other side, you know.'

Stepping off the decking, Millie walked the fifty yards or so down the lawn and looked out across the water, a tranquil wildlife oasis right in the middle of suburbia. Two-thirds of the circumference of the lake was bordered by gardens similar to this one, and a couple of the neighbouring houses even had short wooden jetties with rowing boats moored to them. On the far side, what Ted had called the nature reserve, was a wilderness of trees and reed beds. A heron stood poised on the edge of the water on one leg, watching and waiting for a vulnerable fish, and completely untroubled by Millie's presence. It crossed her mind that dredging that expanse of water would be a major operation and commitment of resources. But she was getting ahead of herself; there was no reason to think it should come to that. She went back into the house. 'I wouldn't mind that view at the end of a busy day,' she said to Ted, as she passed him and made for the staircase. 'Do you mind if I take a sneaky look while I'm here?'

'Who did you say you were, bab?' Ted stopped what he was doing.

'I'm Millie, a friend of Gaby and Sam's,' Millie said confidently. For some indefinable reason, she was reluctant to produce her warrant card in here. Instead she held up the house keys. 'Gaby gave me these and told me to have a look round if Sam wasn't about. You can give her a call if you like.'

'Nah, you're all right,' said Ted, satisfied with the explanation.

Whilst the ground floor of the house was still being worked on, upstairs looked almost finished, the polished wood floors exposed and the master bedroom complete with super king-sized bed, his and hers walk-in wardrobes, and a luxurious en suite wet room. Although bone-dry now, there were some indications that the shower cubicle might have been used, in the form of a couple of dark hairs on the edge of the plug hole.

In what looked like a spare bedroom that was set up to be an office there was a desk, an office chair and two newly constructed shelving units alongside one that was half-finished. Sam's achievements from Saturday night, perhaps.

'It's lovely,' said Millie to Ted, on her way out. 'They're a lucky pair.' It would take a certain kind of man to walk away from this little lot. But if that's what Sam Fleetwood had done, she still had no clues about where he might be now.

Leaving Ted to his work, Millie exited the house through the adjoining garage. It would be a long time before a car could be parked in here. Ted and his workmates were currently using it as a store room, and sheets of plasterboard were stacked against the wall alongside a row of rolls of the heavy-duty plastic, miscellaneous strips of timber and a pallet of leftover ceramic tiles, leaving very little room for anything else. But at one end there was some evidence that the young couple had begun to move in their possessions; either that, or the last owners had left behind the mountain bike, propped up against a surf board, and a faded wetsuit dangling from its hook. Aligned with the garage was a further covered carport. As Millie emerged into this, she saw a man on a driveway on the opposite side of the road washing his car, the old-fashioned way with a sponge and bucket of water. He made eye contact with her, so Millie went over.

'Are you moving in?' he asked.

'Sorry, no.' Millie showed him her ID, which she felt sure would play better out here. 'You haven't met your new neighbours?' she asked.

'Not face-to-face,' he said. 'Are they going to be trouble?'

'There's no reason to think that,' said Millie.

'To be honest, I'm not really sure yet who they are,' the man told her. He looked retired, or close to it, lean with a lined, tanned face and short white hair. 'There have been so many different contractors coming and going to work on the house over the last few months, it's hard to tell who's who. I know it's a young couple, and I've seen him from a distance. I did see a woman there one day who I thought might be the other half, but I couldn't be sure. Women do all sorts of jobs these days; one mustn't make assumptions.'

'Were you aware of anyone about here on Saturday night?' asked Millie.

'Let me think. Yes, it would have been Saturday as we were going out. We saw a man arriving, getting out of his car.'

'What time was that?'

'About ten to seven, I suppose. We were going to a concert at Symphony Hall, so that's the usual time we would be setting off. When we came home later in the evening the car was still there. That would have been at around half past ten.'

'Any idea what kind of car it was; the make or colour?' asked Millie.

'Hm, I only saw it for a few seconds. Once it's under the carport it's partly obscured by those laurel bushes. It looked about the size of a Golf, I think, dark blue or grey. These days they all look so similar. I did notice that it had some kind of rack on the roof, though, for carrying skis, that kind of thing.'

'Was the car still there in the morning?' asked Millie.

'No, in fact, I think I might have heard it leave. At about one in the morning, I heard a car engine, and the headlights swept across our bedroom. Our daughter had gone out, you see, and I thought it might be the taxi dropping her off and turning round. But Lydia didn't get home until much later and when I looked out then, the car over there had gone. Certainly all the lights in the house were off and the light on the burglar alarm was flashing, as if it had been set.'

'One o'clock? Are you sure it was as late as that?' asked Millie.

'Yes, it was thereabouts; past the witching hour,' he smiled. 'I was quite surprised really, because when we saw the chap earlier he had a bag with him, as if he was planning to stay a few days.'

'What kind of bag?'

'Oh, you know, a sort of holdall thing.' He modelled the size of it. 'An overnight bag, with leather finishing. I've got one a bit like it.'

'I don't suppose you'd know which way the car went when it left here?'

He didn't, but that didn't much matter. There were any number of routes Sam could have taken back to Edgbaston, and either direction was legitimate. 'Look, what is this?' he asked. 'Is something going on over there that we should know about?'

'It's probably nothing,' said Millie. 'Mr Fleetwood, the man you saw, hasn't been seen for a couple of days. We're trying to track him down. So far, yours is the last sighting of him.'

'Oh. When I saw you, I thought you might be here because of the Kramers.' Millie waited for him to elaborate. 'They live at number forty.' He gestured a little way down the road. 'They've been worried about a van hanging about, though I'm not sure if this was Saturday. We get the odd spate of burglaries around here, and they thought it might be someone "casing" them.'

'Well, it's helpful to know that,' said Millie. 'I'm not sure that it's related, but I will go and talk to them.'

Leaving the man to his polishing, she went up the road to the number he gave her and rang the doorbell, but the Kramers were not at home. This time when she tried Sam Fleetwood's phone the number wasn't even recognised.

When Millie got back to Granville Lane at lunchtime, most of the office staff were on their breaks and she thought at first everyone was out. Then she spied the top of Brown's thinning pate over his work station in the corner. 'Well, that didn't tell me much,' she said, depositing her bag on the desk.

Brown seemed to startle, and after some light scuffling, a good minute elapsed before he responded. 'Oh, hello,' he said.

There were a number of things she could have caught him doing, but after the briefest hesitation, Millie decided to let it go. 'Is DI Mariner back yet?' she asked instead.

'I think he's still out on the fire thing,' Brown told her, his composure recovered, though gazing at her over his PC monitor, he still looked a bit shifty. 'Oh, and no luck with the hospitals. What exactly is it with this feller?'

Mariner had told Millie to keep things low key, but not confidential, so there didn't seem any reason not to let Brown in on it. As much for her own benefit as for his, she summarised how far she'd got. 'According to the neighbour, Sam Fleetwood had a holdall with him when he went into the house, but he didn't leave it there. Carrying it around with him starts to look to me as if he might have been planning a few days away,' she said.

'Could have been a gym bag,' Brown suggested. 'Does he go to the gym?'

'Not that I know,' said Millie. 'He does triathlons, though, so he must need to stay fit. But wouldn't he leave his bag in the car? Why take it into the house?'

'Perhaps he came straight from the gym, had a shower and got changed.'

Millie remembered that wet room, and her impression that it had been used. 'Maybe,' she said out loud. 'But Sam left Charlie Glover's house at the same time Mariner did.' She hunted through the papers on her desk, before finding Mariner's scrawled notes. 'That was at about twenty past six,' she said. 'Would he have had time to go to the gym but still arrive at the house before seven?'

'Depends where the gym is,' said Brown reasonably. 'Where did he go after that, I mean after he left the house?'

'He should have gone back to his flat, but I don't know which direction he took,' said Millie. 'I need to get hold of any Gatso footage around that area, at and around one a.m., to try and track his movements.' It was one of the most tedious tasks imaginable, and Millie couldn't help herself; she smiled sweetly at Brown. It took him about three seconds to catch on. 'Oh, right. I'll see what I can do, boss.'

Millie wasn't sure if she liked that title. It felt like a lot to live up to. 'How about you just call me Millie?'

'Okey-doke.'

'Can you check too if Sam's got a passport?' Millie asked. 'He's meant to be going on honeymoon to Antigua. So he's left it a bit late if he hasn't.'

Millie didn't then get the opportunity to check in with Mariner until later that afternoon. 'There's nothing from Sam's work or the accommodation to show that anything's amiss,' she told him. 'Although I haven't found anyone yet who's seen him since Saturday night.'

'We've checked with local hospitals?' Mariner asked.

'The first thing I did,' said Millie, 'or at least Brown did it for me, and nothing doing. Also, Sam's phone hasn't been used since Saturday night, when he had the text exchange with Gaby at about eleven, and I'm not getting a signal from it any more.'

'So either the battery's dead or he's taken out the SIM,' Mariner concluded. 'It doesn't necessarily mean much. Fleetwood could have still had some kind of accident. We had a bloke go missing a few years back who was in the habit of spending all night in the pub before wandering back along the canal. We didn't dredge his body up until about six weeks after he disappeared.'

'I don't think that's Sam Fleetwood's style,' said Millie. 'I mean, he might go running, but at that time of night? There's nothing at his flat to signal that he's left unexpectedly or in a hurry. Though I did find a couple of interesting things.' She told him about the make-up and tights. 'They're the kinds of things a woman might keep there, as spares, but there's nothing else belonging to Gaby that I could see; not even a toothbrush. I've looked at Gaby's Facebook page and there are lots of pictures of her with Sam. She's fair-skinned, but the make-up is the sort of colour I might use, for a woman with olive or darker skin.'

'I'm not sure that she even wears much make-up,' said Mariner. 'I'm pretty sure she wasn't on Saturday, and that was a special occasion. She was dressed up.'

'There you go then,' said Millie. 'And how tall would you say she is?'

'She was wearing heels,' said Mariner. 'But even then, she didn't come much past my shoulder. About Suzy's height, I suppose.'

'Suzy's petite,' said Millie. 'But the tights are medium, so for a taller woman.'

'You said a couple of things?' said Mariner.

'Yes, these were in a drawer,' said Millie. 'I'm guessing they're this year's, as Valentine Day was only a couple of months back.' She showed Mariner the pictures of the cards on her phone. 'The handwriting on this one matches Gaby's, but not on this one.'

'*From your little bear,*' Mariner read.

'Then we have one of the neighbours at the new house seeing Sam arrive there on Saturday with what looked like an overnight bag,' Millie continued. 'He heard him drive away again, but not until around one a.m., two hours after Gaby received the text from Sam to say that he was just leaving.'

'So why the delay?' Mariner wondered aloud.

'I was thinking that perhaps he had a specific rendezvous with someone,' said Millie. 'Perhaps it was the only time she could get away. Something else you should know; Gaby told you that

Sam has to work away some weekends, didn't she? Well, not according to his boss, he doesn't. Nobody from his department does.'

'You think Sam Fleetwood's got another woman on the go,' said Mariner.

'That's what it all looks like to me,' said Millie.

'And he hasn't been back to his flat?'

'I don't think so. The guy in the flat below Sam's thought he heard bumping around up there early on Sunday morning, but there was no sighting and he couldn't even be sure about the timing. The flat's all neat and tidy and the wardrobe's a bit sparse, as if he's taken stuff with him.'

'So what next?' asked Mariner.

'I'll start talking to other people who know him and see what that turns up. See if I can find out who "Little Bear" could be.'

'Sounds like a plan,' said Mariner. 'Keep me apprised. But so that you know, I'm on leave all day tomorrow, so anything you're not sure about will have to go to Superintendent Sharp. I don't really want to make a thing of this, so can you let the rest of the team know? If there's anything urgent, I can be reached on my mobile, and I'll be back in on Friday.'

'OK.' Millie was slightly taken aback. She'd never known Mariner to take leave in the middle of an investigation before, and here there were two ongoing. She was tempted to ask what was up, but it was none of her business, so she said nothing.

'Do you think he's ill?' asked Vicky straight away. Millie had waited until people were starting to leave for the day before telling them, and now she and Vicky were the only ones left in the office. 'Or is it a job interview?'

'Whatever it is, I'm sure he'll tell us when he's ready,' said Millie. 'He's not one for secrets, either. Enough of them out there. I just got the impression he didn't want it bandied around the office. PC Brown is a bit of an unknown quantity, isn't he?' She said, changing the subject.

'That's one way of putting it,' said Vicky. 'What?' She'd seen Millie's expression.

'What do you make of him?'

'He seems all right,' said Vicky. 'Why?'

'It's just that – when I came in at lunchtime today, he was all on his own. I think I caught him up to something.'

'Oh yes?' she was intrigued now.

'I thought I might have walked in on him having a wank,' said Millie. 'He jumped a mile, and there was definitely some rearranging of the clothes going on.'

'Ugh, really?' Vicky screwed up her face in disgust.

'I might be completely wrong,' said Millie. 'Perhaps I shouldn't have said anything. But I can't think what else—'

'It wouldn't do any harm to get Max to check the history on Charlie's computer,' said Vicky. She couldn't help herself. 'Maybe that's why Stone calls him what he does,' she giggled.

Millie joined in. 'It might explain the glasses too,' she said.

ELEVEN

J amie's hospital appointments were based on his (and therefore Mariner's) home address so were, conveniently enough
for Mariner, at the QE. He parked in the nearest of the visitor
car parks and walked up the ramp to the main building, where
he caught up with Jamie and Nell in one of the many waiting
areas of the outpatients' department. They stood out, not because
of Jamie, but thanks to Nell's electric blue spiked hair and multiple
piercings. Nell met Mariner with one of her customary smiles;
one of the loveliest Mariner had ever seen, but spoiled today by
a couple of deep gouges down her left cheek. 'Courtesy of Jamie,'
she said, seeing Mariner's reaction.

'God, I'm sorry,' said Mariner, on Jamie's behalf, but Nell
shrugged it off.

'I've had worse,' she said. 'And they're healing nicely given
that it was only a couple of days ago.'

Jamie, to Mariner's dismay, was slumped in a wheelchair,
largely inanimate, apart from tugging listlessly at the bandage
again. He was hunched over like an old man. His eyes grazed
Mariner's fleetingly, but were dull and indifferent.

'What have you given him?' said Mariner grimly.

'I know,' said Nell. 'Creepy, isn't it?' And, she didn't need to
add, further proof that Jamie wasn't himself at all. 'Would you
like me to hang around? It's just that we are pretty short-staffed
at the moment, so they could do with me back at MP.'

'Short-staffed' wasn't a phrase Mariner liked to hear, and he
wondered for a moment if that had anything to do with Jamie's
change of behaviour. But Nell couldn't be held to account for it.
'No, it's fine,' he said. 'It doesn't look as if he's going to put up
much of a fight today. I'll drop him back when it's finished.'

'Great,' said Nell. 'I've put some snacks and a drink in his
bag, and a change of clothes should you need them.' She'd
thought of everything, and when she said goodbye to Jamie, it
was with tenderness, despite the injuries. When she had gone,

Mariner immediately checked his work mobile, but there were
no messages, yet. Everyone was probably out and about. He sat
down beside Jamie for the long wait.

DC Millie Khatoon was on her way to speak to Sam Fleetwood's
church mentor, Laurie McKinnon, who worked from home as
a software designer. He lived in Cofton Hackett, which had
once been a discrete village but was now a far-flung extension
of the city, nestling at the foot of the Lickey Hills. When he
came to the door McKinnon wasn't quite what she'd expected.
In Mariner's notes Gaby had described him as an 'elder', which
Millie had taken literally, anticipating him to be an older man.
McKinnon's hair was greying, but he could only be in his early
forties at most; a quietly spoken Scot.

'Guiding Light?' said Millie. 'Isn't that a bit like stepping
into the Big Man's shoes?'

McKinnon smiled. 'Not at all.'

Once Millie had explained her purpose he had brought her
through to his office, offering her a drink along the way. Millie
accepted it with gratitude; she hadn't quite appreciated just
how many cups of tea she'd drunk when she was at home with
Haroon. She'd gone home yesterday thoroughly dehydrated.
Now they were sitting in the spare room that doubled as
McKinnon's work space, a row of Apple Macs set up along a
worktop. Each one pinged intermittently, signalling an incoming
email, and each time McKinnon couldn't resist checking the
sender.

'So how does this mentoring work?' Millie asked.

'It's much less formal than the title implies,' said McKinnon.
'Our church has expectations. We recognise marriage as a life-
long commitment and responsibility towards another individual.
Modern life can challenge that, so we try to support couples,
especially someone in Sam's situation, whose own parents split
up. I'm there as a kind of sounding board. The idea is that
having married and raised a family myself, I can draw on those
experiences. That's all there is to it,' he said, with a smile.

'And how does Sam feel about that?'

McKinnon shrugged. 'I hope it helps. He comes to the house
about once a week and we talk about how things are going, and

any concerns he might have. We usually start with a passage from the scriptures.'

'Like what?' Millie wasn't really sure why she'd asked that, or what good it would do.

McKinnon reached across to a bookshelf, from which he took down a modern edition of the Bible, opening it to a book-marked page. Millie couldn't think of anyone she knew who kept a Bible in the workplace, though in fairness she'd never looked closely at Charlie's desk. *'And you shall know the truth, and the truth shall make you free. John 8:32'*, said McKinnon. 'That was the one we discussed last.'

'Which was when?'

'Let me think – it'll be two weeks ago tomorrow.'

'So not every week then.'

McKinnon conceded it with a tilt of the head. 'We did have an appointment for last Thursday, but Sam sent me a text cancelling it.'

'Was that unusual?'

'It happens. We all have busy lives. I think he'd had to work late, or was meeting his friends or something.'

'Did anything prompt that particular discussion?' Millie was curious now about how this worked.

'Not that I remember,' said McKinnon. 'Over the weeks we've been discussing the kinds of qualities that go to make up a successful partnership, and I happen to think that honesty is one of them. Are you married, Detective Khatoon?'

'Yes.'

'Then it won't be news to you.'

'When did you last see Sam?' Millie asked.

'That last appointment,' said McKinnon. 'We couldn't make it to Charles and Helen's on Saturday.'

'And how did he seem then?'

'Fine,' said McKinnon. 'He was looking forward to the wedding and getting settled into the new house.'

'Excited?'

McKinnon smiled. 'Sam's pretty laid back. I'm not sure that he really does "excited".'

'Would you say that you're close?' Millie asked. 'In the absence of his father—'

'Oh, I don't kid myself that I fulfil that role,' said McKinnon. 'Nor would I want to. Sam's quite a private person, so I couldn't claim to know him well. Clearly his childhood experiences have influenced his attitude towards his responsibilities as a husband, and his ability to live up to them. He worries about the weight of ensuring someone else's happiness. It's a big deal for him. I think Sam always has at the back of his mind his father's desertion of the family, and is keen that history doesn't repeat itself.'

'Is he having doubts?' asked Millie. It was an obvious question.

'No, not at all,' McKinnon said. 'He's being realistic and that's refreshing in a younger person. I've been in this role a few years now and I'd be surprised if there weren't some nerves about the wedding.'

'And what else did you talk about?' asked Millie. 'After the scripture.'

'As I said, we talked about his expectations when he's newly married and all of that. Look, I'm not entirely comfortable going into details. My meetings with Sam are informal, but they are personal and if he thinks that I've shared the discussion with you, he'll have no reason to trust me again, will he?'

'So Sam wasn't at church on Sunday?' said Millie.

'No, but I know he sometimes has other weekend commitments. I understand he was at Helen and Charles' renewal on the Saturday. There's no compulsion to come along every week, although I understand that will change when he and Gaby are married.'

'You seem certain that Sam will show up,' said Millie.

'Of course I am,' said McKinnon easily. 'His wedding is less than two weeks away and there are other important people in his life. What's always impressed me with Sam is his strong sense of duty. You've spoken to his sister?'

'Not personally,' said Millie. 'But one of my colleagues has.'

'Then you'll know that he has other significant family responsibilities. One thing I have learned about Sam; he's not the sort of man to let people down.'

Millie was down to her last business card; she needed to replenish her supply from the office. 'If Sam does get in touch,

please could you ask him to contact me,' she said. 'Hopefully I
won't need to come back.'

'Of course,' said McKinnon. 'Though I'll be off up to Glasgow
tomorrow for a couple of days. My mother's not been well, so
I have to head up there fairly regularly at present. I'll be back
again early next week.'

As McKinnon opened the door to let Millie out, a people carrier
pulled on to the drive and came to a halt. A woman in tight jeans
and a strikingly patterned shirt climbed out and, calling out a
greeting, went round to the boot, from which she lifted out several
bolts of cloth.

'This is my wife, Tanya,' said McKinnon.

Millie was more attracted by the fabrics, and Tanya noticed
this as she brought them up to the house. 'I'm a dressmaker,'
she said. 'It's something I can do working from home, around
the children, and it supplements the income a bit.'

'This is lovely,' said Millie, stroking one of the rolls of brightly
coloured silk.

'For bridesmaids' dresses,' Tanya smiled. 'Or at least it will be.'

'For Sam and Gaby?'

Tanya was surprised, but shook her head. 'No, those have been
done for a while.'

'Detective Constable Khatoon came to talk to me about Sam,'
said McKinnon. 'He's disappeared.'

'Disappeared?'

'Well, we don't know that yet,' said Millie. 'We're just trying
to find out if anyone has seen him in the last few days.'

An unidentifiable expression crossed Tanya's face. 'He hasn't
been here for a week or two, has he, love?'

'I was just explaining that,' said McKinnon.

'Well, thanks for your help,' said Millie.

Vicky Jesson was at her desk, prevaricating. In Mariner's absence
she needed to attend the Fire Investigation briefing on Wellington
Road, but was disconcertingly fretful about getting it right, so
was preparing excessively by going over and over her previous
notes for anything requiring clarification.

Brown had been watching her. 'You OK?' he asked.

'Yeah,' said Jesson. 'I just want to get this right, that's all.'

'Want me to come, moral support and all that?' Brown offered. 'I could write stuff down; make sure nothing gets missed.'

Jesson weighed it for a moment, trying to put out of her head what Millie had told her yesterday.

'It would make a change to get out from these four walls,' Brown added persuasively.

'All right then, thanks.' Vicky felt ridiculously relieved to have the back-up, even though it was only Brown, and even if he was behaving like a puppy on its first outing.

'You look great,' he told her, as they got out of the car at Wellington Road. He'd caught her checking in the rear-view mirror.

'Something in my eye,' Vicky said, but she could tell from Brown's smirk that he didn't buy it.

Gerry Docherty was waiting for them at the gate of 104. 'There's good news and bad,' he said. 'We've been systematically working our way into that ground-floor room, and the good news is; we've found accelerant, particularly in the area below the front window. Once we suspected it we brought in the dog team to confirm it and search for other traces. When I say team, that's him, Dougal, with his handler, Lance.'

A blue roan springer spaniel, with what appeared to be plastic bags on its paws, was running around on a long lead. Brown immediately knelt down to pet him. 'Clever fella,' he said, as the dog jumped all over him. 'How do you know when he's on to something?' he asked.

'He has an indication signal,' Lance told him. 'He keeps his nose on the spot, whilst repeatedly looking up at me.'

'But hasn't all the water from the hoses diluted any substance you find?' asked Vicky.

'You'd think so,' said Lance. 'But the water actually acts as a barrier to preserve accelerant. Dougal can pick up the tiniest trace; splashes on furniture, carpets or shoes. Once he's got something, we swab the area for analysis then mark it up with spray paint. He's trained to identify almost all flammable liquids.' Lance grinned. 'The irony is, I myself don't have any sense of smell at all.'

'Perhaps you'd like to come and have a look?' said Docherty, keen to get on.

While they got kitted out in forensic suits, Vicky introduced Brown to Docherty. 'DCI Mariner's been called away,' she explained.

'And I'm just here to observe,' said Brown, struggling to get his second foot into the suit and almost falling over in the process.

When they were ready Docherty walked them into the house and through into the charred cave that Mustafa Shah had described as once being his office.

'Might be as well if you wait here,' Docherty said to Brown. 'Not much space where we're going.' He stepped carefully along the inner wall, using a row of stepping plates, through a ravine no more than eighteen inches wide that had been cut between the wall and the mound of debris that was still piled almost up to the ceiling. Once he reached the window, Docherty squatted down, so that Jesson, following behind him, could see over his head, the black circular stain underneath the window sill, high-lighted with fluorescent paint. 'Accelerant has pooled here.' He pointed to further purple marks on the concrete floor that had similarly been marked out. 'Then we've got a few spots trailing to another, bigger pool, back there.'

'So it could have been put through the window,' said Jesson. 'What Mrs Shah reported as glass breaking could have been exactly that.'

'It could,' agreed Docherty.

'But there are more spots over here,' Brown pointed to several other orange marks to the sides of the stepping plates.

'The broken window would allow the perpetrator to throw accelerant deeper into the room,' Jesson speculated.

'That's one explanation,' said Docherty. 'There seems to be less of it in those areas, which could be because it's soaked through the carpet on to the floor below, instead of seeping down the side. But that's the bad news; there's a complicating factor with this room, especially as most of the carpet was destroyed.'

'What's that?' asked Jesson.

Brown was ahead of her. 'It used to be a garage,' he said.

'So there could potentially be all kinds of flammable chemicals on this floor: oil, petrol, white spirit – anything like that,' added Docherty. 'Any of those traces could be there legitimately, and until we've had each swab analysed we can't eliminate it.'

'Shit. Sorry.' Jesson didn't know why she was suddenly self-conscious about her language.

'Shit indeed,' Docherty agreed. 'The Detection, Identification and Monitoring team should be able to identify the constituents of each for us, but that is going to take more time.'

'Wouldn't the Shahs have cleaned up the floor before they laid the carpet?' asked Jesson.

Docherty shook his head. 'It doesn't look as if they bothered much. I guess if it was always intended to be an office or store room it didn't matter. It would have cost money to get it properly cleaned and put down new flooring. Normally we'd take samples of the carpet as a control, but there wasn't much left except for odd scraps of molten underlay, which probably won't yield anything. But as we progress, we'll swab down the concrete for any further traces of accelerant, and when there's enough space for him to move around more freely, we'll get Dougal back in to help.'

'So how sure can we be that this *was* arson?' said Jesson, crouching down to get a better look.

'We're definitely edging in that direction,' Docherty said. 'I can be about ninety per cent certain. It's that stain under the window that clinches it. So far it's unlikely that the residue left over from previous use would be enough to ignite a fire, especially at ground level. It just complicates things for us in trying to determine absolutely what was used to start it.'

'So this attack could relate to the previous one,' said Vicky.

'It could,' said Docherty. 'The porch was unsuccessfully targeted last time, so it's possible that someone got wise to what would work, and this is completely at the other end of the scale. We've collected up the glass from the floor just under there too,' he said. 'Most of it will have come from the window panes, but we'll look out for anything thicker; sometimes you can identify a corner or base that suggests a glass container of some kind; a bottle or jar.'

'Like a Molotov cocktail?' said Brown.

'Exactly,' said Docherty. 'The pieces will get sorted into window glass and "other". Who knows? On some lucky occasions we can even get prints. My lads haven't come across any discarded bottles in the immediate area – it's one of the things we're always on the lookout for in this situation – but you might want to put some of your officers on looking further afield. Any liquid receptacles, like pop bottles that have been thrown away, might be what we're looking for. Arsonists can be surprisingly careless after the event. And if it was an arson attack, it could have been two-pronged. For anyone who knew what they were doing, access to the back of the house would have been easy enough around the side. We'll keep looking for clues.'

'The family have asked us to fetch some of their things for them,' said Jesson. 'Is it OK with you if we do that?'

'Be my guest,' said Docherty. 'We're really only concerned with this side of the property at the moment.'

It turned out to be helpful having two people to collect together the things, as everything taken from the house had to be recorded. Vicky collected each item, while Brown wrote it down and bagged it. Most of what they needed was clothing for all the family and toys for the children, and it didn't take long to locate almost everything on the list and pack it into carrier bags. The one thing they hadn't yet found were spare asthma inhalers for Yousef.

'Bathroom cabinet?' suggested Brown.

Jesson handed him her bags. 'You start taking this lot down to the car, I'll catch you up,' she said. The inhalers were indeed in the medicine cupboard, along with the usual everyday family remedies, but also a couple of packets of prescription medication, which Vicky bagged up too. It wasn't certain at this stage whether the toxicology report on Soltan Ahmed would reveal anything, but they might be helpful if it did.

TWELVE

From the McKinnons' house Millie had gone out into the open air, in pursuit of the man both Gaby and Fiona had nominated as Sam's best mate. Nathan Dornham, who was a landscape gardener, worked for Birmingham City Council parks division, and Millie tracked him down to his base, a park just up the Bristol Road from the police station. He was out working somewhere in the locality, so she had to sit in her car and wait for him to return for his lunch. She watched as a number of mowing machines came and went in the compound, until finally she saw the gaffer approach one of them and speak to the driver, nodding in Millie's direction as he did so. She got out of the car.

'What's this about?' Dornham asked straight away, as he came towards her.

'I just need to ask you a couple of questions,' said Millie. 'It won't take long.'

'Do you mind if we walk down the park a bit?' he said. 'I can have a smoke.' They walked down to a bench overlooking the lake and woodland, where a couple of dog walkers were wandering the footpaths.

'I'm trying to locate Sam Fleetwood,' said Millie. 'Any idea where he might be?'

'At work, probably, like the rest of us,' said Dornham simply. He was a few inches under six feet tall and chunky, with mousy hair and freckles.

'Actually, he's not,' Millie told him. 'And he hasn't been there at all this week. As far as we can ascertain, nobody's seen him since last Saturday night.'

He pulled a face. 'What about Gaby, his girlfriend?'

'She and Fiona reported him missing,' said Millie. 'When did you last see him?'

'Friday week, well . . . nearly two weeks ago. We sometimes have a drink in the Hare and Hounds of a Friday night, though not so much since he's been with Gaby.'

'What about last Friday?' asked Millie.

'He texted me to say he couldn't make it; said he'd got too much to do with all the wedding stuff. She's got him running round all over the place. She'd have me at it too, given half a chance. I'm supposed to be his best man.' Despite the complaint, there was a hint of pride in his voice.

'So you're organising the stag do?'

'Oh, we've already had it,' said Nathan. 'Madam wanted it early so that there was no chance of it ruining the big day.'

'So you know Gaby too?' Millie asked.

'Not that well. She started coming along to things, y'know. She's classy and a good laugh, but the God-bothering's a bit of a turn-off. Not that it would have mattered. She and Sam were pretty tight from the start.'

'So you're not surprised that they're getting married?' said Millie.

'I'm not surprised that she wants the whole big white wedding and all that, but it was a bit of an eye-opener that Sam would go for it. He'd never really seemed that keen on the idea of marriage, on account of happened with his old man. And he's always been a free spirit; likes to keep his options open.'

'But he's what, thirty-two?' said Millie. 'Maybe he thinks he's done all that, and it's time to settle down.'

'Maybe,' said Dornham, but he didn't sound very sure.

'What are you not telling me?'

Nathan took in the scenery. 'I don't know. Sam has a bit of a history of mature, unattainable women, if you get my drift.'

'You mean married?' said Millie.

'Yeah. He had some serious thing going, round about the time he was at uni. It was pretty full-on, and I'm not sure that it's ever completely ended.'

'What makes you think that?'

'Sam didn't even last the course on his stag night. We were all getting stuck in, having a good time, and suddenly, about half eleven, he said he'd had enough and he was calling it a night.'

'Perhaps he was just tired,' said Millie.

Nathan scoffed. 'Not many blokes walk out on their own stag night, do they? It crossed my mind then that he'd got other plans.'

'Like seeing this other woman?'

'Last chance before he's married, isn't it?' said Nathan.

'Tell me about her,' said Millie.

'That's the thing,' said Nathan. 'I can't, because we never knew who she was. Sam was always very secretive about her. We assumed she was married, older than us and more sophisticated. The pattern was that he would disappear for whole weekends, so we always thought whoever it was, was making the most of the old man being out of the way.'

'So what happened?' asked Millie.

'Whatever happens? She dumped him. Not long before he took his finals, Sam went off for the weekend with her, but came back early the next day and said it was over. He was in bits. It really screwed up his exams. Anyway, that stag weekend did make me wonder if he'd arranged to hook up with her again, one last time before he tied the knot, you know? But I'm just guessing. Maybe you're right and he was just knackered.'

'Sam told Gaby he has to work away some weekends, but we know that it's not true,' said Millie.

Nathan grinned. 'There you go then. Cheeky sod,' he said. 'I couldn't be doing with it – all the sneaking around – but I think Sam gets a real buzz out of it.'

'And you really have no idea who this woman might be?' asked Millie.

Nathan smiled. 'One thing about Sam, he can always keep you on your toes. I've known him since we were at school, and he's not an easy person to get close to. He thrives on secrecy and all that. We were all eaten up with curiosity, of course.' He looked suddenly guilty. 'I tried to follow him once, just before it all finished. Managed to stay with him as far as the M42, but then I lost him; didn't know which way he went.'

'What made you think this woman was older and sophisticated?' asked Millie.

'The whole set-up, I suppose. When he was seeing her he always took real care with what he was wearing. She bought him this really smart leather holdall thing. We used to call it his shag bag, because he always took it with him.' He frowned. 'That's the other thing – I hadn't seen it in a while, but the night I picked Sam up for his stag do, it was there, sitting on the floor in his flat. I made some joke about it. That's what made me think about that woman again, I suppose.'

Millie remembered the Valentine cards. 'Did Sam have a pet name for this woman?' she asked. 'Did he ever refer to her as his "Little Bear"?'

Dornham scoffed. 'Not that he told me. But I wouldn't be surprised.' He stubbed out his cigarette on the arm of the bench. 'I should be heading back,' he said, standing up. 'I've got to get over to Highbury this afternoon.'

They began walking back up the footpath. 'Gaby's young and single,' Millie said, pointing out the obvious. 'So not what you'd call Sam's usual type. Have you ever had reason to think he might be regretting the commitment to her?'

'What with her pedigree and her money? I don't think so,' said Dornham. 'There's no future with a married woman, is there?'

'So why would Sam do a disappearing act now?' asked Millie.

Dornham snorted. 'If I had his domestic arrangements, I wouldn't mind having a break from the father-in-law and the obligation to go to church every week.'

'How does Sam get on with Gaby's father?' asked Millie.

'All right, I think,' said Dornham. 'He'd drive me crazy, though. Daddy Boswell wants everything to be perfect for his perfect daughter, so he likes to be in control of everything. And I know he's come the heavy with Sam – *if ever you let my daughter down*, that kind of thing. But if there's one thing Sam is pretty resistant to, it's being controlled. He'll do what he can independently, despite the old man. And he's banking on things being different once they're married. Sam doesn't like to feel obligated to anyone and he's determined to provide for Gaby in his own way. According to him, Gaby feels the same and can't wait to get out from under her old man's grip.'

'Do you believe that?'

'I want to, for Sam's sake.'

Jesson and Brown had dropped off the items for the Shahs and then returned to Granville Lane. Brown went on ahead of Jesson, and as she climbed the stairs, Vicky almost literally ran into Inspector Pete Stone.

'How are you getting on with the Angel of the North?' Stone

sneered, looking up the stairwell as the door banged behind Brown. 'Irritating little tosser, isn't he?'

'He's thorough, if that's what you're getting at,' said Vicky, feeling suddenly protective towards her newest colleague.

'You know he still lives at home with his mum,' Stone went on, spitefully. 'And at thirty-odd that's not good, is it? I saw the pair of them not long ago, going into the Bingo. Jesus.' Stone shook his head. 'I have a feeling he might like musical theatre too.'

'Meaning what exactly?' Vicky moved past him to get up the stairs.

Stone ignored her. 'Has he started telling you all how to do your jobs yet?'

'No,' Vicky called back over her shoulder. 'But perhaps that's because he doesn't feel the need.'

Stone just scowled after her.

Mariner's day had been a long one, that involved mostly sitting in a series of waiting areas, each distinguished by the colour of the chairs, before being transferred to the next, until eventually they saw whichever medical professional was next on the list. He felt like an aircraft being kept in a constant holding pattern. The tests themselves – physical exams, X-rays, the sampling of various bodily fluids – were each over relatively quickly, in inverse proportion to the time spent in limbo, and although Mariner felt guilty even thinking it, things were a whole lot easier given Jamie's current docile demeanour. On a different occasion, with Jamie in a different humour, he might have wanted to take advantage of the multi-sensory room on offer for patients, but today there was no need. The afternoon's finale was a full body scan, which proved the most problematic, no doubt because it was the procedure that was the least familiar to Jamie. He strongly resisted, both verbally and physically, and eventually the solution was to give him an additional mild sedative, which calmed him. Once he was co-operating, Mariner returned to the seating area and, as he did, he heard his name.

'Tom?' Dr Eleanor Kingsley had been involved in a previous case that had centred for a while on the hospital, during the course of which, she and Mariner had become friends. He went over.

'What are you doing up here?' she asked, knowing that his usual hang-out was the basement mortuary. 'Not another serial killer on the loose?'

'Not as far as I'm aware,' said Mariner.

'So this must be a personal visit,' she surmised. 'Are you OK?'

'I'm fine,' said Mariner. 'This is for Jamie,' he added for clarification. 'He's been peeing blood, so they're sticking tubes and needles into all kinds of places, to try and determine the problem.'

She grimaced. 'How's that going?'

'For Jamie, he's doing remarkably well,' said Mariner. 'But that in itself is worrying. Not like him to put up with unsolicited physical contact from anyone, let alone invasive procedures from complete strangers.'

'Well, I'd try not to worry too much. It could be lots of things,' she said, to reassure him. 'Most of them not necessarily life-threatening.'

'I know, but thanks for saying it. And how are you?' Mariner asked.

'I'm good,' she said. 'Life has calmed down a bit for us now that all our lads have shipped out of Afghanistan, but still enough to keep us busy.'

As she spoke, a nurse came into the waiting area. 'Mr Barham?' she called, scanning the room.

Mariner realised then that he was mistakenly being addressed using Jamie's surname. 'Oh, that's me,' he said to Eleanor. 'I've got to go. But it's good to see you again.'

'You too.' She squeezed his arm. 'Let me know how it turns out.'

'I will.'

The sedation had taken its toll, and Jamie slept for most of the journey back to Manor Park, so that Mariner had to half carry him up to his room. His dinner had been kept back for him, so Mariner helped him to eat it before he fell asleep again. Afterwards he sought out Nell. 'The results will be sent through to the doctor here,' Mariner said, relaying what he had been told.

'We'll let you know as soon as we know anything,' said Nell. 'Try not to worry.'

Easier said than done, thought Mariner, getting back into his car. It was rush hour by the time he headed home so he had to sit in traffic queues at all the major junctions, prolonging the journey considerably. By the time he got back, he felt knackered, even though he'd done nothing but sit around all day. Checking his mobile, he found nothing from Granville Lane, so no major developments there, but there were several messages on his voicemail from Gaby Boswell. She could keep until tomorrow, when, with luck, Millie might have some positive news.

THIRTEEN

Overnight he'd made the decision to bring Millie's investigation into Sam Fleetwood's disappearance out into the open. Although they were two quite separate inquiries, in his experience shared discussions could prove fruitful. He convened a joint briefing in a corner of the main office around Vicky's desk, and started with Sam Fleetwood. 'Gaby Boswell's been trying to get in touch with me,' he told Millie. 'Any progress there?'

'He still hasn't shown up, if that's what you mean,' said Millie. 'And honestly? I can't make up my mind. Sam's boss and his mentor at the church agree with Gaby and Fiona that Sam going so comprehensively off the radar is unusual and completely out of character. But according to his best mate, Nathan Dornham, Sam had some cloak-and-dagger relationship going with a married woman, a while back. It was enough of a deal that Nathan thinks Sam could be having one last fling with her again, before he gets married, which would explain what I found in his flat. Or it could be someone else. Dornham made it clear that Sam has form for this kind of thing. The weekends "working away" are not at all what Gaby thinks they are, and Sam did a disappearing act on his stag night a couple of weeks ago.'

'This has gone way beyond a weekend now, though,' said Mariner. 'So where does that leave Gaby?'

'There doesn't seem to be any question about his commitment to her,' said Millie. 'And from what I understand, the whole point about this other woman is that she's essentially unattainable. That's the appeal.'

'Things can change though, can't they?' said Vicky. 'A married woman can always decide to leave her husband. Do you have any idea who this woman might be?'

Millie shook her head. 'All Nathan told me is that she's likely to be older, sophisticated and married, and that it could have been going on a while.'

'A work colleague?'

'I don't think so,' said Millie. 'His boss made a point of saying that Sam keeps to himself there, and it seemed to be a pretty male-dominated environment. It goes back further than that too, to when he was at uni.'

'It's Sam's mother that bothers me,' said Mariner. 'All this time he's been a caring, thoughtful son and supported his sister, so whatever is going on in his private life, why duck those responsibilities now?'

'Because it's getting tougher?' Vicky suggested. 'We all know that people do walk away from their lives and their commitments. They do it all the time.'

'And his mother's got dementia,' Mariner conceded. 'So he may be of the opinion that she won't even notice. According to Fiona he didn't handle the father's desertion very well. He could even blame his mother for the father walking out. And Fiona is clearly very capable and managing things. Perhaps Sam considers it's a small price to pay. I agree. There are people who walk out on much more.'

'What I don't understand is, if this is about another woman, or even having second thoughts about marrying Gaby, why not just come clean and admit it?' said Millie.

'Maybe he didn't plan it this way,' said Jesson. 'Maybe he really was meeting this woman for one last time before he gets married. Then, when it comes to it, they decide they can't live without each other. Depending on who she is, the other woman might not want it broadcast. And if part of the thrill is the secrecy, then eloping would suit them. Never underestimate the power of illicit sex.'

'And we're absolutely certain that nobody has seen or heard from Fleetwood since last Saturday,' Mariner checked.

'The last contact we have with anyone, is still the text he sent to Gaby at eleven, to say that he was finishing up and about to leave the house on Meadow Hall,' Millie confirmed. 'The neighbour there *thought* he heard him leave after one a.m., and a neighbour at Sam's flat said he *might* have heard someone moving about in his flat on the Sunday morning.'

'That's a lot of uncertainty,' said Mariner. 'So we can't be sure where he went after he left the house?'

'The Gatso on the Redditch Road picked up Fleetwood's car heading out of the city going south on the A441 at one twenty-two on Sunday morning,' Brown chipped in.

Mariner turned to face him. 'And you know this . . .?'

Millie took a breath. 'I asked him to look at the footage—'

'In fairness, I offered to look at it,' countered Brown.

'No, I specifically—'

'All right, all right,' said Mariner. 'I'm not really interested in how it happened. But what then?'

'Nothing,' said Brown. 'One minute he's on the A441, and by the next camera, three miles on, he's vanished.'

'That would seem to add considerable weight to the possibility of another relationship going on,' said Mariner. 'If, as his mate suggests, there is another woman, Sam could have been going out to meet her – it might explain the timing and the holdall. Any likely candidates for this other woman at all?'

'Unfortunately not,' said Millie. 'That's where all the creeping around doesn't help. The most I've got is the Valentine card from someone calling herself his "Little Bear". The handwriting is definitely not Gaby's.'

'Little Bear? It's an odd nickname,' said Vicky.

'Perhaps they met on Paddington station,' suggested Brown.

'I might go back and talk to Tanya McKinnon, his mentor's wife,' said Millie. 'There was something about her reaction when she found out who I was. She's an older, pretty woman and her husband is also away on a regular basis at the moment.'

'Worth a pop then,' said Mariner. 'And sometime today we need to go and have a potentially rather awkward conversation with the Boswells about why we probably can't do anything to help.'

Mariner could sense Vicky getting restless, keen to share progress on the fire investigation. He thought he detected developing competition between her and Millie, which wouldn't be a bad thing. He'd already looked over Vicky's input to the policy book from yesterday. 'So Docherty's considering arson after all?' he said.

'Almost certainly,' said Jesson. 'Normally we'd start with the possibility of an inside job, but in this case I think we can discount it because of Soltan Ahmed's death.'

Mariner's expression indicated less certainty, but Vicky

pressed on. 'Everything Salwa and the children have told us stacks up; Salwa tried to get her father out, sustaining nasty burns in the process. And what would be the motive?'

'Have we got any further with the insurance policies?' Mariner asked Brown.

'Not yet, sir, still waiting for Mustafa Shah to let me know the details. His copies were destroyed in the fire, and I think he's waiting for the company to send him something through.'

'Well, stay on it, will you?' said Mariner. 'Both Salwa and Mustafa made reference to how good their policy is, and seemed confident that it would cover the damage. It could be a scam that went wrong,' he went on, 'Salwa told us that her father was physically fit. She could reasonably have expected him to get out safely too.'

'It would be a hell of a risk, though,' Jesson argued, 'and, as it turned out, not one worth taking. If that was the plan, why leave Soltan in that bedroom?' she continued. 'Once the children were asleep it would have been much safer for Salwa to have brought him into the children's room. Then they could all get out together. All they would have to say is that Soltan woke first and raised the alarm, which would make perfect sense given where the fire seems to have started.'

'So, if it's not an inside job?' said Mariner.

Vicky looked at him. So he didn't believe it either; he'd just been testing out her ideas. 'We focus our attention on outside threats,' she said. 'That means the Wright family, and anyone else who may have had something against the Shahs.'

Mariner called across to Brown. 'Any other contenders crawled out of the woodwork yet?' Brown looked up from his PC monitor, pushing up his glasses. 'Jordan Wright is the favourite so far,' he said. 'Along with our mysterious man in the hoodie, supposing of course that they are different people.'

'So start with him,' said Mariner, signalling the end of the discussion.

'You've been helping Millie out then,' said Mariner to Brown, before he left to go back to his office. 'Hope you're keeping up with your own work too.'

Brown blinked at him. 'I had time, sir,' he said.

*   *   *

Millie was following up, as she'd said, by returning to the
McKinnon family home. This time, it was Tanya who came to
the door. 'Ah, you'll want to speak to Laurie,' she said straight
away. 'I'm sorry but he's not here—'

'Actually it's you I was hoping to speak to,' said Millie.

'Oh, OK then.' Initially reluctant, Tanya held open the door.
'Come in. I was about to make some tea. Sam hasn't turned up
yet then?'

'No,' said Millie, following her into the kitchen.

'How strange,' said Tanya. They took their drinks into a living
room overlooking the garden, where a number of small children
were playing. Millie watched them all, in her estimation about
four or five years old, swarming over a climbing frame. She felt
an ache of longing for Haroon.

'Only two of them are ours,' Tanya smiled, glad of the distraction. 'But for some reason our yard seems to be a magnet for
all the kids in the neighbourhood.' As they watched, two little
girls broke away from the group and ran over to a cluster of
dwarf daffodils which they stooped down to pick. Tanya tapped
on the window and wagged a finger at them. They turned and
giggled to each other, before scampering off again.

'And you've got a new baby?' said Millie, noticing the pile
of laundered Babygros.

'Yes, although I thought I'd done with all that.' She raised
her eyebrows. 'Martha was a bit of a surprise. Have you got
children?'

'Yes,' said Millie. 'I only came back to work this week, so
I'm trying to get used to leaving my little boy at home.'

'That's hard,' said Tanya. 'I'm not sure if I could do it.'

It wasn't said at all judgementally, so why did it make Millie
feel bad? 'I need to ask you about your relationship with Sam
Fleetwood,' she said, getting out her pocketbook.

'I don't have one,' said Tanya quickly, 'that is, I only know
him through the church and through Laurie.' She was sitting on
the edge of her seat, as if hoping this wouldn't take long. 'We
just chat a bit when he comes here. You know, just a bit of small
talk.'

'Does Sam ever come to the house when Laurie isn't here?'
Tanya looked down at her mug, away into the garden, anywhere

except at Millie. 'He has done, a couple of times, to bring the measurements for the dresses and to see how they're coming along.'

'Isn't that unusual?' Millie couldn't remember her husband Suli taking the slightest interest in anything like that. It would provide a good excuse, though.

'I don't know,' said Tanya uncertainly. She caught Millie's eye. 'I think Sam just wants to be involved. It's not what you think,' she added hastily. 'We have a cup of tea and a bit of a chat, that's all. Actually we get on quite well. In a way I think Sam finds it easier to talk to me than to Laurie, but then he grew up in an all-female household, so perhaps that's not surprising. He's quite a sensitive soul and good at picking up on people's moods. I've been a bit low since the baby was born.' She was talking too much now, like someone who has something to hide.

'Does Sam ever confide in you?' Millie asked.

'About what?'

'I don't know, anything – his relationships, perhaps?'

'I know he's very happy to be marrying Gaby,' said Tanya. 'He thinks the world of her.'

'Do you think it's a good match; Gaby and Sam?'

'Yes. I think Gaby's a very lucky young woman. Well, they both are – lucky, I mean.'

'You must know Gaby very well?' said Millie.

'Of course. She was just a little girl when we started going to the church. It was always obvious that she'd marry a good man, because she's got so much going for her. But Sam is different from her previous boyfriends.'

'In what way?'

'Gaby's a big personality, and she gives off this impression of being the life and soul of everything, but actually I don't think she's at all confident where her appearance is concerned, or with men. Because of that I think she's always played it safe and gone for boys who are quite shy and not particularly good-looking. But Sam's different. He's handsome, yes, but also very thoughtful; there are a number of older ladies at church and he always takes the trouble to say something nice to them, compliment them on their outfits or hair or something. It makes them feel special.'

'What about any previous girlfriends,' said Millie. 'Has Sam ever talked about them?'

'Why would he?' Tanya seemed mystified.

'I don't know.' Millie kept it casual. 'Perhaps getting married himself might have stirred up memories of old flames, as it sometimes can.'

'No,' said Tanya. 'He's never mentioned anyone.'

'There are plenty of pictures of Sam on Gaby's Facebook page,' said Millie.

Tanya smiled. 'Gaby's always been one for showing off her new acquisitions; new pony, new car or whatever. She's proud of him, that's all.'

'Does Sam ever indicate any doubts about the wedding?'

Tanya chuckled. 'He wouldn't dare.'

'What does that mean?'

'Oh nothing, nothing at all,' said Tanya lightly. 'It was just a throwaway remark. Clive, Gaby's father, has a reputation for being a bit fierce. Completely unjustified, of course – he's a lamb – though he is naturally very protective of Gaby, because it's been just the two of them for so long. I think Sam is a bit wary of Clive, but that's probably wise.'

'Well, that's been really helpful,' said Millie, getting ready to go. 'What are the bridesmaids' dresses like?' she added. 'Could I be nosy?'

'Of course.'

As they climbed the stairs, Millie felt a sudden tug in her chest, as, very close by, a baby started to whimper. Tanya disappeared into one of the bedrooms and returned with a child of about Haroon's age, on her hip. The little girl rubbing her eyes with chubby fingers had pale skin and wisps of dark brown hair.

'Hello,' Millie held out a finger and the baby grabbed it and squeezed hard.

'The bridesmaids' dresses are through here,' said Tanya. She led the way into a bedroom given over to sewing, where dresses in a delicate floral design hung on a rail, each covered in protective polythene.

'They're beautiful,' said Millie truthfully. The intricate beadwork on the bodices must have taken hours. 'Gaby has great taste.'

'They both have,' said Tanya. 'Sam has views too.' They went back downstairs. 'Before you go, would you like to pray together, for Sam?' Tanya asked.

'No, thank you.'

Vicky dropped into Mariner's office to let him know that she was going to talk to the Wright family.

'I'm not sure about you going alone,' he said. By now he'd had time to catch up on Brown's entries to the policy book.

'You think it's unsafe?'

Mariner vacillated. 'Don't take this the wrong way,' he said. 'But I think they might be the kind of family where a male presence would be helpful, especially a uniformed one.'

Vicky told herself that Mariner wasn't questioning her competence. She'd been in challenging situations before, and had come through largely on her own wits and initiative. OK, so there might be something reassuring about having Brown along, and apart from anything else it would be another pair of eyes and ears, but still, she couldn't quite understand it. She went back to the main office. 'Fancy another outing?' she said to Brown. He was up in an instant, or would have been if he hadn't managed to sweep a pile of notes with his elbow and send them floating to the floor. It took him a couple of minutes to gather them up and restore them to where they had been, while Vicky made an effort to keep her exasperation in check.

The Wright family had moved from Wellington Road to Attwood Green, a modern housing development close to the city centre, regenerated and rebranded from a social housing estate that had been practically a no-go area, especially after dark. It was only as Brown drove them nearer that Vicky realised this, and the quickening of her pulse made it suddenly clear why Mariner had been concerned about her going alone.

'You all right?' Brown asked, as they turned into the complex.

'I'm fine,' said Vicky, breathing deeply. 'It's just that the last time I came here was to look at the spot where my husband was killed.'

On the doorstep of the Wright household, Jesson made the introductions, the uniformed Brown at her shoulder, and they were admitted with reluctant scepticism. 'I saw about that fire on the telly,' said the woman they could only assume to be Jordan's mother, when faced with the warrant card. 'I thought it wouldn't be long before you lot turned up.' Apparently familiar with the routine, she wandered off into the house leaving them to follow and Brown to close the door. 'Never mind that it could be an accident; someone's *stupidity*.'

'But we know from the Fire Investigation Team that it wasn't,' Jesson told her, as they came to rest in what was arranged as a sitting room, a vast widescreen TV taking up one wall and playing soundless, scrolling BBC news. The air was a warm combination of cooked food and animal. 'It was down to vindictiveness. Someone broke a window and sloshed around a bit of white spirit, in the hope that they would start a devastating fire. It could even have been started by someone who intended to kill all the people inside, including two small children. So I think we're within our rights to talk to anyone we think might have been involved. After all, it's not the first time the Shah family have been attacked, is it?'

'What, fireworks through the letterbox?' Mrs Wright snorted. 'Any kids could have done that. We don't even live anywhere near there anymore.'

'Nevertheless,' said Jesson pleasantly. 'Is Jordan about?' Though not invited to, she sat down on the sofa, beside a large marmalade cat, leaving just enough room for Brown to squash in beside her.

Mrs Wright went to the door and called up the stairs, 'Jordan! Get down here. You've got visitors!'

By the time Brown had taken out his pad and pen, the lumpen youth had appeared, wearing lurid boxer shorts and a T-shirt. 'Get us a cup of tea will you, Mum?' he mumbled, his eyes heavy with sleep.

'Where were you on Saturday night, Jordan?' Jesson asked, as he plonked down into the armchair next to them, facing the TV.

'I was out with my mates,' Jordan said, his attention already snared by the flickering screen.

'Who's that then?'

Jordan reeled off three names, which Brown had to ask him to repeat, so that he could write them down.

'Will they back you up?'

Jordan shrugged. 'Yeah,' he said petulantly.

'I understand you had a dispute with the Shah family.'

'What?' Jordan's eyes remained fixed trance-like on the forty-inch screen, unmoved by footage of atrocities in the Middle East.

'An argument.' Jesson remained patient.

'That?' He wrinkled his nose. 'It was ages ago. Stupid old duffer shouldn't go poking his nose in, should he?'

'Poking his nose into what?' asked Vicky.

Finally, Jordan turned to look at them. 'He didn't like me cleaning my car on the street. I mean, why shouldn't I? We were there before them.'

'So you're saying he objected to you cleaning your car,' Jesson clarified.

Jordan shrugged. Apparently it was as inexplicable to him as it was to her. Jordan's mum brought in a mug of tea, which she handed to her son while pointedly failing to offer the two police officers any refreshment. 'It was nothing to do with him,' she added.

'I'd like Jordan to tell me,' said Jesson. 'So what happened?'

'He yelled at me, I yelled back. He walked away, back to Paki-land. End of.' Jordan slurped his tea noisily, while his mum stood watching, her arms folded defensively. Further questioning was met either by 'dunno' or a wordless shake of the head. It was as much as they were going to get.

'What have you got against the Shahs?' Brown asked Jordan's mum, as they were on their way out.

'Oh, it's nothing personal.' Mrs Wright blew a stream of cigarette smoke in his direction. 'But you know how it is; once one lot move in the rest of them follow.'

'And why does that matter?' Brown continued, with the tone of the genuinely bewildered.

'I want my children to be safe.'

Jesson scoffed. 'From what?'

'The *Daily Mail*,' said Brown as he and Jesson walked back down the path to the car. 'Alive and well and living in a street near you.'

That lunchtime, over a sandwich, Millie reported back to Mariner.

'So it's not Tanya?' said Mariner.

'No, I think if anything she and Sam have more of a platonic relationship. And Tanya and Laurie seem to be committed to their faith. In a church where the sanctity of marriage is so revered, I can't imagine extramarital affairs amongst members are encouraged.'

'But you still think that's what this is with Sam Fleetwood, an affair?'

'It's what the evidence points to,' said Millie. 'Though admittedly it's all circumstantial. I'm just surprised, I suppose, that with all the surveillance we've got these days, someone like Sam Fleetwood can just vanish.'

'He could have taken on a new identity,' Mariner suggested.

'But why? What would make him go to that extreme?'

'Perhaps he feels backed into a corner, and has taken the coward's way out.' Mariner sighed. 'Frankly, if it wasn't for Charlie's link with the Boswells I'd have already let this one drop. It would have been good to see Sam Fleetwood show up for his wedding at least, but realistically, we should go and talk to Gaby and her father, to try and prepare them for a gentle let-down.'

In the car park they met Jesson and Brown, returning from Attwood Green. They looked despondent.

'Wright's got an alibi,' said Mariner, guessing.

'We'll need to check with his mates that he was where he says he was, but that should be straightforward enough,' said Jesson. 'To be honest, though, he's a slob. I can't quite imagine him bothering to get up off his backside to initiate arson, let alone being smart enough to cover his tracks.'

'So if not him, then perhaps someone closer to home,' said Mariner. 'We need to get Mustafa Shah to think a little harder about who that might be.'

'This help centre that he runs clearly plays a major role in the community,' said Vicky. 'There must be scope there for tensions of some sort or another. I'll go first thing on Monday.'

FOURTEEN

'**B**rown seems to be insinuating himself into this enquiry too,' Mariner remarked, as he and Millie drove over to Kingsmead, late on Friday afternoon.

'That was completely my fault,' said Millie immediately. 'I did my helpless female act and he stepped up. I hope it was OK.'

'As long as the fire investigation doesn't get compromised that's fine,' said Mariner. 'I don't want him being distracted unnecessarily.'

'I'll make sure he isn't,' said Millie. 'For what it's worth, I think Brown's quite good at his job.' She hesitated, wondering whether to tell Mariner about what she thought she might have seen. But something held her back.

'You could be right,' said Mariner. 'How are you going to play this?'

'What do you suggest?'

'We have to leave Gaby and her father with a clear rationale for why we can't launch a full-scale investigation,' said Mariner. 'And bear in mind that these are people who are used to getting their own way.'

'Do we drop the bombshell that there might be someone else in Sam's life?' Millie asked.

'Not if we can avoid it,' said Mariner. 'We don't have conclusive proof yet, and if Fleetwood does show up in the next few days, we'll have really screwed things up for him. What we do is broadly explain what you have found so far. If those are the conclusions they choose to draw, then there's not much we can do about it.'

'I'll take it gently,' said Millie. 'Gaby isn't going to like what she hears.'

Clive Boswell lived with his daughter just a few streets away from Meadow Hall Rise in the kind of house that might have featured on a property design show; all slick concrete angles and plate glass, uniquely designed and built on a couple of acres of prime land. Mariner wasn't sure if anyone would be home from work yet, and was prepared for a wait, but the Mercedes sports car on the drive was an encouraging sign, and he pulled in behind it.

Gaby was at the door only seconds after they rang the bell. 'What's happened?' she asked straight away, obviously fearing the worst. In the few days since they'd last met, it looked to Mariner as if she'd shed a few pounds, and her complexion had lost that healthy glow. The impeccable grooming had been abandoned and her hair hung loose and uncombed, while her clothing could have been assembled from the rejects rack of an Oxfam shop.

'Sorry,' Mariner shook his head. 'But can we come in?'

'Yes, of course,' she stepped aside to let them through. 'I'm in the conservatory. It's warmer in there.' Though it wasn't a cold day, and Mariner would have described the conservatory as stifling. Instead of the lake view, this house had a swimming pool, and Mariner couldn't help but wonder about its practicality, given the English climate. However, the steam rising from its surface indicated that it had the benefit of heating, and there was the added compensation of the hot tub nearby. Spacious and filled with light, the conservatory overlooked the park towards the distinctive steeple of Kingsmead church. The internal fixtures and fittings were high-end luxury; nothing from Homebase here. A book lay open on the coffee table, which Mariner recognised as a modern version of the Bible.

Gaby invited them to sit. 'Would you like some tea?' she asked automatically, though it looked as if the effort of making it might be a bit too much.

'We're fine,' said Mariner. 'This is DC Millie Khatoon. She's been making the enquiries about Sam on my behalf.'

'But—!' The petulant child began to protest.

'DC Khatoon is a highly experienced officer,' Mariner interjected. 'And she and I liaise frequently.'

Mollified, Gaby cast an expectant look at Millie.

'I'm sorry,' Millie said. 'So far I haven't come up with anything. But the good news is that nor have I found anything to suggest that Sam has come to any harm.'

Gaby sat back, her hand fluttering to her chest, and she almost smiled. 'Thank God.' Then the implications of that began to occur. 'But I don't understand, then. Where is he?'

Mariner and Millie exchanged a look. 'There can be lots of reasons why people choose to disappear,' said Millie. 'And in the vast majority of cases, they just turn up again after a few days, with a perfectly rational explanation.'

'Such as what?' she demanded.

'Sometimes people just take a bit of time out to think things through,' said Millie tactfully. 'How is your relationship at present?'

'It's good,' she said emphatically. 'We're getting married. You already know this,' she said to Mariner. Then: 'Oh God!' She was suddenly aghast. 'The wedding! What if Sam's not back in time? There are people travelling from all over the place. What do I tell them? What about the expense?'

'One thing at a time,' said Mariner. 'As Millie was saying, most people surface after a short time.'

'But why would Sam do this?' She was struggling to rationalise it. 'Where would he go when there's so much to do? Why wouldn't he at least let me know where he is, and that he's all right?'

Ignoring questions that right now they couldn't answer, Millie said: 'What kind of man is Sam? Is he tidy, untidy . . .?'

'Oh, very tidy,' said Gaby. 'Much more than me. We joke that it's one of the things that will drive him mad after we're . . .' She tailed off.

'I had a look at Sam's flat,' Millie said. 'It was very organised, but there didn't seem to be much in the wardrobe.'

Gaby rolled her eyes. 'It's something I'm working on. He's not very adventurous when it comes to clothes. He doesn't think they're important. But he's in such great shape, he could wear anything.'

'Do you go there often, to Sam's flat?' Millie asked casually.

'Never,' said Gaby. 'You've seen how pokey it is. And I think Sam's embarrassed about it. I mean, I went to see it when we first met. But since then it's been much more convenient for us to spend time here.'

'So when was the last time, before you were there last weekend?' Millie asked.

'Oh, ages ago. Months. I can't remember exactly.'

'Does Sam ever talk to you about past girlfriends?' Millie asked carefully.

'No,' said Gaby. 'I mean, when we first met we did talk a bit about some of the people we had been seeing before. Everyone does, don't they? Why?'

'We're just getting some background,' said Millie barely pausing. 'I know this might seem an odd question, but what brand of make-up do you use?'

Gaby looked at her. 'You're right, that is an odd question. I don't very often wear make-up; I prefer a natural look.'

'So you don't wear lipstick, mascara?'

'No. What is all this?'

'I found those items at Sam's flat, which might indicate that another woman has been there,' said Millie. 'In fact, could be a regular visitor.' She paused to allow Gaby to process what she was saying. 'Sam doesn't work away at weekends,' she went on. 'Nobody does that where he works.'

'So where does he go?' Gaby asked eventually, innocently.

'That's what we don't know,' said Millie. 'I was hoping you may have some ideas.'

They could see her mind working. 'You think Sam is seeing someone else? That's nonsense. He wouldn't—' She broke off, chewing on a nail. The silence went on for so long that Mariner almost wondered if she'd forgotten they were there. Finally, when she did respond, her voice was small. 'There *was* someone,' she said. 'Someone who had been very important to Sam, in the past. He was quite preoccupied with her when we first started going out.' She looked up at Millie in distress. 'Do you think he might have gone off with her?'

'Not necessarily,' said Millie. 'Perhaps it's a question of closure. It would make sense for him to tie up any loose ends before he marries you, wouldn't it? Did Sam tell you who this woman was?'

'No, he never said her name.'

'What about a nickname? Have you ever heard Sam refer to anyone as "Little Bear"?'

Her laugh was brief and derisive. 'No. Sam really doesn't go in for that kind of thing.'

As she spoke, they all heard the unmistakable sound of tyres on gravel. Gaby's reaction was instant. 'Oh God! Please don't say anything to my dad about this, he would—'

'What?' prompted Millie.

She was beside herself. 'Well, I don't know what he'd do. I've had to work so hard to convince him that Sam is the right man for me. If he found out—'

A key turned in the latch and the front door slammed shut, before the bulky form of Clive Boswell appeared. Having seen their car on the drive, apprehension was written all over him. 'There's news?' he asked Mariner, going over to kiss his daughter. 'What's happened?'

'We haven't located Sam yet,' said Mariner quickly. 'But at the same time, we have no reason to think that he has come to any harm.' Seeing Gaby's expression, he left it there. As he introduced Millie, Mariner thought he saw Boswell twitch. Was that because Millie was female or because of her ethnicity? 'We were just filling Gaby in on where we're up to and clarifying one or two details.'

Boswell sat down beside Gaby, taking one of her hands in his. Millie addressed Gaby. 'At one twenty on Saturday night, Gatso cameras picked up Sam's car driving out of the city along the A441 towards Hopwood,' she said. 'Do you have any idea why he might have been going in that direction at that time of night?'

Gaby frowned. 'I don't know.'

After a moment, Clive Boswell said: 'What about Carter's? Isn't their place out in that way?'

'What's that?' asked Millie.

'It's a waste disposal site,' said Boswell, when Gaby didn't respond. 'One of those that Sam was looking into for the Agency. There were some irregularities, and Sam was trying to gather evidence of what they were up to. He took his camera out there to try and get photographs.'

'He was spying on them?' said Mariner.

'I didn't think it was a very good idea,' said Boswell. 'I have dealings with some of these people. They're not a nice bunch. If they caught him at it, they wouldn't be very pleased.'

'Would he go out there at that time of night?' asked Millie.

Gaby was shaking her head. 'No, he wasn't involved with that any more,' she said. 'He told me, he'd passed it on to his managers, higher up.'

'But Sam told me he was hoping to get more evidence,' said Boswell. 'He felt sure they were up to something.'

'Out of interest, what kind of camera does Sam use?' Mariner asked.

'Oh, it's a good one,' said Clive Boswell. 'A digital SLR. And he knows how to use it.'

'And how does he carry it around? Does he have a proper camera bag?' Mariner was thinking about that holdall.

'Oh no,' said Gaby. 'He usually just throws it into the nearest bag he can find.'

Mariner caught Millie's eye, giving her a nod to move things along.

'Can I just confirm that after the party at the Glovers', you both came back here on Saturday night?' Millie asked.

'Yes.' They spoke in unison.

'And you were here all evening?'

'I went to bed early,' said Gaby. 'I had a really bad headache. Champagne always does that to me. I never learn.' She looked expectantly across at her father.

Boswell seemed suddenly preoccupied, as if he was thinking something through. 'Mr Boswell?' Mariner prompted.

'Sorry,' he snapped out of his contemplation. 'Actually, I went out again. There was a dinner for the Midlands Business Consortium. It went on late.' He smiled. 'Isn't that always how it goes? Weeks without anything and then two social events on the same day—'

'And where did this dinner take place?' asked Millie.

'At the Hotel Du Vin, in the city centre.'

'And what time was it when you left there?'

Sensing Boswell's hesitation, Mariner chipped in. 'It will save time if we can rule things out as we go along,' he said.

'Why?' Gaby demanded suddenly. 'Why is any of this relevant?'

'It's fine, darling,' Boswell said, before Mariner could reply. 'They're just establishing some facts. If we want to find out where Sam is, we need to help as much as we can.'

'Sorry, yes, of course.' All the while they'd been talking she was chewing on her fingernails, now, eventually she must have punctured the skin, because she had to go and get a tissue.

Boswell watched her go. 'I can't be very precise about the time,' he said. 'Rather a lot of alcohol was drunk. But I think I got back at about midnight. I got a taxi, of course,' he added quickly.

'I think I heard you come in,' said Gaby, returning to her spot on the sofa. 'I sort of half woke up, if you know what I mean. I think it must have been about midnight.'

'And what time did you go to bed?' Millie asked Gaby.

Gaby was still watching her father. 'Early, but I was just dozing really until Sam sent me the text.'

'And that was at eleven, is that right?'

'On the dot.' Gaby smiled wistfully. 'Sam is nothing if not precise. Oh God,' she said again. 'What about the wedding?'

'Try not to worry, sweetheart,' said Boswell. 'There's still a week for Sam to turn up, then, well . . .' He was unable to end the statement satisfactorily, so he turned to Mariner. 'So where does this leave us; you?'

'I'm afraid there's not much more we can do at this stage,' said Mariner. 'Unless there's a clear indication of foul play, all we can do is watch and wait.' He turned to Gaby, who was lost in thought. 'Do you know who Sam banks with, and what type of credit card he holds, or would Fiona have that information?'

'Why do you need to know that?' she asked.

'When someone uses their bank or credit cards then it can give us a clue to as to their whereabouts,' said Millie reassuringly. And if, as time went on, they weren't used, it would point to the possibility of something having happened to Sam. Clive Boswell looked across at Mariner, though he said nothing. Mariner sensed that Boswell senior had worked it out, but was relieved that he didn't add to Gaby's distress by forcing them to make it explicit.

'Oh, OK,' Gaby revived a little. 'Well, he banks with HSBC, same as me. I'm not sure about his credit card; Fiona might know.'

'I noticed there was no computer in Sam's flat,' said Millie.

'He keeps his laptop with him. It will be in his car.'

With a signal from Mariner, Millie wrapped things up with the usual undertaking that they would be in touch if there was

any news, and asked Gaby and her father to do the same. Clive
Boswell walked them out. 'Did I miss anything important?' he said.

'Not really,' Millie hedged. 'Gaby will be able to fill you in.'

'What do you think is going on?' he pressed Mariner, his
dismissal of Millie implicit.

'It's really hard to tell,' said Mariner. 'It may just be with the
wedding coming up that Sam needs some space. How do you
get on with him?'

Boswell stroked the back of his head. 'Well, to be honest, to
begin with I didn't think he was good enough for my daughter,
but then I imagine all fathers feel like that.'

'Was there any special reason?' Mariner asked.

'Truthfully? Early on, I had some concerns about his commitment to Gaby. As time has gone on they seem to be unfounded,
but you know.'

'Anything in particular that made you think that?'

'Nothing I could put my finger on,' said Boswell. 'It was just
a feeling. Apart from anything else, we know hardly anything
about him or his family.'

'Everyone we've talked to describes Sam as loyal and
trustworthy—' Mariner began.

'So why is he bunking off work, and shirking his responsibilities to his mother and sister?' Boswell clearly wasn't in the
mood to be charitable.

'It's early days,' Mariner reminded him. 'There's still time for
him to show up and explain himself.'

On the drive back Millie phoned through Sam's bank details to
Brown. 'Do you buy that about Sam going to the waste disposal
site,' she checked her notes, 'Carter's?' she said, when she'd
finished the call. 'I mean, why would he, if his part of it is over
and the case is being taken up with the agency itself?'

'Good question,' said Mariner. 'Clive Boswell seemed keen
on that idea, though, didn't he? And he's the first person we've
spoken to who has questioned Sam's loyalty.'

'So what now?' asked Millie. 'You think we'll have to drop it?'

'Not entirely,' said Mariner. 'To tie it up once and for all, it
would help to get some background checks authorised. I'll go
and talk to the gaffer.'

Superintendent Sharp's concern, as Mariner had known it would be, was the demand this might place on time and resources. She was understandably sceptical about the need for background checks. 'In the absence of a body we're on dodgy ground,' she said, pointing out the obvious. 'We have to bear in mind data protection. And it's not as if Sam Fleetwood is in any way vulnerable, is he, or have I missed something?'

'He's not,' Mariner conceded. 'But this behaviour is out of character, given his responsibilities.'

'What about mental health issues or relationship problems?' Sharp asked.

Mariner shifted in his seat. 'OK,' he said. 'This is where it gets a bit murky. If Fleetwood was having doubts about his commitment to the marriage there are plenty of people he could confide in, yet he doesn't seem to have intimated that to anyone. Other than a pushy father-in-law, there don't seem to be any issues with his fiancée. I saw them together last weekend and they were all over each other. However, there are some indications that despite this, Sam might have rekindled an old relationship.'

'Any ideas on who she might be?' asked Sharp.

'All we have is a nickname. I understand that in the past, secrecy has been an important factor. All I want to do is put a flag on his financial, phone and online activity. Hopefully it will help to confirm that Sam Fleetwood is OK, and we can let it go. On the other hand, if it should turn out to be something and the IPCC come knocking, we will have covered all the bases right from the off. Plus, these are Charlie's friends. I feel a certain obligation.' That was the clincher.

'That seems reasonable in the circumstances,' said Sharp. 'It's been less than a week. Let's give it until Monday, then see where we're up to.'

'It's a sound decision,' Mariner told Millie back in the ops room. 'If we're going to pursue this further, we need to establish absence of proof of life, and demonstrate that Sam Fleetwood has stopped doing the ordinary, everyday things we all rely on, like withdrawing cash and using his phone. Meanwhile we will start a policy book, alongside the fire investigation, to document what we find.' He looked across at Brown. 'Are you all right to run those two in parallel?'

Brown flushed slightly, but didn't immediately respond.

'You already are,' deduced Mariner.

'I just thought it might help to set up the MisPer electronic tracking system, so that we're ready to raise actions.'

Mariner couldn't fault him. 'So then, we watch and wait,' he said.

It had been a long and testing week which had left lots of unanswered questions. There was still no definitive evidence of foul play in the Wellington Road fire. Jordan Wright's alibi was so far standing up, in that his mates had vouched for him. So, short of any fresh evidence from either the fire investigation or from Sam Fleetwood's background checks, there was nothing urgent to attend to and Mariner had no compunction about letting his team go for the weekend. Millie stopped by his office on her way out.

'So how's it been, your first week back?' Mariner asked.

'Good,' said Millie, with a grin.

'You look knackered,' said Mariner.

'That obvious, eh? I'm glad to be getting back to my little man, too.'

'Off you go then. And Millie?'

'Yes?'

'It's good to have you back too.'

FIFTEEN

When Millie had gone, Mariner phoned Fiona Fleetwood to apprise her of the situation. She took it calmly, as he'd known she would, but he could hear the strain in her voice. He then checked in with Gerry Docherty that the situation there was ongoing. All this meant that Mariner left the building late enough to walk out with Superintendent Sharp. 'How did Millie take it?' she asked him.

'She's fine,' said Mariner. 'She knows how it works.'

'Always good to keep the overtime down too,' said Sharp, with a wry smile. 'And is Bingley settling in?' she asked.

'Who?'

'Kevin Bingley, from uniform.'

'Bingley? Pete Stone told me his name was Brown,' said Mariner.

'I think that might be Stone's little joke.' Sharp waited.

It took Mariner several seconds, as finally he managed to pinpoint the constable's accent. 'Oh I get it,' he said. 'Newcastle Brown. Hilarious. But why hasn't he corrected us? We've all been calling him that.'

'I'm guessing he's just keeping his head down,' said Sharp. 'And is he working out?'

'Seems to be,' said Mariner. 'He's done everything that's been asked of him so far, and more.'

'Good,' said Sharp. 'Perhaps we can hold on to him after all.'

'Meaning?'

'I understand he was thinking about a transfer before he came up to CID,' said Sharp.

'Really, why?'

'Getting sick of being Pete Stone's whipping boy. I'm glad he's found his way to your team.'

'What is it between him and Stone?' asked Mariner.

'I'm sure he'll tell you if and when he wants to.' They'd

come to the car park. 'Anyway, have a good weekend, Tom. Try to switch off.'

Mariner laughed. 'That's rich coming from you.'

'Yeah, all right.'

On the drive home Mariner realised he'd heard nothing from either Manor Park or the QE, both of which he took to be positive signals. He spent the evening at home. Although he looked forward to seeing Suzy, they had long given up on trying to share the narrow bed in her student room. In addition, the kitchenette in the postgrad block was quite inadequate and there was nowhere to sit, so, by mutual unspoken agreement, Friday nights had become their own. But first thing on Saturday morning Mariner drove over to the university, with an OS map on the seat beside him, and an idea for where they could have lunch. Suzy greeted him with her usual enthusiasm, but looked tired; the strain of getting to know a whole bunch of new colleagues and working procedures telling. Mariner couldn't imagine it; it was something he hadn't done for a very long time.

'You look as if you need a break,' he said. He had to raise his voice above the rowdy group of students who chose that moment to pass by. 'I thought we'd have a walk and find a good Warwickshire pub for something to eat.'

'I like the sound of that,' said Suzy. 'Just give me a minute.' She disappeared into the tiny bathroom.

'So how's the first week been?' Mariner called after her as he sat down on the bed.

'Good. I'm going to like it,' came the reply. 'They're a really interesting crowd, plus I found out something pretty amazing.'

'Amaze me,' said Mariner, deadpan.

Suzy stepped into the doorway, back where he could see her, at the same time threading an earring into her left ear. 'Yes, well, I'm not sure that you'll appreciate it in quite the same way,' she said.

'I might,' said Mariner, hurt.

'You remember I told you about my part-time colleague, Rosalind?' Mariner did, just about. 'Well,' said Suzy. 'It turns out that she's married to none other than Gideon Wiley.'

'Astonishing,' said Mariner.

'You have absolutely no idea why that's significant, do you?' Suzy challenged. The earring in, she went across to the book-shelves they'd erected the previous weekend and took down one of the door-stop books, which she handed to him: *Religious Icons of Ancient China* by Professor Gideon Wiley. 'You must be impressed by that.'

'Mm,' said Mariner, trying to muster some enthusiasm. Inside the flyleaf was a black-and-white photograph of a distinguished-looking middle-aged man.

'It's so exciting,' said Suzy.

'I'll take your word for it.'

Replacing the book, she picked up her coat and bag. 'Right, I'm ready.'

'I have more good news,' Suzy said, as they drove off the campus. 'It's possible that I've also found somewhere else to live. Rosalind and Gideon have got a cottage available for rental. They had trouble with a previous tenant, so had made the deci-sion not to let it again, but since they know me . . . It's adjacent to theirs in a village called Woolford, about eight miles away. Do you know it?'

'I do,' said Mariner. 'Very smart. She sounds a gem, this Rosalind.'

'She is,' Suzy agreed. 'Everybody loves her, including the students. In fact, I understand that one of them last year had a rather unhealthy attachment, but that's one for another time. Apparently the cottage has been empty for a while, so I've arranged to go and look at it this afternoon. I thought we could call in there after lunch? I'd like you to see it too.'

'Sounds interesting,' said Mariner.

'I might even get the opportunity to meet Professor Wiley face-to-face too, which would be wonderful. Anyway, enough of me, how's your week been?'

'Slow,' said Mariner. 'We're still waiting on Fire Investigation. Not that Vicky minds that. I think she's developing a thing for their lead investigator.'

'You know what they say about firemen,' said Suzy.

'Well, Docherty seems increasingly convinced that it was an arson attack, so we're trying to work out who might have been behind it.'

'You mean a deliberate attempt to kill the old man?' Suzy was understandably horrified.

'Or someone else in the family,' said Mariner. 'And I had another strange thing: a phone call. You remember your property developer, the one who turned up at Charlie's house?'

'You mean Gaby? The girl who is determined to find me somewhere to live? I suppose I should contact her now, to let her know I'm fixed up.'

'You won't need to, I can tell her,' said Mariner. 'She called me on Tuesday evening, at home. Her fiancé seems to have gone AWOL.'

'That's worrying,' said Suzy.

'Maybe,' said Mariner. 'He hasn't been seen since last Saturday night, so it's a week now, but we don't know for sure yet that he hasn't disappeared voluntarily. We're getting some strong hints that there may be another woman, past or present, who's distracted him. But obviously the longer it goes on the more concerned people are getting about him.'

'There seemed to be some tension between him and his prospective father-in-law,' Suzy remembered.

'Yes, there was, wasn't there?' said Mariner.

'So what will you do?'

'As an adult male, he's not a high risk, so there's a limit to what we can do at this stage, beyond monitoring the situation,' said Mariner. 'I've got Millie working on it, making some enquiries.'

'Yes, of course, Millie's back. How's she getting on?'

'She's good. Missing Haroon, naturally, but she's picked up again remarkably quickly. And then we've got Bingley, aka Brown, who's a catastrophe on legs, though paradoxically, quite a resourceful one, as it turns out.' He told Suzy about the name confusion. 'I can't work out what's going on with him,' he admitted. 'It's almost as if he's afraid to own up to his own competence.'

'And what about Jamie?' asked Suzy.

'I haven't heard anything yet, from either his doctor or the hospital. I'm taking it as a good sign.'

After a walk and lunch, they drove over to the picturesque Warwickshire village of Woolford. The sky was pale, with the occasional glimpse of a bright sun and some signs of early spring, though the air was sharp, and foggy-smelling. They parked next to the village green and followed Rosalind's directions along a winding lane past the church, to the Forge, where Rosalind and Gideon lived. Following along the high perimeter wall, they could hear the grunting sounds of exertion, and turned into the path of a wide, untamed garden to find a woman engaged in a tug of war with a deeply embedded tree root.

'Rosalind!' Suzy called to her.

Rosalind broke off from what she was doing and waved. 'Suzy! How lovely to see you.' As she straightened to ease her back, Mariner saw she was tall and rangy, with startlingly blue eyes and a ready smile. She'd made a largely unsuccessful attempt to tie her nest of rust-coloured hair back with a bandana. She came over, still breathing hard from the effort and wiping her hands on her jeans. 'And you must be Tom?' It was heavy work, but even so she seemed lightly dressed for the time of year in jeans and a loose cotton top under which 'her breasts swung freely.

'Is there anything I can do to help?' asked Mariner.

'Well, I've nearly got it, but it's a stubborn brute,' she said. 'I daresay you're stronger than I am. If you don't mind applying a bit of force?' The accent was pure cut-glass.

'Not at all.' Mariner gave his jacket to Suzy, and while Rosalind applied some leverage with the spade, he managed to wrench the root out of the ground, staggering backwards as it finally gave way.

'That's wonderful,' gasped Rosalind. 'Thank you so much. I was sure I'd have to pay someone to come and finish the job. Oops, sorry, you've got dirt all over you now.' She reached over and brushed a chunk of loose soil from his thigh. 'Let's get cleaned up, then I'll take you round to the cottage.'

The house was a long, irregular, half-timbered building with a traditional farmhouse kitchen that was chaotically untidy. Mariner sluiced his hands under the tap then cast around for something to dry them on, settling eventually on what looked to him more like a drying-up towel. Rosalind meanwhile had gone to change into corduroys and a more substantial jumper, and at the same time check on her husband who was resting.

They walked round the corner to the cottage, even though it shared a gated back fence with Rosalind and Gideon's house. On the other side it became clear why. Its garden was like a jungle, growing high and effectively blocking the narrow path. A fraction of the size of the Forge, the cottage was almost literally two-up two-down, with a faded sign to the right of the front door that announced, in alarmingly modern text-speak 'Y worry'.

'Why indeed?' murmured Mariner, as Rosalind unlocked the door and they crossed the threshold and into a musty atmosphere. 'It's all a bit retro,' said Rosalind encouragingly. 'It was a shepherd's cottage originally.' She sniffed the air. 'It's been empty for a few months, so I'm afraid it does smell a bit damp. But once the air gets through . . .'

Inside the furniture and rugs were mismatched and harked back to a bygone era, crowding the small, dimly lit rooms. The floorboards creaked underfoot as they walked, and everything was slightly off-kilter. Rosalind watched Mariner duck his head to get through a doorway. 'There's a concussion waiting to happen,' she said cheerfully. 'There's no central heating, I'm afraid, but you have got a cosy open fire. There's hot water from the geyser in the kitchen, and we put in an electric shower for the last tenants.'

An electronic bleep brought them back into the twenty-first century, and Rosalind hunted her pockets, coming up eventually with a paging device. 'Gideon,' she smiled. 'I need to get back to him.' She held the keys out for Suzy. 'Why don't I leave these with you and you can have a good look round and test things out without me breathing down your neck. Then stop by the house to let me know what you decide. I hope you'll have time to have a cup of tea and say hello to Gideon, too. Once he's managed to get up and about, he'd love to meet you both.' And she disappeared back around the side of the cottage.

'Are you sure about this?' said Mariner after she'd gone. He ran his fingers over the flaking paint on the window frames, feeling cool air wafting through where the fit was far from snug. 'It's a bit isolated.'

'Good. I'll be able to practise my violin, without driving the neighbours insane,' said Suzy. 'Rosalind's right about the smell, though.' She wrinkled her nose. 'Body under the floorboards, do you think?' she murmured as they climbed the narrow stairs.

'I think it might be the drains,' said Mariner. She'd always had a stronger sense of the macabre than him.

Upstairs were a bathroom, circa 1950, and two tiny bedrooms with low, uneven ceilings. 'It's all so quaint!' Suzy exclaimed.

'That's one way of putting it,' said Mariner. His own place was far from modern but he did like some comfort.

Having had a good look around, they came to the larger of the two bedrooms overlooking the jungle of a back garden, where they could see the ivy creeping over the gate in the fence that led into Rosalind and Gideon's garden. This room was furnished with an old mahogany wardrobe and chest of drawers, but the brass bed frame and its bare mattress looked brand new.

They were, through necessity, standing close together and now Suzy slipped her arms around him. 'What do you think?' she asked, leaning back so that he could feel the pressure of her hips against his.

'Rosalind or the cottage?' asked Mariner.

'Both, I suppose. Rosalind's sweet, isn't she? A free spirit. No bra today, but of course I don't suppose you noticed that.'

'Can't say that I did,' he lied.

'Oh really?' She reached down between them and gave him a squeeze. It had an instant effect. Suzy glanced over at the bed. 'Rosalind told us we should try things out,' she said artfully.

On another occasion Mariner would have resisted, afraid of disappointment, but this time, caught up in the moment, he didn't. And perhaps it was the adrenaline rush of removing the tree stump, maybe it was Rosalind's attire or the frisson of something slightly illicit, but this time he didn't falter, not even distracted by the banging of the bedstead against the wall.

Afterwards Suzy stretched luxuriantly. 'A welcome return to form, DCI Mariner,' she said. 'If this is what the place does to you, I need to move in right away.'

'So what do you think?' When they got back to the Forge, Rosalind smiled expectantly, looking from one to the other of them. Mariner wondered if she could tell what they'd been up to, perhaps from the look on his face.

'I love it,' said Suzy. Mariner thought it best not to say anything. He wasn't the one who would be living here, after all.

'I'm so glad,' Rosalind beamed. 'As I said, you can move in whenever you like.'

'As soon as possible, as far as I'm concerned,' said Suzy, casting a mischievous glance at Mariner. 'It will be good to get out of the noisy halls. I could start bringing over some of my things tomorrow?'

'Wonderful,' said Rosalind.

They both turned to Mariner.

'Fine by me,' said Mariner, knowing that Suzy was reliant on his much bigger car.

They were standing in the kitchen, and as they talked, Rosalind had been moving around, putting tea things on a tray. 'Now, come and meet Gideon,' she said, adding the newly filled teapot. 'He'll be cross that I'm keeping you to myself.'

Gideon was sitting by French windows in an armchair, a rug over his knees, looking out over a beautifully tended garden; a stark contrast to Y Worry. He'd diminished somewhat since the photograph in the book had been taken, and Mariner would have placed him at about seventy years of age, so twenty or thirty years older than his wife. He was slight but unfolded from his chair would have been tall, and his dark, intense eyes under bushy brows would have made him imposing. Sparse white hair grew down over his collar, and his beard growth probably owed more to the inconvenience of shaving than a conscious style decision. His movement was limited, but his face remained expressive, and it looked as if intellectually he was still sharp; a research journal, with tiny, close-packed print, was set up beside him on a kind of lectern. He seemed delighted to see them, especially Suzy.

'I've told him all about you,' said Rosalind. 'And this is Suzy's partner,' she added.

Gideon's hands lay loosely in his lap, so, unsure of whether a handshake would be appropriate, Mariner simply raised a hand in greeting. 'Tom Mariner,' he said.

Gideon murmured something unintelligible in response.

'Oh yes, that's right,' replied Rosalind, though Mariner was at a loss. 'Like Sir Neville, the conductor,' she repeated for his benefit. 'Are you musical?'

'Not at all,' said Mariner, thinking that his back catalogue of the Sex Pistols probably didn't count.

'Gideon does like his Radio Three,' Rosalind replied, confirming this. She urged them to sit on a rather sagging sofa and, when she had served them, fussed over Gideon, helping him to sip tea through a spouted cup, finishing up by wiping the saliva that trailed from his mouth.

'Right,' said Rosalind, 'now we can switch on ARNIE.' ARNIE turned out to be Gideon's electronic aid that spoke for him, with rather a forthright delivery. 'Don't know what I would do without it,' the robotic voice said, in its slightly belligerent monotone. Suzy cued into how the machine worked straight away, but it took time for Gideon to compose his sentences, so conversation was stilted. 'You do get used to it after a while,' said Rosalind, in one of the lengthy pauses.

'Where were you?' the machine demanded, and Mariner realised that Gideon was addressing him.

'Sorry?'

'He wants to know which university you studied at,' said Rosalind.

'Oh, I didn't,' said Mariner, to Gideon.

'He's a police officer,' Suzy told him.

Gideon inclined his head politely, but it was obvious that as of that moment, Mariner ceased to be of any interest. Suzy, though, more than made up for his shortcomings and before long she and Gideon were discussing the finer points of the article Gideon had been reading, while Mariner and Rosalind sat looking on, their presence irrelevant. Mariner listened for a while, feigning an interest, but when Rosalind got up to clear the tea things, he picked up the tray and carried it out into the kitchen for her.

'Sorry, that must have seemed rude,' said Rosalind. 'Gideon's always been very academic, but since he's been ill his focus is even more on the cerebral. I suppose it's the one area that is still within his capabilities.'

'It's completely understandable,' said Mariner. Normally it would have rankled, but nothing this afternoon could dent his good mood. He felt like a different man. 'It must be hard work,' he went on. 'Taking care of Gideon, I mean. Do you have help?'

'Oh yes. There's a carer who comes in to enable me to go to

the university. That's an absolute godsend, I'd go mad without it. And the local doctors are regular visitors, of course. Gideon's in quite a lot of pain, so needs powerful relief. But the GPs are often locums these days and I'm not sure of the extent to which they really understand his condition.' She and Mariner returned to the conservatory and sat for a further half hour before Gideon suddenly seemed to deflate, the energy draining out of him, and Rosalind announced that he needed to rest.

'I hope you weren't too bored,' said Suzy as they drove back towards Birmingham to stay the night at Mariner's place.

'Don't worry about it,' said Mariner. 'You and Gideon seemed to hit it off.'

'It was fascinating,' said Suzy. 'He's thinking of writing another book, and asked me if I might like to co-author it.'

'That sounds like a commitment,' said Mariner.

'I know, but it would be tremendously exciting to work with him, not to mention the kudos.' She frowned. 'I'm just not sure if I'd be up to it.'

'Of course you would,' said Mariner. 'Don't undersell yourself.'

On Sunday morning they returned to Coventry and packed up Mariner's car to drive Suzy's things over from the university accommodation to Y Worry. Overnight, Rosalind had added some homely touches to make Suzy feel welcome; flowers from the garden, a bottle of wine and from somewhere she'd got hold of a child's hard-hat, to which she'd added a Post-it: *For Tom – only thinking about public liability!*

'Nice sense of humour,' said Mariner.

'That's why I took to her so quickly,' said Suzy. 'She's such a good mimic too; she takes the piss out of the students something rotten.'

Mariner deposited Suzy and her belongings at Y Worry, and, leaving her to empty boxes, went across to the self-storage facility where she had left the rest of her library. By the time he'd returned and unloaded the car, most of the little spare bedroom was taken over by books. 'This is a complete fire hazard,' said Mariner, thinking of that ground-floor room in Wellington Road. 'Don't go dropping any lit matches anywhere here, will you?' He stood up. 'Fuck!' And for the third time, banged his head on the beam.

'There's a good idea,' said Suzy, coming up behind him and slipping her arms around his waist. 'What do you think, shall we commemorate my first day here?'

In truth, Mariner thought he might be pushing his luck, but, as it turned out, he was gratifyingly wrong. That evening they christened the Aga too, and Suzy cooked while Mariner re-assembled some of her furniture.

'Now that I'm a bit settled, I'll ask Mum and Dad to come and stay,' said Suzy, as they sat at the rickety little kitchen table to eat. 'And it's about time you met each other. They've known about you for ages and I'm sure they're starting to think you're avoiding them.'

It was jokingly said, but Mariner recognised that meeting Suzy's parents was long overdue. It was meant to have happened at Christmas, but then his work had got in the way, and for some reason he'd been happy to defer it. The whole idea of family had been so alien to him for such a long time now that the prospect of it made him feel slightly claustrophobic. 'It's a pity I won't be able to reciprocate,' he said.

She smiled. 'Not your fault if both your parents are gone, is it?' Mariner had told her all about his mother, who had been a formidable and unique individual, but he'd played down what little he knew of his father, a public figure, whose identity Mariner had only discovered quite recently, and after his death.

SIXTEEN

On Monday morning Mariner returned to Granville Lane, knowing that with Millie off now until Wednesday, they'd be more stretched than ever trying to pursue two separate enquiries. What would make things simple, and allow them to focus on the fire investigation, would be if Sam Fleetwood's bank account had seen some activity over the weekend, putting an end to the uncertainty.

'It hasn't,' said Bingley, his disappointment reflecting Mariner's own. 'According to the bank, he's been financially inactive since the Friday before he went missing.'

'Crap,' said Mariner. 'It might not mean anything, of course. If he is off with some rich, married woman somewhere, she might be paying all the bills for him. Have we made any progress with his phone?'

'I've used the number to retrieve his calls from the provider,' said Bingley. 'There are no numbers showing up that can't be accounted for.'

'But that doesn't mean he hasn't got another pay-as-you-go phone,' said Mariner. 'What about social media?'

'Fleetwood doesn't seem to be that into it,' Bingley told him. 'He's got a Facebook page but there's hardly anything on it, and it hasn't been looked at for months. But I know DC Khatoon has looked at Gaby's page, which is covered with pictures, mostly of her and Sam. Neither of them do Twitter, unless they're using really obscure account names. I even did a quick search for "Little Bear". That threw up some weird stuff, but nothing I could see that was relevant for us.'

Mariner had been reluctant to believe that this was as simple as Fleetwood going off with another woman. It didn't seem to fit the profile of the man he had built. But he couldn't deny the evidence, or Fleetwood's reported history. 'That's how we nail it,' he said to Bingley. 'If we can find this unknown woman, we'll find Fleetwood.' And, thanks to Suzy, he now had a good idea of where to start. 'That old flame Nathan Dornham described, it was while he was at university, wasn't it?'

'Yes,' said Bingley. 'An older lady, probably married, according to Dornham.'

'So how about one of his lecturers?'

'That could work,' said Bingley.

'Do we know where Fleetwood studied?' asked Mariner, hoping it didn't turn out to be Canterbury or Aberdeen.

'I can find out,' said Bingley. 'Gaby or his sister will know that.'

'While you're doing that, I'm going out to Fleetwood's flat to see if there's any indication that anyone's been there over the weekend,' said Mariner.

Vicky Jesson had gone to talk to Mustafa Shah, in the hope of finding out who, if anyone, might want to attack his family. He was not at his sister's house, but already back at work, so that was where she sought him out. The Yemeni Advice Centre was a religious and welfare centre and inhabited a small building, once a shop, that had been converted into two small offices on the Ladypool Road running through Sparkhill. Although Jesson arrived only minutes after the doors opened, the room was already half full, with men, women and children, and there seemed to be no organisation. The walls of the waiting room were plastered with posters, some in English, some in Arabic, but all of which advertised assistance of all kinds, drawing attention to people's rights and entitlements. A closed door to one side bore Mustafa Shah's name, and when Jesson asked one of those waiting, she was told that he was inside, in conference with clients. So she took a vacant seat beside a shabby desk covered with neat stacks of paperwork and picked up a magazine while she waited.

Shortly after Jesson's arrival, the door from the street opened again, and a young woman came in, unwinding a scarf from around her neck. Like a flock of birds disturbed, all those waiting surged towards her, clamouring for attention, each pleading his or her case loudly and vocally. She deftly side-stepped each of them, and, removing her coat, hung it on a hook behind the desk and sat down, only then responding to the demands, calmly and firmly. Gradually order was restored. At an opportune moment Jesson laid down the magazine and discreetly passed the woman her warrant card, saying: 'I need to speak to Mr Shah as soon as possible.' The woman studied the card and Jesson, before nodding acquiescence. 'Busy place,' said Jesson sympathetically.

'It's always like this,' said the PA, starting to address the papers on her desk. 'Especially first thing in the morning.'

'And are you the only assistant?' asked Jesson.

'Yes, although I don't think Mr Shah really wanted me; he's not very good at delegating. The pay's not bad, and I get to drop the kids at school before I come in. But then it's always chaos when I get here. I've tried telling him that we should open at ten, but he won't listen to me.'

'How many people do you see each day?'

'Oh, I've given up counting,' the PA said. 'In theory there's an appointment system, but of course people come in when there's an emergency and Mr Shah insists on trying to fit everybody in. A lot of the people who come over here are hoping to make a better life, so they have very little in the way of resources. They rely on us.'

'Mr Shah and his family must be popular,' said Jesson.

'Yes, although there's always someone who isn't satisfied with the help they get.' As she spoke the door to Mustafa Shah's office opened and he ushered out a young couple, shaking them each by the hand as he did so. The woman was tearful. Glancing towards the desk, Mustafa Shah caught sight of Jesson, whose clothing and skin colour made her conspicuous. He smiled: 'Please, come in.'

It was probably for the best that Jesson couldn't understand Arabic, but she caught the mood of the room in the facial expressions as she jumped the queue and followed Mustafa Shah into his office. 'I didn't expect to find you back at work so soon,' she said, taking one of several chairs arranged in front of Shah's desk.

'People don't stop needing help because of our misfortunes,' said Shah. He waited until Jesson was seated before sitting down. 'And it helps me to stay busy. My sister's house is rather a crowded place just now. To be honest it is a relief to get away.'

'You must miss your father-in-law too,' said Jesson.

'Yes, although Soltan only worked here part-time, usually in the evening for an hour or two.'

'So what exactly is it that you help people with?'

Shah waved a hand across all the papers on his desk, and a stack of overflowing in-trays. 'Whatever they are having issues with: finance, housing, employment, family issues. Anything and everything can walk through that door and does so on a daily basis.' But he clearly didn't mind. His relaxed, easy manner said that everything was under control. Jesson imagined that he was good at his job; people would find it easy to trust him.

'Anyone you fall out with in the course of your work?' she asked.

'Ha! Where would you like me to start?' Shah sat back. 'My job is to try and secure for people what they are entitled to. There are many people who want to stop that from happening, because it costs them. I spend a good proportion of my time on the phone, harassing local councillors and private landlords.'

'Do any of them take that harassment personally?'

'Why do you ask?' He was suddenly wary.

'Despite what we first thought, it's looking increasingly likely that your wife was right, and that the fire at your house was started deliberately. It could have been a random attack, but the odds are that it was started by someone you know.'

Shah sighed. 'You're aware that it has happened before?'

'The Wright family.'

'The son is a thug. He spat at my wife while she was walking in the street, pretending that it was just an accident, and he argued with my father-in-law. It was very upsetting.'

'We have spoken to Jordan Wright regarding this latest incident,' Jesson said. 'But it looks as if he has an alibi. For the record, what exactly was the argument about with your wife's father?'

'Soltan was proud to live in this country. He thought it was important to look after the environment and to keep things neat and tidy. This boy used to clean his car on the street, which involved tipping out all the rubbish from it – tin cans and crisp packets – and leaving it lying there for others to dispose of for him. Soltan took issue with him about that.' It hardly sounded like grounds for murder.

'How many people knew that you were going to be out of the country last weekend?' Jesson asked.

'Not many; Aisha here, my wife, of course. I may have mentioned it to a couple of clients, to explain why I wouldn't be able to see them for a week or so.'

'So it could reasonably have been assumed by anyone else that you would be in the house too?'

'Perhaps,' said Shah. 'The trip was arranged quite suddenly. It's not always easy to get flights at a good price.'

'It's likely that any arson attack would be directed at you or your father-in-law,' said Jesson. 'Is there anyone you think would want to harm you or your family?'

Shah was affronted. 'Enough to set fire to my house with my wife and children inside? Enough to kill members of my family? No. No one I know would do that.'

'Not even some of the people you rub up against here?' Jesson pressed.

Shah was pensive. 'We have instigated court proceedings against a couple of private landlords on behalf of clients,' he said. 'But I really don't think they would go to such lengths.'

'All the same, it would help to have details of those cases.'

The outfit wasn't sophisticated enough for an intercom, so Shah got up and went out to the waiting room, where Vicky heard him in conversation with his assistant. 'I've asked Aisha to print off some of the correspondence,' he said, coming back into the office. 'But I would ask that our clients' details remain confidential.'

'Of course,' said Jesson. 'And there is no one else you can think of? You must come across some unsavoury individuals at times.'

Shah snorted with disbelief. 'There are of course people we challenge, but I can't imagine that they would resort to—' He paused. 'Except . . .'

'Yes?'

'The couple that just left here – they are in trouble with their finances and their debts are spiralling out of control because they have taken out a loan with an outfit called Going for Gold; it's a place on Bethel Street.' Turning towards the window he gestured to the right. 'We have had trouble with them in the past.'

'Loan sharks?' Jesson speculated.

'From the outside the business is a legitimate pawnbroker's cash-for-jewellery kind of thing,' said Shah. 'But it's become apparent in the last few months that they also offer short-term loans with punishing interest rates. It's not a service they advertise; instead they just take advantage of the desperate customers who go into their shop. The problem is that as far as I can work out they are not doing anything illegal, simply preying on already vulnerable people in the way that's become so commonplace. My strategy has been to publicise what they are up to and discourage our clients from doing any kind of business with them. And I know they're aware of this, because a couple of months ago we had a nasty note put through the door.'

'Did you keep it?'

'No,' said Shah. 'I barely even looked at it. The tone was threatening but I didn't take it seriously.'

'Who runs the outfit?' asked Jesson.

'It's a couple of white Englishmen. I don't know their names, though I think they might be brothers.'

'Well, that's a good start,' said Jesson. 'But it would help if you and your staff could—'

Shah smiled again. 'My staff? It's just Aisha and me.'

'Well, it would be useful if you could think back over the last months, or even years, in case there's anyone else you remember who might have sufficient grounds for carrying out an attack like this,' said Jesson. 'What was the purpose of the visit to Sana'a?'

'I was meeting with business associates. We have donors there who support our work.' He smiled. 'I went to sweet-talk them.'

On her way out, Aisha presented Jesson with a slim folder containing details of the cases against the landlords. 'Good luck,' she said.

Exiting the Advice Centre Jesson turned right and walked along to Bethel Street. This was a thriving community of businesses that reflected the diversity of a city with no majority population, and the pavements were busy with mothers and their children and elderly people. Some way along the street she found Going for Gold. The windows were protected by permanent mesh grilles, the door was locked and the premises looked empty and dark inside. She went into the sweet shop next door to ask about it.

'It's been closed for at least a week and we haven't seen the men who worked there,' the girl serving behind the counter told her.

When Mariner got to Sam Fleetwood's flat, everything looked pretty much as Millie had described it, although in the last few days a substantial amount of post, much of it junk, had built up in the mail box. Mariner took out the pile and sorted through it. He found two items of interest. The first was an invitation from Oxfordshire police to a Speed Awareness course, as an alternative to paying the speeding fine that Sam Fleetwood had incurred three weeks ago, on a stretch of the A3400. Mariner knew that road. Unless a driver was familiar with the section that ran through a series of small villages, it was easy to get caught out by the sudden drop to thirty miles per hour. Sam Fleetwood had been clocked, late on a Sunday evening, doing thirty-seven mph.

Then, further down, Mariner came to a printed postcard advertising special weekend deals at a Cotswold hotel. Although addressed only to 'the occupier' at Fleetwood's address, the message on the reverse began '*To all our valued customers . . .*' The two items were not incompatible with one another.

Walking back to his car, Mariner phoned Bingley. 'If anyone needs me I'm on my way down to north Oxfordshire,' he said. 'I've got a lead on where Sam Fleetwood might have spent some of his weekends away.' It even crossed his mind that Fleetwood might be there right now. If he was, Mariner would be having sharp words with him.

It took Mariner an hour to drive down to the Rookery Hotel at Eccrinton, but it wasn't quite the typical Cotswold boutique hotel he'd expected. Instead, it was a former country house, set in its own grounds, and now run by a national chain known for its themed holiday-camp-style activity weekends. It wasn't at all the kind of place he could imagine Gaby wanting to stay for a little romantic getaway, but perhaps it was suitably anonymous for an illicit assignation of the kind that Sam seemed to be leaning towards. One of the regular weekends featured on the programme in the lobby was a 'singles weekend'. Mariner couldn't help glancing around, in the hope that Fleetwood might suddenly materialise before his eyes, but most of the clientele on this weekday morning looked like retired couples. Identifying himself, Mariner showed the Eastern European receptionist Sam's photograph. The man took it and studied it for a minute or two. 'Yes, I think I have seen him,' he said, eventually.

'His name is Sam Fleetwood,' said Mariner. 'We are keen to speak to him. Is he staying here now?' He half expected to meet some resistance on the grounds of guest privacy, but his warrant card apparently overruled such concerns. After a search of the registers, however, he was told that Sam Fleetwood wasn't on the system, either for today or going back over the last six months, which was as far as records went.

'Do you remember seeing him with anyone, or if he was here for any particular event?' Mariner asked, but unsurprisingly the receptionist's memory did not stretch to those details. He was apologetic nonetheless. 'We have so many guests staying here.'

CCTV was deleted on a weekly basis and Mariner didn't want to waste time trawling through it, though he asked for a copy of the last week's material to be emailed to him, just in case. He couldn't then think of anything more. It was annoying to come so tantalisingly close to Sam Fleetwood, but to leave with nothing.

He'd only been back in the car a few minutes however when his phone rang. Bingley was beside himself. 'Sam Fleetwood's debit card has been used to draw out two hundred quid,' he said. 'His bank has just been on to let us know.'

'When and where?' said Mariner.

'This morning, from a cash machine in Redditch.'

So perhaps they were closing in; geographically at least. Hopwood and Redditch were within spitting distance. 'Are they sure it was him?' Mariner asked.

'The pin number was used too,' said Bingley. 'So unless he's pretty stupid . . . Anyway, turns out there's CCTV on the machine, operated by Redditch district council and monitored by West Mercia. I thought as you were down that way, you might want to go and see.'

'You thought right,' Mariner told him. 'Let them know I'm on my way, will you?'

'I'll text through the details,' said Bingley.

At Redditch police station Mariner met local bobby Sergeant Ron Wheeler, who found him coffee and a spare interview room, where he could wait while the CCTV was located and sent across. Sitting waiting reminded him of his time at the QE and he took the opportunity to check in with Nell at Manor Park. They hadn't heard anything from the hospital either, and Jamie was much the same. Nell was in the middle of recounting to Mariner what Jamie had been up to the previous day, when Wheeler appeared again, signalling that the CCTV had come through.

When Mariner and Wheeler watched the footage, it was immediately obvious that it wasn't Sam Fleetwood who had used his card. 'Chantelle Brough,' Wheeler said straight away. 'She's one of our regulars, but petty theft and shoplifting are more her line. She must think her luck has changed. We know her usual haunts; I'll get the area cars looking out for her and let you know when we've brought her in. I'll get the CCTV clip sent to you for exhibits too. Do you want to wait around?'

Mariner decided he'd give it an hour. If Chantelle Brough wasn't brought in during that time, he'd have to rely on Wheeler to pass on any intel. Fifty-five minutes later, just as he was thinking about returning to Granville Lane, Wheeler had a call to say that Chantelle was on her way.

Chantelle Brough may have thought her luck had changed for the better, but it wasn't going to last. She claimed to have found Sam Fleetwood's wallet, completely by chance. She was bony and pasty-skinned, with lank brown hair, and Mariner guessed that most of the money had gone on some or other intoxicating substance. Certainly Chantelle seemed oblivious to or ignorant of the trouble she was in, but was delighted with her good fortune, and grinned inanely at everyone throughout the interview.

'Where did you find it, Chantelle?' asked Wheeler.

'It was just lying there, on the ground,' she said, her eyes wide with wonder.

'Really.' Wheeler's voice was heavy with scepticism.

'I know! I couldn't believe it either.' Chantelle beamed, displaying stained and crooked teeth.

When asked to be more specific, she identified a street close to Redditch town centre and the cash machine she'd used. 'And you didn't think to hand it in to us, that someone might be looking for it?' Wheeler asked.

For the first time Chantelle's face clouded a little, as if that thought had genuinely never occurred to her. 'Well . . . no. Finders keepers, innit?' She looked up at Wheeler, perturbed. '*Are* they, looking for it?'

Wheeler rolled his eyes at the two-way mirror. 'How did you get the pin number, Chantelle?'

'It was written down on a piece of paper in the wallet. How lucky is that? That's how I knew, you see.' Chantelle sat back, satisfied.

'Knew what?' asked Wheeler, suspiciously.

'That the wallet was left there for me to find.'

'Why?'

'The number! It was 1993, the year I was born.'

Wheeler expelled a heavy sigh. 'What else was in the wallet, Chantelle? How much cash?'

She pouted. 'Not much – a couple of notes is all. That's why I used the card.'

'And what did you do with the rest?'

'I chucked it away. Weren't no good to me.'

'The wallet belonged to a man called Sam Fleetwood,' said Wheeler. 'Do you know him?'

'No. Why would I? I didn't steal it!' She was outraged by the suggestion.

Afterwards there was time for Mariner to have a few words with Wheeler. 'I've known Chantelle a while now,' he said. 'And I believe her.'

Mariner trusted Wheeler's judgement. Someone smart could have done far more damage with those bank cards by buying expensive goods online, but Chantelle hadn't thought of that, or maybe she didn't have access to the Internet. 'I don't think she'll be able to tell you anything about where your MisPer is,' Wheeler went on. 'I've got a couple of PCSOs looking for the wallet in the area and I'll let you know if they find it.'

On his way back to Granville Lane Mariner considered the implications of Sam Fleetwood's wallet having turned up as it had, combined with the fact that he had been last seen heading out of Birmingham on the A441, the Redditch Road. The most likely scenario was that he had been in Redditch and had dropped or lost his wallet. It could have been stolen, but why would the thief then discard it, along with its contents, for Chantelle to find? And why would Sam Fleetwood, a seemingly intelligent man, include his pin number conveniently written down alongside the bank cards? Unless it had been planted; a deliberate ploy, to cast off his old life, and conceal his true whereabouts. The other, less palatable alternative was that something untoward had happened to Fleetwood. It was a possibility that had lurked at the back of Mariner's mind, but so far with no evidence to support it.

Mariner was considering all this when his phone started going off like a Geiger counter at Chernobyl, texts and calls coming through simultaneously. As soon as he could, he pulled over and returned the first call to Vicky Jesson.

'Where are you?' she said. 'We need to get down to Wellington Road right away. They've found another body.'

SEVENTEEN

As Mariner arrived at Wellington Road, he pulled in behind a line of cars that included one he recognised; this wasn't going to be good. The find had effectively suspended the operation in the ground-floor room, and the investigation and forensic teams were kicking their heels out in the front garden. Someone had done a tea run to the nearby McDonald's and the cups and donut bags were lined up on the garden wall. Jesson was already on-site, deep in conversation with Gerry Docherty as she got suited up. Mariner cleared his throat as he approached, clearly interrupting a more than professional chat. 'What do we know?' he asked.

'Nothing much yet,' said Docherty. 'We sent Dougal in to locate any further accelerant sites from the newly excavated areas, but he was going nuts, trying to drag Lance under that one last area that we haven't cleared. Come and see for yourselves. Stuart Croghan's in there having a look at the moment.' So Mariner had been right about the Land Rover.

Mariner and Jesson trod the now familiar route into the house behind Docherty, as far as the door into the ground-floor room. More headway had been made since the last visit, and it presented a surreal sight. Look to the left and the room was forensically clean back to the grey, stained walls and floor. Look to the right and debris was still heaped up like a snowdrift, ten feet high against the far wall. Underneath this pile, a crude kind of cave had been hollowed out, its roof held up by steel supports. It was inside this cavity that Croghan squatted on his haunches, while the photographer took shots from various angles. With a brief greeting to the two police officers, Croghan shuffled back to allow them to see, and Mariner heard Jesson draw breath. The body, resting on a blackened slab, was burned beyond recognition, a skeleton of brown stretched skin, with just a few sparse strands of black hair sprouting from its scalp. It looked like one of those perfectly preserved prehistoric beings, periodically discovered in peat bogs. 'Not pretty, is she?' said Croghan. 'All I can say for sure at this stage is that she's female, and that's mainly from the jewellery she was wearing.'

'To be honest we're lucky we've even got that,' said Docherty. 'Given the intensity of the fire, she could have been cremated to nothing.'

'So why didn't that happen?' asked Jesson.

'When the ceiling collapsed, some of the debris fell at an angle and created a small pocket of space that would have halted the fire's progress.'

'So who the hell is it?' said Mariner, looking at Jesson. 'The only person Salwa Shah was concerned about that night was her father. No one else was mentioned as being in the house.'

'And when we talked to her, she didn't give any impression that she was hiding anything, or anyone, from us,' Jesson agreed.

'We're pretty certain now that the fire was started deliberately?' Mariner checked with Docherty.

'As sure as we can be,' Docherty answered.

'So this gives us a whole new dimension,' said Mariner, turning to Vicky. 'Only Salwa Shah can tell us who she is.'

They left Croghan to his investigations and made their way out to Mariner's car. 'How did you get on with Mustafa Shah?' he asked, once they were on their way.

'He gave me some files relating to people they've crossed swords with at the advice centre,' said Jesson. 'I haven't had a chance to read them yet, but Shah also mentioned an outfit called Going for Gold. They're on Fraud's radar, but the brothers behind it haven't been seen now for about three weeks. The consensus is that they've scarpered. Apart from them, all we've got is possible professional conflicts of interest.'

'I don't think this is about a professional disagreement,' said Mariner. 'This is personal.'

'So what were you doing in Redditch?' asked Vicky. 'Has something happened with Sam Fleetwood?'

Mariner told her about the wallet. 'I'm still trying to work out what it means,' he said.

'And you're certain that this Chantelle Brough just happened upon it?'

'I've got to trust Wheeler on that,' said Mariner. 'He seemed pretty confident that her involvement could be innocently explained – if that's the right word.'

'Does Fleetwood have links with Redditch?' Vicky asked.

'Not that anyone's told us, but we know he was heading in that general direction the last time he was seen. If we work on the assumption that Sam Fleetwood is seeing another woman, who's to say that he hasn't just taken off with her, and somewhere along the way left his wallet for us to find.'

'But we still don't know who this other woman could be?' asked Jesson.

'Not really,' said Mariner. 'I left the boy wonder doing a bit of digging.'

'Well, if anyone can come up with the goods it'll be him,' said Jesson.

And so it proved. As they waited at traffic lights to cross the Moseley Road on the way to Sparkhill, another call came through from Bingley. Mariner put him on speakerphone.

'You'll be relieved to know that Sam Fleetwood went to university in Birmingham,' Bingley said, naming one of the newer rebranded establishments. 'His sister couldn't remember the exact subject he studied, except that it was to do with environmental science.'

'Brilliant,' said Mariner, meaning the opposite.

'Well, it's a start,' said Bingley cheerfully. 'I've found four different programmes that seem to meet that criterion,' he went on. 'Supposing that the titles haven't changed since Fleetwood left. And the staff profiles help too – only four females out of twelve tutors, so that narrows the odds.'

'So what are you going to do?' asked Mariner. 'Phone each of them to ask if they had an illicit affair with Sam Fleetwood? That will make you popular.'

'That's one idea,' said Bingley, missing the irony. 'But I think I might have cracked it. One of them is called Ursula Kravitz.'

'Should that mean something?' Mariner asked.

'Well, I've got this telescope at home,' Bingley explained.

'Why does that not surprise me?' murmured Jesson, just loudly enough for Bingley to hear.

'It's relaxing watching the stars,' he said. 'You should try it before you make a judgement.'

'Is this going somewhere?' said Mariner. 'We're nearly at the Shahs'.'

'Well, that's it really,' said Bingley. 'The Little Bear – Ursa Minor. Ursa and Ursula are similar, and it's not that common a name. From her photograph she looks exotic, if you like that sort of thing, so she fits the bill.'

'I don't suppose it tells you where she lives, or can you divine that from the stars?' said Mariner.

'Unfortunately not,' said Bingley. 'But I thought maybe I could go and talk to her? DC Khatoon won't be in again until Wednesday, and it would save her having to . . .'

Mariner mulled it over. 'Why not?' he said eventually. 'Tread carefully, though, Bingley. Oh – and you can take today's prize for lateral thinking.'

'Bingley?' said Jesson, after Mariner had ended the call. 'I thought—'

'As did we all,' said Mariner. They had come to the house belonging to Salwa's sister-in-law, Ettra Shah. Things were quieter today; the crowd of mourners dispersed.

'How are we interviewing Salwa?' Vicky asked, before getting out of the car. 'Is she a witness? A suspect?'

'Let's just gauge her reaction for now,' said Mariner. 'At the very least she's a significant witness, and depending on what she has to say, we might then need to interview her formally in a witness suite, to get it all down on tape.'

Mustafa Shah was at work, and the children had gone back to school, so they were able to speak to Salwa on her own. Ettra brought refreshments again, but Jesson waited until she had left the room before explaining to Salwa why they were there. 'The jewellery on the body leads us to believe it's female,' she said.

By Mariner's calculation, it was at least four seconds before Salwa Shah reacted, during which time her face was blank with incomprehension, while she scrabbled for a mental foothold in what Jesson was saying. 'I don't understand,' she said finally, her voice hoarse. 'Oh God.' Her head swayed from side to side. 'No, no, no!' She jumped up and walked to the window, wringing her hands. She sat down again. If this was fake surprise she was a brilliant actress. 'It can't be,' she said, distraught. 'She had gone.'

'Who?' asked Jesson. 'Who do you mean?'

'Talayeh, my husband's cousin. She came to stay with us. She had to sleep in the store room because we had nowhere else to put her.'

'But why you haven't mentioned her before?' Now Jesson was incredulous. 'You're saying you forgot that she was there?'

'But it's not possible. She *wasn't* there. *She had gone!*' They waited her out. 'Talayeh left us on the day before the fire,' Salwa said. 'She went to stay with her aunt and uncle, in Bradford.' Her eyes gleamed with intensity. 'I put her in a taxi that afternoon with the money for her coach ticket. She had *gone*. Please. You must believe me!'

Although far-fetched, her explanation wasn't entirely implausible. 'Have you had any contact with Talayeh since, or the people she went to stay with?' Mariner asked.

'No.' Salwa shook her head. 'We don't really know them. Even my husband has never met them. They are her mother's relatives.'

'So you don't know if she got there,' said Mariner.

'In all that had happened I just thought she must have. I put her out of my mind.' Silent tears made wet trails down her cheeks.

'And up until Saturday, Talayeh was sleeping in the downstairs front room,' Jesson verified.

'It was the only room where there was space. We put a mattress on the floor. It wasn't perfect but in an emergency—'

'What kind of emergency?'

'No, not emergency, that's too strong,' Salwa corrected herself. 'I just meant it was a sudden decision for her to come here. She just needed a place to stay quickly.'

'Why didn't she go straight to her relatives in Bradford?' Jesson asked.

'She flew into Birmingham airport and my husband hadn't seen her for a long time, so . . .' She tailed off. 'And she said she had a friend she wanted to visit.'

'But as far as you were aware she had left your house earlier in the day,' said Mariner. 'What time did she go?'

'It was in the afternoon,' Salwa said. 'Soon after lunchtime. It was a rush at the end. I thought her coach left at two fifty, but

when I checked the timetable it was two thirty, so I had to call
a taxi quickly to take her to the coach station.'

'Which taxi firm did you use?' asked Mariner.

'I don't know. We had some cards next to the phone. I had
to try several because I had left it till the last minute and they
had no one free.'

It would be tiresome but shouldn't take too long to track the
company down; another little task to keep Bingley busy.

'Did anyone else see Talayeh get into the taxi that afternoon?'
Jesson asked.

'I don't know. The children were here at my sister-in-law's.
My father was there!' Salwa said, suddenly hopeful, before realising her mistake. 'I gave the driver her fare,' she went on.
'Talayeh doesn't understand English money, so I didn't want him
to take advantage of that.'

'And he was clear where he was taking her?'

'Yes.'

'You described Taleyah's visit as sudden,' said Jesson. 'Why
was that?'

'She wanted to come to England to visit family.'

It sounded hollow to Mariner, but there were more important
things to establish. 'I'll need to have contact details for the
relatives in Bradford,' he said. 'And for Talayeh's immediate
family, to let them know and to arrange for confirmation of
identity. Unfortunately, her body is badly burned, so this may
need to be done through DNA.'

'Oh God.' Salwa left the room, and was gone for several
minutes, returning with a page torn from a reporter's pad. Her
hand shook as she passed it to Mariner. 'It's all I have.'

'I'd like you to wait here until I have checked with them,' said
Mariner. Leaving Salwa and Jesson sitting in a painful silence,
he stepped out of the house to make the call immediately. If the
death turned out to be suspicious – and right now it was hard to
see how it could be otherwise – any delay would give the Shahs
and anyone else an opportunity to confer and get their stories
straight. He spent a few impatient minutes pacing the pavement
outside the house until he finally managed to get through to the
number Salwa had given him. Talayeh had not arrived in Bradford,
but the woman he spoke to, Talayeh's aunt, was unperturbed.

She just had assumed that Talayeh was staying longer with the Shahs and had only been expecting her 'in the next week or two'. She had seen reports of the fire in Birmingham, but as they knew little about the Shahs, she'd been unaware that it would have had anything to do with Talayeh. Mariner's news was greeted with a shocked silence at the other end of the phone. Expressing his condolences, Mariner ended the call.

When he returned to the house, Salwa Shah appeared to be in a trance. 'We will need to speak to you again,' said Mariner.

She snapped back to the present. 'Prayers are to be said for my father at the mosque tomorrow,' she said. 'So we will not be here.'

It would be an opportunity to observe her and her husband. 'We would like to come and pay our respects,' said Mariner.

'Yes, of course,' she forced a weak smile. 'We would be honoured.' As they left, Mariner saw her with Ettra, watching out of the window.

'She didn't seem too keen on that,' remarked Jesson, as she and Mariner headed back to Granville Lane. 'What do you think is going on?'

'Two possibilities,' said Mariner. 'Either Salwa Shah's an expert at faking it, and was covering the fact that Talayeh was there, or she genuinely didn't know. If it's the latter, then it's pretty weird.'

'That's what I can't get my head around,' said Jesson. 'How could she have been there without anyone realising?'

'Beats me,' said Mariner. 'Something interesting, though: Salwa didn't seem to feel an immediate need to tell her husband, and I'd have thought she'd want to do that. Is that because he didn't need to be told?'

EIGHTEEN

Having established that Ursula Kravitz still taught at the university, it then took Bingley some time to locate on which of the several campuses she worked. If Sam Fleetwood had eloped, it wasn't with Ms Kravitz, who was still very much around. She agreed to meet Bingley at her office, in between student tutorials. This was not a hallowed institution set in its own grounds, but one cobbled together from upgraded further education facilities, and whose buildings were scattered across the north of the city in an urban setting.

'Much less daunting for some of our students,' said Kravitz, as she and Bingley sat in her fifth-floor office in a modern block, the sun streaming in and making the small space uncomfortably warm. Somehow this wasn't how Bingley ever pictured academia. In his mind they should be looking out over lush green lawns, not the number 997 bus meandering past the dog track and on towards the Aldridge Road. Ursula Kravitz was making coffee for them both, taking advantage of this snatched opportunity between appointments. She was, as Bingley had deduced from her photo, glamorous; pale and sleek with shoulder-length hair and features perfected by flawless make-up. More than a little intimidating, in fact. 'So, Constable Bingley,' she said, passing him a bone china mug. 'Are you *sensible, good humoured and lively*?'

'Eh?'

'Not a fan of Austen then,' she concluded.

'My dad drove an Austin Metro for a while,' he offered.

'Never mind.' As she sat down beside her desk, her knees, exposed by her short skirt, were almost touching his. 'Now, what was it you wanted to ask me about?'

'It's a bit tricky,' said Bingley, sliding back a couple of inches. 'Do you remember a student called Sam Fleetwood? He would have been here between about six and nine years ago, on your Environmental Studies degree.' He passed Kravitz a copy of Fleetwood's photograph.

'Yes,' said Kravitz, examining the picture. 'I do remember him, though it would have taken me a while to recall his name. We see so many students each year. But he was a bright boy and worked hard. Sensitive, as I remember. He did well, I think, perhaps a first or at least a two-one, although – no, that's right, he was on track for that, but had disappointing results after all.'

'Have you any idea why that was?' asked Bingley.

'Not at all.'

'When did you last see him?'

She chuckled. 'Oh gosh, now you're asking. It would have been at graduation, if he was there. I mean, he probably was, but I don't specifically remember.' She looked at Bingley. 'Is he in some kind of trouble?'

'Not necessarily,' said Bingley. 'It's just that he hasn't been seen for a few days.'

'What on earth makes you think that I would be able to help, after all this time?' Kravitz seemed genuinely perplexed.

'It was suggested to us that while Sam was here, your relationship with him might have been more than just that of a student/teacher.'

'By whom?' Despite the incredulity, she seemed highly amused. It was not the typical response of the guilty.

Bingley felt slightly foolish now. 'It's been suggested that the two of you might have been having a . . .' Bingley grappled for the right word. 'Relationship.'

Kravitz's well-defined eyebrows arched a fraction. 'That's outrageous, and absolutely not true. Quite apart from anything else, behaviour like that would be professional suicide and I've still got rather a large mortgage to pay – even bigger back then.' She broke off in response to a knock on the door. 'Yes?' she called.

The door opened and a man's face appeared, bespectacled, with grey, thinning hair. 'Sorry to interrupt. Just checking if you're coming to lunch,' he said, his gaze lingering on Bingley.

'Can't, I'm afraid,' said Kravitz. 'But you should hear this, Scott. This is my husband,' she added for Bingley's benefit.

'What have you done now?' asked Scott, jokingly.

Kravitz gleefully recounted the conversation. 'Could you imagine it?' she said. 'You remember Sam Fleetwood, don't you?'

Bingley passed the picture across and Scott frowned at it. 'He does look vaguely familiar,' he said. 'But I couldn't tell you anything about him. Pleasant lad, as I remember. But to be honest, once you've been doing this job a while all the students start to look like one another.'

'Now,' said Kravitz to Bingley. 'My next student will be here shortly, and I need to prepare.'

Bingley could see no reason to detain her further. 'Before you go, though,' he said. 'Could I just ask where you live?'

Kravitz looked bemused. 'If you must; we live in Alcester.' Off the M42.'

Bingley left the university a disappointed man. He'd felt sure he was on to something and had hoped that he might be able to hand DCI Mariner a clear breakthrough, but now he was going back empty handed. Neither Mariner nor Jesson was there when he got back to Granville Lane, so he carried on with updating the policy book. There were still a number of actions that needed following up on. If he couldn't solve anything, at least he could be efficient at what he was meant to be doing. He was entering data when Mariner and Jesson returned, soon after.

'How did you get on with your lecturer, PC Bingley?' asked Mariner.

'She was flirty,' Bingley said, with slight disapproval. 'She quoted Jane Austen at me. But I don't think it's her. She was too relaxed. And besides, I saw her at work, so where's Sam Fleetwood, unless she's abducted him and is keeping him locked in her cellar?'

'Wouldn't be the first time,' said Mariner. He paused. 'Why have you let us keep calling you Brown when it's not your real name?' he asked.

Bingley shrugged. 'I've been called worse.'

'By Pete Stone?' Mariner speculated. 'What's he got against you?'

'I don't really know,' said Bingley, turning back to his monitor, though Mariner felt sure that wasn't true. 'Anyway,' Bingley added, 'the joke's on him, cos I'm from County Durham.' And that seemed an end to it.

'There's been a further, rather unexpected development at Wellington Road,' Mariner said, and filled the constable in on what had been found.

'Crikey,' said Bingley. 'I don't know if it's relevant, but I'm sure that in the house-to-house notes, one of the neighbours said something about raised voices in the street earlier on the day of the fire.'

Mariner and Jesson exchanged a look, as they waited for him to locate the record.

'Yes, here we are,' said Bingley eventually. 'Mrs Grant at number eighty-nine. That afternoon she heard shouting in the street and looked out to see her neighbour Mrs Shah "in loud conversation with another young woman, who then got into a waiting taxi". We didn't probe any further because Mrs Grant didn't think it was an argument, only a lively discussion. And she didn't think there was anything wrong as such.'

'Does she specify a time?'

'It's a bit vague. Sometime in the afternoon, so she says.'

'Well, it at least might confirm that Salwa is telling the truth, in that Talayeh went off in a taxi,' said Mariner. 'We need to follow up with the taxi driver. If we can find him we need to make sure he took her to the bus station and find out if he has any idea what happened to her once she got there, and if there's a reason she didn't get on the bus.'

'The bus station will have CCTV too,' said Bingley. 'Shall I get hold of that?'

'Yes, and I'll ask the press office to put out a description of Talayeh, and appeal for anyone who may have any information about her last known movements.'

'There's something else Mrs Grant said,' said Bingley. 'She was asked the usual questions about anything out of the ordinary that she might have seen recently, and she couldn't say exactly when, but sometime not long back she saw Mustafa Shah unloading boxes of papers into that downstairs room. An accident waiting to happen is what she called it.'

'Well, that's easy, with the benefit of hindsight,' said Jesson.

'Mustafa Shah,' said Mariner. 'Have we established that he was definitely out of the country that weekend?'

'We have,' said Bingley. 'He's confirmed on the passenger lists going out on the third and coming back in on the seventeenth.'

'We'll need to ask him to provide a witness statement,' said Mariner. 'Even though he wasn't there at the time of the fire. He will be able to confirm the details about Talayeh's presence. It's made me wonder why Talayeh had the sudden urge to visit her relatives in this country, especially given that she apparently ended up sleeping on the floor in what was basically a storage room. Not exactly a warm welcome, is it? It will be interesting to see if she gets a mention at the gathering tomorrow.'

Both Mariner and Jesson attended Soltan Ahmed's funeral at the mosque. The place was packed out, with more than two hundred people, confirming what Mustafa Shah had told them about his father-in-law's popularity. Mariner said as much to Shah as he greeted them at the entrance.

'Soltan was a traditionalist,' he said. 'I think in these uncertain times a lot of people in our community appreciated his wisdom. Salwa has told me about what you found yesterday. I can't believe it.' He looked genuinely stunned. 'Poor Talayeh, I don't know what we will say to her family.'

Many of the mourners also seemed subdued and in a state of shock, and Mariner wondered how quickly the latest news had circulated. 'It is a sad day,' said the man standing beside Mariner. 'I can't believe anyone would want to do this to Mr Shah's family,' the man went on. 'He's such a good and faithful person.'

Mariner nodded sympathetically. As he turned back, Vicky was waiting to catch his eye. 'Over there,' she said, gesturing subtly towards a woman standing nearby. 'That's Aisha, Mustafa Shah's assistant.'

'Perhaps you should go and talk to her,' said Mariner. 'Express your sympathy.'

Afterwards as they went outside, Vicky did exactly that. 'It's a good turnout,' she said. 'Easy to see how popular Mr Ahmed was.'

'Oh, that's true,' Aisha smiled and lit up a cigarette. 'He was lovely. It has been a real shock about the girl, though.'

'Did you know her?' asked Vicky.

'Not really,' Aisha said. 'I just met her a couple of times when Mr Shah brought her to the office.'

'What was she like?'

'She was all right,' Aisha smiled. 'A bit of a live wire. I'm not sure if Mustafa and Salwa knew quite what they were taking on.'

'What do you mean?'

Aisha glanced around to see who was nearby. 'I don't know if I should be telling you this, but between you and me, I think Talayeh had caused problems back home, and the hope was to get her married off and out of trouble. But when she got here she wasn't particularly co-operative and well, let's just say things didn't exactly go to plan. I know the first meeting didn't go too well and Mustafa was pretty annoyed about it.'

'What meeting was this?' Jesson asked casually.

'The family had fixed her up with one of Mustafa's friends. He's quite a bit older than her, so I think basically she turned him down. I don't think she was very tactful about it either.' She pulled a face.

'Do you know who this man was?' asked Vicky.

'His name is Kaspa Rani. He's well known in the community because he's so successful.'

Vicky glanced around the people still milling about. 'Is he here today?' she asked.

'I wouldn't think he'd show his face,' said Aisha. 'It was pretty embarrassing for him; this poor kid from a village in the Yemen, refusing him. I mean, there was obviously going to be an age gap, and he's not much to look at, but he's *loaded*. Stupid girl.'

'How did Talayeh get on with the Shahs?'

Aisha smiled. 'She was a handful. Maybe because she was from this remote village in the mountains, but I think she just went a bit wild when she got here and Mustafa was constantly getting phone calls at work from Salwa about her. A couple of times she just disappeared without telling Salwa where she'd gone. I think after she turned down Mr Rani, everyone was terrified that she might hook up with someone completely unsuitable instead. That's why Mustafa ended up bringing her to the office, but even then we had to watch her all the time. Soltan was kind to her, though. He had a real soft spot for the underdog. I think everyone was relieved they could pack her off to Bradford.' She paused a moment. 'Except they didn't, did they?'

'When was the last time you saw Talayeh?' asked Jesson.

'It would be the Monday before last.' Five days before the fire and when Mustafa Shah was still in the country. The grandfather would have been around then too. A man came towards them calling across something in Arabic. His tone was sharp. 'Sorry, that's my husband. I've got to go,' said Aisha.

Jesson reported back to Mariner what she had learned.

'So Talayeh was a bit of a liability then,' he said. 'How interesting.'

PC Kevin Bingley received a call, on Mariner's behalf, from Sergeant Wheeler, confirming that Chantelle Brough's contacts had been looked at, and there was nothing they could find to connect her, or any of her associates, with Sam Fleetwood. Every indication was that she had, just as she'd told it, stumbled across his wallet purely by chance. Another big fat waste of time, as had been Ursula Kravitz, and Bingley's frustration was growing. He was already quite enjoying this foray into CID, they seemed a good team, and they treated him – well, like one of them. If he could do something to prove his worth, over and above what any other workhorse could do, he might get to stay up here a bit longer. But his best opportunity would be in the next twenty-four hours, before DC Khatoon came back on duty.

Like DCI Mariner, Bingley liked maps, which meant he'd already noticed that the boss had a whole load of them in his office. He felt sure Mariner wouldn't mind lending him one for a few minutes, while he took a break from the constant screen-staring. He went and fetched the largest scale map of the local area he could find, spread it out and, taking care not to drop any sandwich crumbs on it, began to work out from the point where Sam Fleetwood was last seen, just outside a village called Hopwood. It was mostly rural countryside around here and what sprang out at Bingley almost immediately was a collection of structures in a whited out patch labelled 'waste disposal'.

One of Bingley's great strengths was his memory. He recalled from the policy book, what Clive Boswell had told DC Khatoon and Mariner about Carter's; the operation that Sam Fleetwood had under surveillance. A Google search proved ineffective, so instead Bingley looked back at DC Khatoon's notes from her visit to the Environment Agency. He picked up the receiver to call Sam's boss, Mike Figgis. 'Do you know an outfit called Carter's?' he asked, after identifying himself. 'It's in connection with the disappearance of Sam Fleetwood. Tell me a bit more about the situation there.'

'Carter's?' Figgis sounded surprised. 'It's a waste disposal station and breaker's yard. They were brought to our attention for a couple of possible infringements, but they're old news. Sam Fleetwood was trying to build a case against them, attempting to gather enough evidence to bring them to court. But when we looked at what he'd got, it wasn't enough. Plus, the owner is getting on a bit and suffers with his health. To go ahead with any kind of prosecution would have risked having them sue for distress caused. Sam was advised to drop it, and he took that advice. Like I told your colleague who came here, he's a smart lad.'

'So there would have been no reason for Fleetwood to have gone out to Carter's last weekend?' said Bingley.

'None at all,' said Figgis.

Bingley hung up, and was about to give that up as another dead end, when he noticed DC Khatoon's note: *has more to say??* beside the name Zara. He rang the agency switchboard and asked to be put through to her. Fortunately for him, there was only one Zara in the department. 'I'm just following up on your conversation with my colleague,' Bingley told her carefully. 'In which you expressed a particular opinion about your boss, Mike Figgis.'

There was a pause. 'Is this about Sam?' said Zara cautiously.

'You told DC Khatoon that you didn't trust Figgis,' said Bingley. 'Could you elaborate on that?'

Silence. Then, exhaling, Zara seemed to come to a decision. 'It's our job to collect evidence of malpractice and build cases against companies that can go to court, much in the same way as you do, I suppose,' she said.

'And?'

'Mike Figgis reviews each case and makes the decision about whether it can go further.'

'So he gets the last word,' said Bingley. 'And there's a problem with that?'

'It's just that in the past there were some cases that on the face of it were watertight that Mike threw out for insufficient or weak evidence,' Zara told him. 'At first the feeling was that he was just lazy. But then there were a couple of instances when, shortly after cases were rejected, he happened to go off on an exotic holiday, or change his car. This job doesn't pay massively well, not even at middle management level.'

'He was taking backhanders?' said Bingley.

'I don't think anything was ever proven,' said Zara. 'But management must have got wind of the rumours because about six months ago he was hauled upstairs on a disciplinary.'

'And since then?

'I think he must be on some kind of probation, because ever since then he's been super-efficient.'

'Could Figgis have taken a pay-off from Carter's?' asked Bingley.

'It's possible,' Zara said. 'Certainly Sam found infringements of regulations. And he was sure there was a lot more going on. Mike didn't think what he'd got was enough, but Sam was on a kind of crusade. He was convinced Mike was wrong. They had heated words in the office more than once.'

'So what's the position with Carter's now?'

'I think officially Sam dropped it, but I'd be surprised if he really did,' Zara told him. 'Sam can be like a dog with a bone.'

'And what would be the outcome of a prosecution, if the Carters are violating regulations?' Bingley was trying to keep up with all this and take useful notes.

'They'd get a hefty fine,' said Zara. 'And there's an outside chance they might get closed down. In the most serious cases the owner might even get a custodial sentence.'

'What kind of fine are we talking about?' Bingley asked.

'The last successful prosecution we brought was for £200,000.'

Bingley whistled; that was big money. 'And Sam Fleetwood is sure the Carters are up to all this?'

'You develop a nose for this stuff after a while,' said Zara. 'There's another complication there too. Carter Senior is an old guy and shortly after Sam started poking around he had a heart attack and had to undergo major surgery. Given his age it's probably no more than coincidence, but his sons don't see it that way. I think Sam had some threatening emails from them. All a bit pathetic really.'

'Would it be possible to get hold of those emails?' asked Bingley.

'I doubt it. Sam would have deleted them. But he reckoned on Danny, the youngest son. He's an inarticulate thug.'

'Did Sam report these threats to the police; to us?' Bingley asked.

'He wouldn't have bothered,' said Zara. 'It's not really that uncommon in our job. Usually it's people just venting their frustration. I take it Sam hasn't shown up yet then?'

'No, but we're following a number of lines of enquiry,' said Bingley, giving the standard neutral response. But Zara wasn't an idiot. She'd draw her own conclusions.

NINETEEN

Following the call, Bingley sat back, chewing his pen, until the top came off and he almost swallowed it. In the short space of one conversation, two possible leads and motives had emerged. No surprise in the circumstances that Mike Figgis had been less than candid about his conflict with Sam Fleetwood, especially when Fleetwood's persistence might have threatened his lucrative little sideline. Equally if Sam was still pursuing the Carters then they wouldn't think much of that either. Out of interest, he did a quick search on Crimint and turned up one Carter in particular. They were a lively lot, but Danny had a number of previous cautions, including one for assault.

Bingley tried Mariner's mobile, but he must still be in the mosque because it was switched off, and there was no telling when he would be available. Instead, Bingley made his way apprehensively along to Superintendent Sharp's office, but he could hear from halfway down the corridor that she was engaged in a conversation of her own, and probably wouldn't welcome the interruption. He didn't need anyone's permission to go and take a look at Carter's. He was following a legitimate line of enquiry, so if an area car was available that's what he would do. If it turned out to be nothing, he wouldn't be gone long, and no one need ever know. 'I'm just nipping out,' he told one of the admin staff.

As he travelled out towards Wythall and bumped over one of the many canal bridges along the way, Bingley remembered that not so long back there had been problems with pollution in the water around here, when the canals had turned orange. He wondered if that had anything to do with the Carters.

What came into view first was the sign announcing 'Carter's Waste Management and Reclamation Facility'. Yawning steel gates opened on to two great slag heaps of rubbish, monuments to twenty-first-century consumerism, and behind them was the grey cube of an industrial incinerator. This area was part of

the green belt and he'd passed a number of large country properties, whose owners were no doubt thrilled to have an operation
like this ruining their rural idyll. Bingley wondered how they'd
even got their licence. He drove on past and parked a little further
down the lane. Getting out of the car, he considered the wisdom
of putting on a stab vest, but decided against it. He wasn't looking
for confrontation.

Walking back, Bingley could see that the complex stretched
over several acres and comprised two separate sites: one for
general waste and the one next door a typical breaker's yard,
with flattened vehicles piled high in precarious-looking stacks.
Between the two sites, behind a screen of conifers, was what
looked like a family home, while in the yard itself a couple of
caravans seemed to double as offices. Towards the back of the
main compound, material was being shunted around in a seemingly random fashion by a single mechanical digger, and to one
side three Dobermans prowled in their cage.

To avoid alerting either the dogs or the digger driver, Bingley
slipped into the scrap yard first. A caravan in the corner of this
yard had curtains at the windows as if someone lived there, and
he felt obliged to knock on the door, but as he'd anticipated
and hoped, there was no response, so, out of sight of the digger
operator, he began his patrol. He didn't know exactly what he
was looking for, and after several minutes staring at rusting junk,
he was starting to think this had been another wasted effort. But
then the sun emerged from behind a cloud and glinted off something in the far corner of the yard that stood out from all the dull
brown metal around it. It was the shiny bodywork of a gunmetal
grey Vauxhall Astra, not unlike like the one he'd recorded as
belonging to Sam Fleetwood.

Bingley went across to take a closer look. The registration
plates had been removed, but attached to the roof was what he
recognised as a bike or ski rack. The front end of the car looked
in tip-top condition, but from close quarters, he saw that the
windscreen was opaque from smoke, with a large crack running
across it from one side to the other. Looking in through the side
windows he could see that the front and rear seats were burnt
out, the upholstery melted away from the springs.

'What the 'ell are you doing?' said a voice right behind him.

Bingley turned and found himself face-to-face with a hulk of a man, with untidy dark hair and a leathery complexion coloured by years of outdoor working. Faded tattoos covered forearms that were as thick as shoulders of lamb. One of the Dobermans strained silently on the leash beside him.

'Mr Carter?' said Bingley, wishing he had a bit of Mariner's authority in his voice. He fumbled for his warrant card and held it up for Carter to see. 'PC Bingley,' he said. 'Is this your scrap yard?'

'It belongs to the family,' said Carter, displaying a couple of gold fillings. 'My brother, Danny, manages it.'

So this must be George, Bingley concluded. 'Does he live in the van?'

'Yes, but he'll be out right now, doing the rounds in the pickup.' One of those, no doubt, whose crackly loudspeakers were part of the city soundtrack. It never ceased to amaze Bingley how quickly they appeared when something of interest had been left outside a house. He turned back to where the Astra sat. 'How did you come by this?' he asked Carter. From his reaction, Bingley would have guessed that Carter was as surprised to see the car there as he was. Bingley wondered if he recognised it.

'I expect it was abandoned somewhere,' said Carter, trying hard to sound unconcerned. 'It happens. We pick up quite a few vehicles that way. You'd be astounded.'

'But this one in particular?' Bingley persisted.

'I don't know.' Carter shrugged. 'You'd have to talk to Danny. Him or one of the other lads will have come across it. People know where we are, so they dump stuff nearby in the hope that we'll pick it up and save them the bother of getting rid of it. The boys don't need my permission to go and get it. They will have used their initiative.'

'And brought it here without your knowledge?' Bingley queried.

Carter raised an arm. 'Look around you. Do you think I monitor every single item that goes in and out of here?'

'You're supposed to,' Bingley reminded him. 'Especially items as big as this. It looks like the latest model too. Isn't that a bit strange?'

'I expect it was stolen and dumped by kids, joyriders,' Carter replied. 'We get all sorts. And it will be down in the record book. I expect I just hadn't clocked it yet.'

'Have you had a visit from the Environment Agency lately?' Bingley asked.

'Not for a while.' Carter stared at him, weighing the significance of that question.

'Well, I have reason to believe this vehicle may relate to a missing persons' enquiry,' said Bingley. 'So in the absence of any clearer explanation about how you came by it, I'll need to impound it for further examination.'

Carter regarded him evenly. 'Knock yourself out, mate. I'd be careful, though,' he added. 'These sites can be dangerous. Wouldn't want any accidents to happen.' And with a last long glower at Bingley, he walked away, tugging the Doberman after him.

It took just a couple of phone calls and Bingley scrabbling about on his hands and knees with a torch for a few minutes, to establish that the chassis serial number of the Astra in Carter's yard matched the one belonging to Sam Fleetwood, so seizure of the vehicle was, to his relief, fully justified. It seemed to him to be the first strong indication that Sam Fleetwood was not missing of his own volition. Careful not to touch anything, he scrutinised the inside of the vehicle as best he could through the murky windows, but it was too much to expect that there would be anything of value left there.

Next Bingley contacted the forensic service, and learned that it would be at least an hour before they could get across to Carter's with a low loader. He had no choice but to stick around until it got here. Finally, he left a message on DCI Mariner's phone: 'I'm at Carter's waste disposal site by Wythall,' he said. 'I've found Sam Fleetwood's car.' Now at least, should George Carter get threatening, someone would know where he was. There was another cause for anxiety too. He'd been out of the office a while now and had come unprepared. But he had no other option than to stay close by the Astra. He couldn't give Carter the opportunity to tamper with or destroy the evidence. Great, and now he wanted to pee.

Mariner had naturally put his phone on silent whilst in the mosque. He'd checked it when he came outside again, but saw nothing of any importance, and now he and Jesson had come to the mortuary, so it was back on silent. Bingley had missed him by mere minutes.

Mariner and Jesson were observing Stuart Croghan as he carried out the post-mortem on Talayeh.

'This is a funny old business,' said Croghan, who was no stranger to the anomalies of human existence.

'It is,' Mariner agreed. 'She took us all by complete surprise, poor girl.'

'Well, the first thing to tell you is that there's a blunt trauma injury to the skull.'

'Is that what killed her?' asked Mariner. 'Could she already have been dead before the fire started?'

'It's hard to say,' said Croghan. 'Unfortunately what little tissue is left is not in a good enough condition to be able to tell if it was pre- or post-mortem. The damage could have been caused by debris falling on top of her. Some of those joists might still have been pretty solid when they collapsed, and part of the metal bed frame from the first-floor room was close to her head when we found her. I'll know more when I've opened up her lungs. But the toxicology is interesting and something you might want to pursue,' Croghan went on. 'She was in such a state I didn't think we'd get much in the way of readings, but what we have got in the initial screening is traces of alcohol. For that to have even registered, she must have consumed a substantial amount not long before she died.'

'The Shahs are Muslim,' said Jesson straight away. 'There's no alcohol in the house.'

'But we already know that Talayeh didn't like to conform,' Mariner reminded her. 'We're still trying to establish her last known movements,' he told Croghan.

'Well, my bet would be that they involved a drinking session,' said Croghan. 'What are we doing about formal identification?'

'Her sister is flying over from Sana'a,' said Mariner. 'She was able to positively identify the jewellery from photographs we emailed to her, and when she gets here we'll follow up with DNA confirmation.'

'Well, I've told you as much as I can at this stage,' said Croghan. 'I'll let you know anything else as I find it.'

Mariner and Jesson left the hospital. 'Say Talayeh did go off in the taxi as Salwa told us, with her coach fare in her pocket, but went to a pub instead and came back to the house roaring drunk,' said Jesson. 'She could have crept back into the house with no one knowing, zonked out from the booze, and then been overcome by smoke when the fire started. That would explain how Salwa didn't know she was there.'

'It's possible,' Mariner conceded. 'But how many drunks do you know who can creep into a locked house, with no one hearing them? And it still doesn't help explain who started the fire.'

'Unless she started it herself.'

'But how?' Mariner asked.

'If she was drinking over here, perhaps she'd tried smoking too,' said Jesson. 'Or maybe Gerry Docherty was right at the outset, and the fire was caused by electrical overload. It hasn't entirely been ruled out.'

Mariner remained sceptical. 'I'd like to look at the coach station CCTV and try and fill that gap between Talayeh leaving and returning to Wellington Road.' He took out his phone. 'I'll see if Bingley has got anywhere with that.' But before he could do so, he saw that he had a missed call from the constable. He returned it, but got no response. And when he rang back to Granville Lane, Bingley hadn't checked in for a while either.

'When did he go out there?' he asked the admin.

'A couple of hours ago at least,' she said. 'He took an area car.'

'Where is he?' asked Jesson, trying to follow Mariner's side of the conversation.

'Carter's waste site,' said Mariner. 'We've had dealings with them in the past. They're not nice people. And Bingley's not responding to his comms or his mobile. Shit, he's out there with a hostile Carter and an incriminating piece of evidence.'

'I'm sure he'll be fine,' said Jesson, with more confidence than she felt.

'Maybe,' said Mariner. 'But I think we'll go and make sure.'

They drove at speed, hastened by blues and twos, with Jesson continuing, unsuccessfully, to try and raise Bingley on his mobile. When they got to Carter's they saw the squad car parked a little way down the road, but the waste site was unnervingly deserted, and the Astra stood unguarded. Mariner felt a chill of apprehension as he noticed the thin trail of smoke rising from the incinerator chimney. After some shouting, George Carter appeared, wiping his hands on a filthy cloth. 'All right, keep your hair on, what's all the noise?'

'Where's PC Bingley, the officer who was here with the Astra?' Mariner demanded.

'I don't know.'

Mariner held his gaze. 'Try his mobile again,' he said to Jesson, knowing full well that if something had happened to the constable, Carter would have destroyed that too. But very faintly, and at some distance, an incongruous tinkling came back at them, not from the breaker's yard, but from the neighbouring compound. The ringtone echoed around the space and it was some minutes before they located Bingley, by clambering over piles of rubbish to get to him. He lay on his back, eyes closed and perfectly still, with not a mark on him. 'Oh God,' said Vicky. 'What's happened? What have you done?' She glared at Carter.

'Nothing to do with me.' He wiped the perspiration from his upper lip with his thumb and forefinger.

'Call for an ambulance,' ordered Mariner, then to the unconscious constable: 'Bingley, can you hear me? Kevin?' Kneeling down he started to loosen Bingley's collar, and in doing so his fingers caught on a chain around his neck. He pulled it out. 'Shit,' Mariner said. 'He's diabetic. He's gone into a coma.'

There was the beat of a pause before Jesson said: 'Oh God; he wasn't wanking, he was injecting himself.' Mariner looked at her askance, just as, over her shoulder, the forensics team low loader pulled into the compound.

Part way through her second week at the university, Suzy was beginning to feel more settled, and for the first time in a while she was looking forward to going home. She'd woken up on Tuesday morning after yet another fantastic night's sleep, feeling rested and refreshed. She had taken to the foibles of Y Worry more easily than she'd expected, not least because of the wonderful peace and quiet. Apart from the odd car passing by, all she heard on waking in the early morning was the sound of birdsong. After living in Cambridge city centre and then the university halls of residence, it was blissful. What had been harder to adjust to was the darkness, but the daylight hours were lengthening and soon that would just seem normal too. She was also encouraged that somehow, bizarrely, the move seemed to be getting her relationship with Tom back on track. And the drive in to work was something to be relished; just fifteen minutes, door-to-door, on a good day. Life felt good.

Driving through the village this morning, though, she'd been brought up short by the sight of a man in clerical attire emerging from the gate of Rosalind's house. She went cold inside – it wasn't yet eight o'clock. Why would a vicar be visiting them at this hour? She slowed a moment, wondering whether she should stop to see if there was anything she could do. But the reality was that she hardly knew Rosalind and Gideon, and if something had happened, she wouldn't want to get in the way.

When she got to the faculty there was so much to do that Suzy didn't have time to give Rosalind and Gideon much more thought, until now. Late in the afternoon there were a number of references she needed to collate, but the software that would enable her to do this hadn't yet been loaded on to her new machine by IT. Suzy felt sure that in her absence, Rosalind wouldn't mind if she borrowed her computer. As Suzy booted it up and logged in, a news alert appeared from an organisation called Journey's End. It looked faintly religious, so she ignored it and carried on with her work. It did, however, serve to remind her of what she'd seen this morning, so after work Suzy drove home to Y Worry, then walked round to Rosalind's house, all the time wondering what she would find. Only Rosalind's car was on the drive, so Suzy tentatively knocked on the door.

'It's open!' she heard Rosalind call, so she went in. Rosalind was in the kitchen loading the washing machine.

'Is everything all right?' Suzy asked.

Rosalind seemed surprised. 'Yes, why?'

'I saw a clergyman coming out of your house this morning when I was driving by,' said Suzy. 'Actually, I feared the worst.'

Rosalind laughed. 'Oh no, Gideon's fine. He's sleeping now, otherwise I'd—'

'No, please, don't disturb him,' said Suzy. 'You're busy, and I've got work to do anyway.'

'The man you saw was Father Peter,' explained Rosalind. 'I'd asked him to call in to see Gideon, and he's very good at coming in at odd times, when Gideon is at his most alert.'

'I didn't realise Gideon was Catholic,' said Suzy.

'We both are,' said Rosalind. 'I try to get to Mass and confession when I can, but it's difficult to get away, of course. Gideon's carer comes in to cover while I'm at work, but I can't really ask her to do any more.'

'I'd be happy to come and sit with him,' Suzy offered.

Rosalind's eyes lit up. 'Really, would you? It's on Saturday morning. I wouldn't want to mess up your weekend.'

'That's fine,' said Suzy. 'I'd love to talk to Gideon some more. I can pick his brains.'

'That would be wonderful. I used to go at about ten, is that OK?'

'It's a date,' said Suzy.

TWENTY

The drama at Carter's was over quickly. Bingley was taken off in an ambulance, while Mariner and Jesson saw Sam Fleetwood's car transported away by the forensic service. That evening Mariner phoned the hospital to check on how Bingley was doing, but learned that he'd been discharged, so he went to see him at his home. Wherever possible Mariner avoided putting his officers at risk and he felt bad about it. He didn't think Bingley was the sort to make a complaint, but Mariner had to accept that he'd been negligent in finding out the facts about his restricted duties. Bingley himself came to the door of the small Edwardian terrace, and he looked OK, which was encouraging. 'What are you doing here, sir?' he asked, casting a glance behind him.

'I just came to see how you are,' said Mariner.

'I'm fine,' said Bingley, and they stood awkwardly for a moment until he finally added: 'Did you want to come in? I'm sorry, it's not very—'

'Don't worry about it,' said Mariner. 'Remember, I'm a sad git who lives on his own. Sometimes I don't even do the washing up.' It was meant as a joke but he wasn't sure that Bingley got it. He took Mariner through to a living room where an older lady sat watching TV. Seeing Mariner, her face lit up. 'Hello, pet.' She scrutinised him carefully. 'Are you one of our Kevin's friends?' Pride in her son was evident all over the walls and mantelpiece: Bingley as a baby with a stuffed animal as big as him; Bingley in his first school uniform; Bingley in the not-too-distant past, at his passing out at Hendon.

'No, Mum,' Bingley blinked at her. 'This is my boss, DCI Mariner.'

'Tom,' Mariner told her, leaning forward to shake her hand.

'Oh. Nice to meet you, Tom. How's our Kevin—'

'We'll go through to the kitchen,' Bingley cut in. 'Would you like a beer, sir?'

'It's Tom when we're off-duty,' said Mariner. 'OK, I'm driving, but one won't hurt.'

Bingley disappeared into a pantry. 'Hobgoblin, Speckled Hen or Marston's IPA?' he called.

'Speckled Hen,' said Mariner approvingly. 'And out of the bottle is fine.'

He took a seat at the kitchen table, forcing Bingley to follow suit. 'Is everything all right?'

'That's what I'm supposed to ask you,' said Mariner.

'I'm sorry about this afternoon,' Bingley said. 'I didn't mean to cause a fuss. Usually I manage, and while I'm on restricted, I didn't think I would ever get into a situation where it would matter. When I had to wait, I knew I was pushing it, but I thought I could get away with it. I didn't want to—'

'You're not in any trouble,' said Mariner. 'I'm honestly just here to make sure you're all right. It's my fault for not fully discussing your health issues with you. We have a duty of care.'

'You can't discuss what you don't know,' Bingley pointed out. 'I was only diagnosed last year, and I don't want it to stop me doing my job, so I suppose I try to play it down.'

'And the metal plate in your head?'

'An argument with a baseball bat – in someone else's hands, not mine,' he added, with a wry smile.

'Is that why you're thinking of bailing?' Mariner asked.

Bingley stared at him, wondering where that had come from. 'I always wanted to be in the police,' he said. 'I would have joined from school but my dad wasn't having it. A lot of his family were miners.'

'Something else we've got in common then,' said Mariner. 'My mum was a peace protester. It wasn't exactly what she had in mind for me either.'

As Mariner was leaving, he called out: 'Nice to meet you, Mrs Bingley.'

He was met with another broad smile. 'Lovely to meet you too, pet.'

'This isn't my ideal set-up,' Bingley said, at the door. 'Dad died not long ago, and it was rough towards the end. I came down to help her out. I think she'll move back up north eventually, but meanwhile . . .'

'Nothing wrong with taking care of your mum,' said Mariner, knowing that he'd fallen some way short in that respect. 'I'll see you in the morning, Bingley.'

Millie was determined to get in early on Wednesday morning, as she knew she'd be playing catch-up with what she'd missed on her days off. It felt oddly disorientating to see that there had been some significant progress while she wasn't here, most of it recorded by Mariner only the night before. 'I see you had quite a day yesterday,' she said to Bingley when he arrived.

Bingley groaned. 'It was embarrassing.'

Millie looked quizzically at him. 'You found Sam Fleetwood's car, didn't you?'

'Oh, that.'

Millie regarded him curiously. 'What did you think I meant?'

Bingley explained the dramatic turn things had taken.

'Well, you're OK now, aren't you?' said Millie pragmatically. 'Did you find anything useful in the car?'

'Not yet,' said Bingley. 'But I'm hoping forensics will get back to us later in the day.'

'That's optimistic,' said Millie. 'What made you go out to Carter's in the first place?'

Bingley summarised his conversations with Sam Fleetwood's work colleagues.

'So that's what Zara meant when she said Figgis couldn't be trusted,' said Millie.

'It made me wonder if Fleetwood went to have another look at Carter's, to try and get something incriminating; something watertight. It's what we would do. If he did, there are at least two people who wouldn't want that to happen; Carter and Figgis. And if Figgis knows Carter's well enough to have been paid off by Carter, they could be in collusion.'

'That would make sense,' said Millie. 'So what do you think happened?'

'Fleetwood goes out there, in the middle of the night. George Carter catches him snooping around. Maybe an argument gets out of hand, or maybe it's a cold-blooded murder. Whichever it is, Carter disposes of Sam's body – conveniently they have an industrial incinerator on-site – then sets fire to Sam's car to make it look like joyriders stole it, and to get rid of any incriminating evidence. It might actually be true that Danny Carter just found it, without knowing it was his older brother who dumped it.'

'You're not bad at this,' said Millie. 'And Figgis?'

'Might or might not have been involved,' said Bingley. 'Danny Carter has a history too,' he added. 'He didn't go to a regular school; he finished up at a PRU.'

'What's one of those?' asked Millie.

'A pupil referral unit. It's for kids who get excluded because of their behaviour. There were some incidents of arson. He's quite the expert fire-setter, is our Danny. I've come across the name Danny Carter before, too.'

'It's probably not that uncommon,' said Millie.

'No, I mean in the last week,' said Bingley. 'The fire on Wellington Road. Jordan Wright and Danny Carter are mates. I saw it on Facebook.'

'You might want to run that by Tom and Vicky.'

The phone on Bingley's desk rang and he picked it up. 'It's the forensic service,' he said, covering the mouthpiece. 'They've got something on the car.'

'That was quick,' said Millie, also feeling slightly miffed that they'd called through to Bingley and not directly to her.

'Well, maybe they think it's important.'

'Or . . .?'

'I sort of know one of the technicians there, Sasha,' Bingley blushed. 'I'll transfer it.'

'Thanks.'

Sasha turned out to be a woman. 'We've got some good samples,' she told Millie. 'Predominantly two sets of prints all over the front interior. They're a match for the ones you sent through from your MisPer and his fiancée. But we've also got some additional smudged prints on the steering wheel. They're partials, so I'm not sure what help they'll be. Could be joyriders. They tend not to have the foresight to wear gloves. What's much more interesting is what we've found in the boot: blood and quite a bit of it.'

'Like someone's cut themselves?' asked Millie cautiously.

'Could be,' said Sasha. 'But it's a significant amount; more than you might expect for just a straightforward cut, and it has pooled in several different places, as if it's leaked out from something. I can't give you any more detail at this stage, but of course we'll get it all off to the lab pronto. And if you can get some DNA material to us for comparisons, we might be able to tell you whose blood it is.'

Millie went straight to Mariner, and caught him just as he was leaving his office, on his way down to a viewing suite, along with Vicky Jesson.

'Surely this is a game changer,' she said. 'It's the first solid indication that Sam Fleetwood might have come to grief.'

Mariner was in agreement. 'And given that there have been no sightings of him for more than a week now, it puts him in the high-risk category. You need to start verifying movements and alibis.'

'And I'm going to pay the Carters another visit,' said Millie.

'Be careful,' said Mariner. 'A lot of these outfits have links to organised crime. Don't underestimate how dangerous they might be.'

'I'll take Bingley.'

'Oh, that'll be a help,' said Mariner, with a touch of sarcasm, before realising it was probably true.

The taxi driver who'd taken Talayeh to Digbeth had not yet surfaced, but transport police had contacted Mariner to say that they had retrieved and sent through footage from the bus station on the afternoon before the fire. Now he and Vicky Jesson were studying it, watching for Talayeh Farzi to appear. The recovery parameter was broad, with several cameras picking up the outside waiting area, the ticket office and the coach parking bays. It was here that they spotted Talayeh as she walked into the station after being dropped off by the taxi. 'Look at the time,' said Mariner. The digital clock in the right-hand corner of the screen said 14.38. 'She's already missed her bus.'

Talayeh looked anxious and glazed over and Mariner wondered about what kind of person it was who would send a young woman hundreds of miles away from home, when she knew little of the country or the people she was going to stay with. As if to under-line this, both he and Jesson winced as Talayeh stepped right into the path of an incoming coach and its horn blared, sending her scuttling to the pavement.

Jesson sucked in air. 'That was a close one.'

They watched Taleyah go into the ticket office, emerging minutes later. Then, after some apparent uncertainty, she turned and went into the cafeteria.

'Well, it confirms that she got to the bus station, but clearly she didn't get on the coach to Bradford,' said Mariner.

'Do you think the whole charade could have been staged to give an impression that she had left?' Jesson speculated. 'She might have been told to get a ticket to make it look as if she was leaving.'

'Possible,' said Mariner. 'But why? It's a lot of trouble to go to.'

They couldn't see Talayeh's movements inside the cafe, and had to fast-forward through the footage for more than half an hour. Finally, almost off-camera, they spotted her again, coming outside. She was with a man in a suit, with dark hair.

'Who's that?' Jesson wondered aloud. 'Anyone we know?' They couldn't get a clear view of his face. 'It's not Mustafa Shah; we know he was out of the country.'

'Kaspa Rani is the only other man we know for certain she met in Birmingham,' said Mariner. 'We need to talk to him as a matter of urgency.'

Kaspa Rani's success was founded on a large cash and carry empire, based largely in Hackney, but with further branches in Coventry and Birmingham. Mariner and Jesson went to interview him there in his office, having agreed that Jesson would lead. They wanted to rattle him.

Wherever the profits went for his enterprise, it wasn't on decor, the only extravagance being a well-stocked drinks cabinet for loosening up clients. There were however indications that this was about to be addressed: dust sheets were folded on the floor in a corner, weighed down by white spirit and tins of paint.

Rani, on the other hand, was a walking gold mine, and a considerable amount had been invested in the Rolex – if it was real – and the chunky chains around his neck and wrists. When he stood up to greet them he was, Jesson noticed, shorter than her and barrel-shaped. What was left of Rani's hair was slicked back over his ears. He looked about fifty.

'Tell us about your relationship with the Shah family,' said Jesson first of all.

'Mustafa is a good friend,' Rani said, addressing Mariner. 'We have known each other many years, and I knew his father-in-law Soltan. A good man.'

'And Talayeh?'

'That is very sad,' Rani said, with no emotion whatever, and as if no further comment was required.

'Especially since, not long ago, she was presented to you as a potential wife,' said Jesson.

Rani smiled. 'It was discussed,' he conceded.

'But I understand that Talayeh had come to this country specifically with the aim of marrying you.'

Rani's eyes narrowed a little, and he finally looked at Jesson. 'Then you have been misinformed. Talayeh and I were introduced, but it quickly became clear that she would not be a suitable wife. She did not display any of the qualities that I admire in a woman, like modesty and respect. I have no time for women like her.'

'You must have already known something about her,' said Jesson. 'So why did you agree to meet her?'

'It was a favour to my friend Mustafa. I knew the family wanted her off their hands, and I thought perhaps I could help.'

'So your interest was nothing to do with her being pretty and half your age,' said Jesson.

'I don't appreciate your tone,' said Rani, a muscle in his jaw pulsing.

'In that case, why don't you tell us what really happened between you and Talayeh, Mr Rani?' Jesson pressed on. 'We have been told that she turned you down. Isn't that how it went? That must have been humiliating; so humiliating that you stayed away from your good friend Soltan Ahmed's funeral?'

'I have already told you. It was me who decided that *she* was unsuitable. It was obvious to everyone who met her. You should ask Salwa Shah how much she liked having Talayeh in the house so close to her husband,' he said nastily. 'Ask her why Mustafa made that trip to Sana'a when he did.'

'When did you meet Talayeh?' asked Mariner.

Rani consulted the diary on his desk and gave them a date. It was ten days before the fire.

'And is that the last time you saw her?'

There was the slightest beat of hesitation before he said: 'Yes.'

'Are you sure about that?' asked Mariner. 'Where were you on the evening of Saturday the eighth?'

'I was at a business dinner in Birmingham. It went on until late.'

'Can anyone confirm that?'

'I'm sure that many of my associates will be happy to vouch for me.'

'We'll need their details,' said Mariner.

'Of course,' said Rani. 'Now, if you'll excuse me I have an appointment in London that I need to keep.'

'He's a cold fish,' said Jesson as they left the premises. 'He didn't seem particularly upset or surprised about what had happened to Talayeh.'

'No,' Mariner agreed. 'But it's not him on the CCTV at the bus station; he's neither tall nor slim enough, so we've got nothing to connect him to Talayeh on the day before she died.'

'So what now?' said Jesson.

'We need to talk to Salwa Shah again,' said Mariner. 'I think we should do it formally and see if that focuses the mind.'

Carter's had got themselves organised. This time, when Khatoon and Bingley went back, the paperwork for the Astra had mysteriously appeared and George was able to produce it. The Astra was down in the book but noticeably entered after items brought in that morning. 'Can you tell us any more about it?' Millie asked George Carter.

'I told him,' said George, looking at Bingley. 'Our Danny found it.'

'If he's here, we'd like to talk to him,' said Millie.

'He's in his van,' said George, walking them round to the breaker's yard.

Millie was curious. 'Does Danny not live in the family home then?'

'Not any more,' growled George. 'He's got to learn some independence.' He hammered with his fist on the caravan door. 'It's the police,' he said, when Danny appeared. 'They want to ask some questions about that car.'

'Where did you find it?' asked Millie.

They weren't invited in, so stood in the yard, while Danny leaned indifferently against the door of his caravan. He was what was commonly termed in police parlance 'a streak of piss'; skinny and undernourished. Like his older brother, Danny went in for tattoos, but his looked more like the home-made variety. 'About half a mile from here,' he said. 'It had been set on fire. That's how I spotted it in the first place.'

'When was this?'

Danny's lips moved silently as he worked it out. 'Week ago last Sunday,' he said eventually. 'I saw the fire in the middle of the Saturday night, so next morning I went out to see what it was.'

'Do you remember what time on Saturday night?' asked Millie. But all he could say was 'late'.

'You must have realised that it was stolen,' said Millie. 'It was in good nick. Did you notify the police?'

'I was going to, but I hadn't done it yet.' Danny gave them a sullen glare. 'Don't need to now, do I?'

'Where are the plates?' asked Bingley.

He shrugged. 'Didn't have any,' he said, though he couldn't meet Bingley's eye when he said it.

'Right, I need you to take us to where you found it,' Millie said, heading back to the car. Bingley followed, but not before taking a discreet photo of the white van parked beside Danny Carter's caravan. He was about to pocket his mobile again when he noticed another photograph, one he'd taken yesterday, just before he'd passed out. Running to catch up, he presented Millie with the phone. 'You should see this,' he said.

At first Millie couldn't see what could possibly be of interest in that pile of miscellaneous rubbish, but then she saw the name printed across a scrap of plasterboard: 'Boswell Construction.' 'Hm,' she said, her voice low. 'I wonder just how well he knows the Carters?'

With both Carter brothers in the back seat, Danny directed them through narrow country lanes for about a mile and a half, until they came to a fork in the road, backing on to woodland, that served as a rough parking place.

'It was there,' said Danny Carter and Bingley drew to a halt a little way off.

'Stay in the car, please,' Millie said to their two passengers, while she and Bingley walked down to the spot indicated. There was a patch of blackened grass that had burnt down to the soil, but at first inspection no sign of any blood. Bingley took a wide circle around the site, and Millie looked up to see him squatting down. She thought for a moment he might be having another funny turn, but then he stood up and came back with an evidence bag, which he passed to her. It contained a cheap gold lighter, the plate wearing off at the corners. 'Does Sam Fleetwood smoke?' he asked.

'No one's said that he does,' said Millie. She stopped. 'But I know someone who was looking for his lighter, around the time that Sam Fleetwood disappeared. I'll get a forensic search of this site and the surrounding area organised.'

On the drive back to Granville Lane they had time to discuss the significance of what they had found.

'If Sam has been playing away his father-in-law wouldn't think much of that, would he?' said Bingley.

'But who's he doing it with? That lecturer from uni?'

'I'm sure she was telling the truth,' said Bingley. 'In a way, though, the identity of the woman doesn't matter. Cheating is cheating, isn't it?'

'I don't suppose you've had the chance to check Boswell's alibi?' said Millie.

'I've made a start,' said Bingley. 'There was definitely a business consortium dinner on that night, and Boswell attended all right. But I haven't got as far as finding anyone who can confirm what time he left, or what kind of state he was in.'

'I think now might be a good time to update Clive Boswell on what we've found,' said Millie.

Salwa Shah still seemed to be reeling from their last visit, when Mariner and Jesson brought her into a station interview suite, to conduct more formal questioning. Her reactions seemed slow, and when Mariner first greeted her, she struggled to make eye contact.

'We know now that Talayeh went to the bus station, as you told us, but we're trying to reconstruct her movements after she missed her bus,' he said. 'It looks as if she might have met someone instead, a white man in Western dress.' Jesson placed a still photograph from the CCTV on the table. 'Do you have any idea who this might be?' Mariner asked. The image was grainy and indistinct, and he wasn't surprised when Salwa shook her head. Even if she did recognise the man, she had every excuse not to acknowledge it.

'Is this an arrangement Talayeh might have made?' Jesson asked. 'Could she have contacted someone?'

'No,' said Salwa. 'Talayeh didn't know anyone in this country apart from us and her relatives in Bradford. Unless—'

'What?'

'A couple of times she went out on her own, before I could stop her. She could have met someone then.' It was conveniently vague.

'What was it like having Talayeh to live with you?' asked Mariner.

'It wasn't easy,' Salwa admitted. 'She was disrespectful towards my father, and towards me.'

'In what way?'

'Talayeh was immature in her attitude towards men. She grew up in a small village and made trouble there by having a relationship with a man who was older than her. It was thought that if she came here, to England . . . But she was no different. We tried to match her with a friend of my husband, but it did not go well.'

'Mr Rani,' said Mariner. 'We know about that. How did Talayeh get on with your husband?' he asked, holding her gaze.

Salwa looked down into her lap. 'It was embarrassing,' she said. 'She flirted with him all the time. She would walk around the house sometimes, inappropriately dressed. Mustafa tried to ignore it, of course. We knew that she had had a difficult time so we tried to tolerate it. If I'm honest, I was relieved that she had moved on. But I didn't wish her any harm,' she insisted.

'Was Talayeh the reason your husband went to Sana'a?'

'No,' she said, a little too quickly. 'He had business to attend to anyway. Taleyah was just a silly girl.' Her eyes filled, but she seemed determined not to succumb.

Mariner suspended the interview at that point, and he and Jesson convened again outside.

'She seems more upset about this than she did about her father's death,' Mariner observed.

'I suppose she was in shock then,' said Jesson. 'She's had more time for this to sink in.' But there was nothing to hold her on, so Mariner arranged for a car to take her home.

TWENTY-ONE

'There is now enough concern for us to open an investigation into Sam's disappearance,' said Millie, without preamble. 'We have significant fears for his safety. His car has been found.'

She was in the conservatory of Clive Boswell's home again, and Millie was glad they were sitting down. Gaby stared at Millie for a moment, processing the words, then seemed transfixed, her attention switching to a spot on the floor that commanded her interest. Her father was immediately at her side. 'Where did you find it?' he asked.

'I can't tell you that just at the moment,' said Millie. 'But what we also found is staining in the boot that looks like blood. Can either of you think of an explanation for that?'

Suddenly raising her eyes, Gaby made a high keening sound. She looked tiny on the expanse of leather sofa, sitting hunched over, as if to minimise her presence.

'Look, is this necessary?' Clive Boswell pleaded, seeing his daughter's distress. 'Couldn't I—'

'I'm sorry, sir, it is important,' said Millie. 'I'll ask again; do you have any idea?'

'What about that fall Sam took, a few weeks ago?' said Boswell.

At that point, Gaby seemed to tune in. 'Oh yes,' she said vaguely. 'He had this road race and he came off his bike, round near Church Stretton. He made a real mess of his arm; took all the skin off the underneath, elbow to wrist.' She lifted her arm to indicate. 'It bled a lot. I told him he should go to A and E, get it properly cleaned up and dressed, but you know what men can be like.'

'OK, that's helpful,' said Millie.

'You think something has happened to him, don't you?' Gaby said, catching on.

Boswell was sceptical. 'You really think that?'

'We're keeping an open mind, but certainly this development is serious,' said Millie calmly.

'We've done the sensible thing and postponed the wedding,' Boswell told her. 'I'm beginning to phone round people to let them know. It's heartbreaking, though of course we still hold out hope that it will go ahead in the end.'

'Mr Boswell, I have to ask you to be a bit more precise about your movements on the—' Millie began, but Boswell was already on his feet.

'Is that all, sergeant? Can I show you out?' Gaby seemed not to notice.

Millie had no option but to follow. Once they were in the hall, Boswell closed the door and lowered his voice. 'Actually, I have a slight amendment to make to what I told you about that Saturday night. Stupid really, but I suppose it's not something I'm very proud of.'

'Go on,' said Millie blandly.

'Well, the truth is, I wasn't drunk when I left the dinner; far from it. But I didn't come home straight away. I went to see a friend.' He cleared his throat.

'Which friend would this be?' asked Millie, though she'd guessed by now what was coming.

'Well, when I say friend . . . She offers a service,' said Boswell, with a weak smile. 'It's one of the ways I've coped since my wife died.' He paused. 'Actually, that's not quite true either. It started before that, when Emma was ill. Anyway, I see her about once a month and that Saturday was one of those occasions. I'm sorry, I know I should have said at the time, but Gaby doesn't know anything about it. It would devastate her. She'd think I was betraying her mother.'

'We will need to verify this with your friend,' said Millie.

'Can it be done discreetly?' pleaded Boswell. 'I have the church to think about too.'

'As long as this information has no direct bearing on Sam's whereabouts, there's no reason to share it at this stage,' Millie said. 'How well do you know the Carters, who run the waste disposal station Sam was investigating?'

'Not at all really,' said Boswell. 'One or two of my site managers use them, because I've seen the name on invoices. But it wasn't until Sam started talking about them that I put two and two together.'

'Do you believe him?' said Mariner, when Millie reported back what she'd learned.

'I'm not sure,' said Millie. 'I keep thinking about the religion. It wouldn't be a very Christian thing to do, to bump off your prospective son-in-law, would it? And it was Boswell who pointed us in the direction of Carter's in the first place.'

'That could be an elaborate double-bluff,' said Mariner. 'As could acknowledging his links with them. And besides, if Clive Boswell wanted to get rid of Sam Fleetwood, I doubt he'd sully his own hands. He'll have plenty of loyal employees who might help him out. You and Bingley need to check out this revised alibi, and some of his contacts.'

Talayeh's sister had arrived from the Yemen and Vicky Jesson went to meet her from Birmingham airport, along with an Arabic interpreter. Until they had established what had happened, Maimoonah ('but everyone calls me Mai') was to be accommodated in a basic hotel; something for which she seemed grateful. 'I hardly know my cousin's family,' she said of Mustafa Shah. 'And I am afraid of what happened to my sister.'

In her mid-twenties, she was a pretty girl and the photograph of Talayeh she showed Jesson was of a young woman who looked very like her, in obscene contrast to the girl Jesson had seen on Croghan's mortuary slab. Jesson offered to wait with the interpreter in the hotel lobby while she settled into her room, but Mai asked them to come up with her. She did not want to be left on her own. So Jesson and the interpreter stood by and watched, while she unpacked her few things. It was a strange dynamic.

'What was Talayeh like?' Jesson asked.

'My sister was a sweet girl, full of life and with big ambitions,' said Mai, haltingly, via the interpreter. 'She always thought the best of people. She was so pretty that even when she was little she had attention wherever she went, from men and women. At first my parents liked it. They were proud of their daughters. It was only when Talayeh was older and began to respond to the men who admired her that things changed. Talayeh formed—'

The interpreter broke off while there was a brief discussion about the precise word. 'An *inappropriate* friendship with a man in the next village,' she went on, 'he was older than her, and already promised. My parents tried to stop Talayeh from seeing him, so they ran away together. They were missing for nine days. When she was found, my parents decided that Talayeh should be married as quickly as possible to a man who she could look up to and who would take care of her.'

And control her? Jesson wanted to ask. But it was too soon to ask such a loaded question. 'I suppose they wanted to put some distance between Talayeh and this man too?' she surmised instead, waiting patiently while her words were translated.

'Talayeh craved excitement,' said Mai wistfully. 'I think they really thought if she came to England it would make her happy.'

'We're going to go to the mortuary,' said Jesson, via the interpreter. 'You don't have to see your sister, she was very badly—'

'No,' Mai looked directly at Jesson, even though it was the interpreter who spoke. 'I want to.'

At the hospital Mai provided a DNA sample. She was also able to positively identify Talayeh's jewellery, and kept her composure right up until she saw her sister's body, at which point she broke down, great sobs wracking her body, and Jesson stepped in to support her.

'Did you have any communication with Talayeh while she was in England?' Jesson asked as they sat in the visitor's room afterwards. She had brought Mai some sweetened tea.

'We spoke on the phone when Mrs Shah would allow it. Talayeh didn't much like it in Birmingham. She didn't feel safe.'

'Safe how?'

'I don't know. Our village is very small and it's in the hills. We go to Sana'a, of course, but just for a few hours at a time. Talayeh told me that the city was exciting but too much; overwhelming.'

'And what about the man she was to marry, Kaspa Rani?' said Jesson. 'What did she tell you about him?'

'Only that she had met him and that he was old and ugly,' Mai let out a giggle that turned into a sob. 'She didn't want to marry him, but my father had threatened that if she didn't, he would disown her. I don't think that's true but Talayeh believed it, and she was miserable.'

Jesson asked the next question carefully: 'Did Talayeh indicate that she felt in any danger, either from her proposed husband or from the Shah family?'

'I don't know.' Mai looked intently at Jesson. Clearly it was something that she had thought about. 'When we spoke Talayeh was in the house of Mr and Mrs Shah. I don't know if she could speak freely.'

'What was the last contact you had with her?'

'She tried to phone me on the night of the fire.' Mai's lip wobbled. 'But I didn't answer her call. The time in Yemen is two hours in front of here, so it would have been night time, maybe ten or eleven o'clock. Talayeh left a message. There was noise in the background and she sounded strange; upset.'

'Why do you think that was?' asked Jesson.

'I thought that perhaps she regretted turning Mr Rani down. Talayeh was stubborn. She would never have admitted it. But I think when they sent her to Bradford she realised she'd missed her chance. Talayeh always had dreamed about living in London or New York or Paris.'

'Could she have gone back to Mr Rani?' asked Jesson.

Mai cradled the mug in her hands. 'Perhaps. I don't know.'

When the detailed forensic report on Sam Fleetwood's car was sent through to Millie, it confirmed the blood as his, but the quantity as inconsistent with the injury Gaby had described. Millie rang Sasha to check.

'Yes, it definitely suggests more than just a graze, however severe,' Sasha told her. 'You'll see too that we also found a scrap of thick polythene caught in the boot's locking mechanism. It's no more than a centimetre squared, but has got two layers, outer and inner. The inner layer is also smeared with blood. My guess would be that Sam Fleetwood's body was wrapped in polythene and put in the boot, where the blood leaked out in several places.'

'From the lack of blood at the deposition site, it's not possible that he was killed there,' Millie told Mariner. 'There's lots of polythene at the house, and that's where we have the last definitive sighting of Sam. It all points to Sam being killed at the house, wrapped in polythene, then driven out to Wythall in the boot of his own car. We made the assumption that Sam was driving his car, but when Bingley looked back at the Gatso footage, honestly, it could be anyone.'

'We've been caught out by that before,' said Mariner, thinking back to a case the previous year. 'So if Fleetwood isn't driving, then who is?'

'It's impossible to see,' said Millie. 'The more we magnify the best image the grainier it gets. We need to do a more thorough search of the house on Meadow Hall Rise. One of the neighbours there also expressed concern about a van seen hanging around. I'll go and get some more detail on that.'

'Are you thinking about the Carters for it?' Mariner asked.

'I'm sure they'd be capable,' said Millie. 'And they'd have the means to dispose of the body, so the question is whether someone else put them up to it, Figgis or Boswell?'

Millie took Bingley with her to Meadow Hall Rise, and while he made a start on the house, Millie went to talk to the Kramers. She rang the bell of the large, rambling house and Mrs Kramer, a small, neat, middle-aged woman came to the door.

'I understand you've had concerns about a vehicle hanging about on the street,' said Millie. 'Could you describe it for me?'

'It's one of those vans that workmen drive, a white one, though it's not very clean,' Mrs Kramer told her.

'You mean a transit van?' Millie checked.

'No, not as big as that. It was the same size as a car, but with storage at the back.'

Millie held up Bingley's phone, showing her the picture he had taken of Danny Carter's van. 'Like this one?' she asked.

'Yes, that's more like it.'

Millie asked, more from hope than expectation, if Mr or Mrs Kramer had taken down the registration number.

'Oh no,' she said. 'We couldn't see it from here in the dark and my husband wasn't going to risk going outside to check. There could have been anyone in it. You hear about people being attacked in front of their own houses for no reason at all, don't you?'

'So it could have been Carter's van, but it could also have been about half a million others,' Millie told Bingley, when she caught up with him back at the house. Bingley was on the ground floor, walking from room to room studying the floors, still covered in their protective layer. 'Can you see the difference between the plastic in here, and in here?' he asked, going from the living room to the kitchen.

'Yes, the stuff in here looks a bit cleaner and newer,' she said, standing in the living room.

'And what do you think about this?' Bingley crouched down by the freshly painted skirting board.

Millie squatted down beside him and peered at the paintwork. She could hardly see the row of fine specks. But it was definitely there, and next to it another, even finer.

'It might not be blood,' said Bingley. 'But luminol will sort that out one way or the other—' He stopped, as Millie held up a hand.

'Wait. Did you hear that?' she asked.

TWENTY-TWO ✏

Bingley had heard the noise too. Someone was speaking in a low voice, very close by. They got out on to the drive to find a man letting himself into the garage, singing tunelessly to himself.

It was Ted, the plasterer Millie had met on her first visit, but today he was on his own. 'Hello, bab,' he said, recognising Millie. 'You back again? I've just come to pick up the rest of my stuff.' He was eyeing up Bingley's uniform, so this time Millie showed him her warrant card.

'Oh, I see,' he said. 'I thought there was something funny—'

'Did your friend find his lighter?' asked Millie pleasantly.

Ted was a little wary now. 'D'you know, I don't think he did. He was hacked off about that. His girlfriend gave it to him and it was a nice one.'

'He and Sam Fleetwood had a falling out, I understand,' Millie reminded him.

Ted was dismissive. 'Ah, it was nothing.'

'What was it about?'

'Robbie annoyed Mr Fleetwood because he'd gone off a couple of times, of a weekend, to work on another job. So then Mr Fleetwood started nit-picking about the way Robbie had done some of the work; wanted him to do a better job. Robbie took the hump, so no surprises there. He knew he wasn't supposed to smoke in here – standard practice these days – so he started doing it just to be awkward. Fleetwood caught him at it. He let rip but Robbie's got a temper on him too, so he wasn't going to back down, was he? He has a chip on his shoulder about what he sees as rich kids living off their parents.'

'Well, he's wrong about Sam Fleetwood,' said Millie. 'Do you know where Robbie is now?'

'Nah, he's finished here now, so he's off on that other job, somewhere down south, I think.'

'Does Robbie have a van?' asked Millie.

'Yeah, a beaten up old thing, on its last legs.'

'Is it white, by any chance?'

'If you'd call it that,' quipped Ted. 'He never cleans it.'

Ted was able to furnish them with a mobile number for Robbie. When they tracked him down he was, as Ted had predicted, pleased that his lighter had been found, but his alibi for the night Sam Fleetwood had disappeared was unassailable. He'd been moonlighting on the other job in Sussex, which he'd been doing every weekend for the last couple of months. The most he could be accused of was not declaring the work for tax purposes.

By the weekend they seemed mired in both cases. Clive Boswell's revised alibi was also sound. 'And I've checked his phone records,' said Bingley, in the Friday afternoon briefing. 'There's no evidence that he made or received any calls that evening, which you might have expected him to do if he was orchestrating things.'

All right,' said Mariner. 'Let's come back to it fresh on Monday morning.'

When Suzy's mobile rang early on Saturday it took her a few seconds to orientate herself. It was Tom. 'Hi, I wondered if you wanted to go for a walk?'

'I could after half past eleven,' said Suzy. 'I've offered to keep Gideon company while Rosalind goes to confession.'

'Really? God-botherers too, eh? I'm surprised that a man with such a sharp intellect buys into all the religion nonsense.'

'I suppose I was too at first,' said Suzy. 'But it's true. And if it helps him cope with his illness, then I suppose it's all to the good. I'll see you later.'

At the appointed time, taking reading matter and a notebook with her, Suzy went round to Gideon and Rosalind's house.

'I'll be about an hour,' said Rosalind. 'Are you sure that's OK?' She seemed different somehow, and Suzy realised she was wearing a little make-up and had put her hair up, as if she was going to work.

'It's fine,' she said. 'Tom's coming over a bit later, but we've got nothing special planned. Take as much time as you like.'

'It's so kind of you,' said Rosalind. 'I'm not sure if Gideon will be very good company. He's been in quite a lot of pain overnight, so the doctor has been round to give him a morphine injection. He bucks up a bit at first but then it tends to knock him out a bit. Between you and me I'm not convinced that this doctor altogether knows what he's doing. He's a locum, you know, and his English isn't that great.'

'I'm sure he wouldn't be employed if he wasn't up to the job,' Suzy said, in an attempt to reassure her, though really she knew nothing about it.

Rosalind's calculation was entirely accurate. Gideon chatted to Suzy for around half an hour, mainly about the latest article he had been reading, after which he did indeed seem inclined to sleep. So having helped him to his room, where he lay down on the bed to rest, Suzy settled into the sunny lounge with her book. She'd barely sat down when the doorbell sounded. On the doorstep was a woman of about her own age, her greying hair cut severely short. Naturally she looked surprised to see Suzy, who explained that Rosalind wasn't there. 'Well, I'm Kirsten, Gideon's daughter,' she said abruptly. 'And as I expect you are wondering, I'm the product of my mother's marriage to Gideon; the one Rosalind wrecked.'

'Oh.' Suzy was at a loss about how to respond to that. But, as seemed to be expected, she held the door open so that Kirsten could come in.

'Rosalind seduced my father; that's all there is to it,' Kirsten went on, pressing home her point. She took off her waxed jacket and hung it on one of the hooks on the wall. 'And now she's made her bed, hasn't she?'

'I'm sure that's not how she sees it,' said Suzy tactfully.

Kirsten didn't reply. 'Is my father awake?'

'Not really, he was dozing when I looked in on him a few minutes ago. We spent some time talking, but that seemed to tire him.'

Kirsten fixed her with a stare. 'Sorry. And you are?'

'Suzy Yin. I'm a friend of Rosalind's. That is, we work together at the university.'

'Lucky you,' said Kirsten, managing to sound utterly insincere.

'I'm just sitting with Gideon while Rosalind goes to confession.' Suzy was annoyed with herself for sounding defensive.

'Oh, she still keeps up with the charade, does she?' Kirsten scoffed.

'I'm sorry?'

'Rosalind only converted because it was one of my father's requirements when they married,' said Kirsten. 'As a matter of fact, she did it at about the same time as Tony Blair, so that tells us something, doesn't it?'

Kirsten, clearly at home, went through to Gideon's room and Suzy heard her greeting her father: 'Hello, Daddy!', before their voices dropped to a murmur. Shortly afterwards, with a curt 'goodbye' to Suzy, Kirsten left again.

Suzy went in to Gideon, to see if he needed anything. He seemed half asleep, but as she approached he mumbled something that sounded to Suzy like 'scheming witch' but she must have been mistaken. Seeing Suzy, he seemed to start. 'Oh, it's you,' he said, and drifted back to sleep.

When Rosalind came back Suzy began to wonder if there might be something to this confession business; she seemed brighter and more relaxed. 'Has everything been all right?' she asked.

'It has,' said Suzy. 'I think it took a while for the medication to kick in, but after that he was fine. He's sleeping.'

Rosalind's face clouded a little. 'He's in so much discomfort. It's no life for him.'

'That's not true, and you know it,' said Suzy. 'Oh, and Gideon's daughter stopped by. She said she was passing.'

'Oh. I'm sorry to have missed her, but Gideon will have been pleased. Did she stay long?' The acrimony Kirsten held towards Rosalind didn't seem at all reciprocal.

'About twenty minutes, I think,' Suzy told her. 'I left them to it. There seemed to be things she wanted to discuss.'

'I'm sure there were,' said Rosalind. 'Kirsten always prefers to talk to her father when I'm not around. She must have been delighted. I expect she managed to convey her disapproval of me.' It didn't seem to bother her in the slightest. 'Well, I've kept you long enough,' she went on. 'Your date will be here soon.'

Mariner was already waiting at the cottage when Suzy returned. By prior arrangement she'd left a key for him under a pot, even though he'd chided her for lax security. 'Just because you're in a village, you're not immune, you know,' he said. 'I saw Rosalind as I drove through, just coming out of the church. She looked a bit different from the last time I saw her, but then it probably offends the Almighty to go into church not wearing a bra.'

Suzy told him about the visit from Kirsten. 'She seemed fairly bitter about Rosalind, although it wasn't mutual. Funny how affairs are always perceived as the woman's fault, aren't they?' she said. 'As though Gideon had no control over his actions.'

Suzy put together a hasty picnic and they set off on a walk around the village. Mariner had brought along his OS map of the area, and they turned into an expanse of deciduous woodland. 'Shakespeare's Forest of Arden,' said Suzy. 'Speaking of which, I've invited Mum and Dad to come and stay with me for the weekend after next. You'll be able to finally meet them. Mum in particular wants to go to a play at the RSC, though I'm not sure how they'll get on with the Bard.'

Mariner pulled a face. 'Nor me. Do I have to come?'

'Yes, you do,' said Suzy. 'Don't be such a philistine.'

'That's always supposing that these latest cases don't get any more complex,' said Mariner. 'It's almost certain now that Sam Fleetwood has come to grief. We're treating his disappearance as suspicious.'

'That young man we saw at Charlie's?' said Suzy. 'But that's horrible. What do you think has happened to him?'

'His line of work has brought him into contact with some undesirables who he's rubbed up the wrong way, so that's where our focus is now. Millie's handling it, along with our new boy, Kevin Bingley. She's very thorough.'

'You're pleased to have her back,' Suzy commented, wandering off the path and into the woods a little way.

'Of course,' said Mariner. Suzy was almost out of sight. 'Are you scouting?' he called. It was something she hadn't done in a while, partly because the weather had been too cold, even for her, but also for other, less palatable reasons.

'Of course I am. And this looks perfect.' He caught her up as she was taking a rug out of her backpack. Spreading it on the ground, she sat down on it and completely unselfconsciously took off her top.

'That Rosalind's a bad influence on you,' said Mariner, sitting down beside her and starting to unbutton his shirt.

'I've got rather less to worry about than she has.'

Mariner cast an anxious look around. 'We're not that far from civilisation here, you know.'

'All the more reason to get on with it then,' said Suzy, turning to help him.

They got back to the cottage pleasantly weary, and after they'd eaten, Mariner struggled to stay awake for the TV programme they were watching.

'This is stupid,' said Suzy eventually. 'We're both shattered, let's go to bed.'

The plan had been to get some much needed sleep, but once in bed another more interesting alternative presented itself.

'I really must move this bed away from the wall,' Mariner gasped.

Suzy froze. 'No, it's not that,' she said. 'Listen, it's still going. There's someone banging on the front door.'

'Christ, what time is it?'

Suzy reached for her phone. 'It's after eleven,' she said. 'I should go and see.'

'No, I'll go.' Mariner sighed, rolling on to his back. Pulling on his jeans, he went downstairs and opened the door to find Rosalind, her hair all over the place and her eyes wild, an over-sized robe pulled around her and Crocs on her bare feet. 'It's Gideon,' she said, panicked. 'I can't wake him up!'

Shit. 'Have you called the doctor?' asked Mariner, grabbing his jacket.

'He was here, just a couple of hours ago, to give Gideon his evening morphine injection. He said everything was fine. Gideon dozed off, as he often does, but I've just gone to get him ready for bed and I can't rouse him.'

By now Suzy was halfway down the stairs. 'Call an ambulance!' Mariner shouted back to her. 'I'll go and see what I can do.' Leaving Suzy to make the call, he followed Rosalind round to the house. Gideon was lying fully clothed on the bed in his room, his eyes closed, and Mariner was experienced enough to know from his pallor and the feel of his skin that they were probably already too late. Nonetheless he began putting his training into practice by administering CPR, while Rosalind stood silently by, wringing her hands.

Suzy appeared, breathless. 'The paramedics are on their way.'

Even then it seemed to Mariner that he was pumping on Gideon's lifeless chest for an eternity, until suddenly there was another pair of hands there, and a young female paramedic said: 'Thank you, sir, I'll take it from here.'

'What has he had?' her colleague asked, already setting up an intravenous drip. After a brief hesitation Rosalind recited the list of Gideon's regular drugs. He listened as he inserted the line into Gideon's forearm.

Suzy slipped an arm around Rosalind. 'Let's go downstairs,' she said. 'And let them do their job.' She guided Rosalind out of the room.

'I must call Father Peter,' said Rosalind suddenly.

'I'll do it,' said Suzy. The priest arrived shortly afterwards, clothes hastily thrown on and his hair standing on end. He was younger than Suzy had first thought and was white-faced. She wondered if it was his first experience of such an emergency.

Upstairs Mariner stood, watching and waiting, but after five minutes the female paramedic sat back and reluctantly declared Gideon dead. They made Gideon presentable and allowed Rosalind, and the priest, some time alone with him, after which Suzy made tea for everyone. The locum doctor arrived to confirm the death, before hurrying off to another emergency call, and after that, Suzy took Rosalind up to try and get some sleep. Mariner had found a bottle of whisky and offered a glass to Father Peter. The two men sat in the kitchen, in companionable silence.

'It's such a shock,' said the priest eventually. 'Poor Rosalind. Gideon was her life.' When he had gone, Mariner slept fitfully on the sofa downstairs until the early morning when, on Rosalind's behalf, he could phone the undertaker and arrange for the mortuary van to come.

Suzy helped Rosalind to make some phone calls, including one to Kirsten, who arrived just as Mariner and Suzy were leaving. Suzy was heartened to see the two women spontaneously embrace, their animosity put to one side, if only temporarily. After that

Mariner and Suzy went back to the cottage to try and take in what had happened. Incongruously the church bells were ringing merrily out for the Sunday service as they made their way along the lane. 'I can't believe it,' said Suzy. 'I mean, Gideon was unwell, but I don't think anyone expected this. What a terrible shock for Rosalind.'

'There will need to be a post-mortem, as it's an unexpected death,' said Mariner. 'That won't be easy either. She'll need your support. It would be a good idea for us each to make a note of everything that happened last night,' he went on.

'What do you mean?' said Suzy.

'Well, I'm sure it won't come to it, but if there's anything that doesn't add up about Gideon's death, the local police may want to speak to us,' Mariner said.

Suzy rounded on him. 'Really, Tom. Can't you stop doing your job just for a moment? We're here as Rosalind's friends!'

'I know, but—' He was wasting his breath. Was there something wrong with him, that he automatically took a professional perspective?

The day passed in a blur. They went up to bed, but Mariner couldn't sleep and, despite Suzy's protests, spent an hour writing down his account of what had happened. After that, when Suzy woke, they went for a long walk, during which they hardly spoke, each of them trying to come to terms with what had happened.

TWENTY-THREE

'Y ou look like crap,' said Sharp, when she saw Mariner on Monday morning.

'Yeah, well, it wasn't the most relaxed of weekends.' Mariner described the events of Saturday night.

'God. Are you all right?'

'I'm fine,' said Mariner. 'It's not as if I even really knew the old boy, or his wife. Suzy's only known them a short time.' And there was far too much happening here for Mariner to dwell on it. From Sharp's office he went straight to the bull pen. Vicky Jesson was on the phone, but waved him across as she ended the call. 'I've done some digging on Kaspa Rani,' she said. 'He's known both to the Met and the Met fraud squad. Incident one was a fire at one of his warehouses, queried as an insurance job, though nothing was proven.'

'And incident two?'

'Aggravated assault on a young woman,' said Vicky. 'Again, no charges were brought and curiously there was nothing on file, so I phoned one of the officers at the PPU. They recorded it as an honour-based incident. Kaspa Rani is the victim's brother and he attacked his sister for consorting with a man from outside their community. Rani didn't like it, and subjected her to a beating.'

'But she didn't press charges?'

'No,' said Vicky. 'She chose to elope with the man instead. As far as the PPU officer was aware, they are still on the run. Do you think that's what Talayeh's death is – an honour killing?'

'Honour?' Mariner was contemptuous. 'Violence is violence, killing is killing. Sticking the word "honour" in front doesn't make them legitimate or justifiable. But it's basis enough to talk to Kaspa Rani again.'

'We can't yet,' said Vicky. 'That was his PA on the phone. He's driving up from London as we speak, expected later this morning. I've asked her to confirm when he gets here.'

'How's his alibi looking, for the night of the fire?' asked Mariner.

'That's a weird coincidence,' said Vicky, and she looked across at Bingley. 'Do you want to tell him?'

'Looks as if he was at the same dinner as Clive Boswell,' said Bingley.

'Do they know each other?' asked Mariner.

'No reason to think that they do,' said Bingley. 'They've each named different individuals to vouch for them, and Clive Boswell's list is longer. But the hotel offers valet parking, and according to them, Kaspa Rani requested his car just after ten thirty.'

'That kid who witnessed the fire,' said Mariner. 'Didn't he also give a description of the vehicles that came and went?'

'Some of them,' said Bingley. 'But he admitted that there were whole chunks of the evening that he missed.'

'Have a look at—' Mariner began.

'Already on it,' said Bingley, disappearing for a few minutes behind the monitor. 'Assorted vehicles, mostly family cars, pizza takeaway delivery, but at about eleven thirty, and I quote: "a massive great big silver thing, flash, like, you know, a Merc or something".'

As he was speaking, Jesson's phone rang. 'Thanks,' she said to the caller, then: 'Out of interest, what car does Mr Rani drive?' Replacing the receiver, she turned to Mariner. 'Kaspa Rani's expected in the next half hour,' she said. 'And he drives a silver Lexus saloon.' Mariner was faced with a dilemma. The weekend search of Danny Carter's caravan had turned up the personalised number plates belonging to Sam Fleetwood's car, so implicating him further. And on the back of that he was coming in for further questioning. Ordinarily, Millie would have handled this, but it was her day off. 'Are you all right to talk to Kaspa Rani?' he asked Vicky.

'I get right up his nose,' she smiled. 'It's perfect.'

And at that moment Mariner saw out of the window that Danny Carter had arrived. Clearly they were beginning to rattle a few cages, because he was accompanied by brother George and another man who could only be their solicitor. 'To clear this up once and for all,' said George, though for Mariner it was the reaction of a guilty man. He politely asked George to wait outside.

Mariner began the interview with the photograph of Sam Fleetwood. 'Do you know this man?'

'No, why?' Danny was immediately on his guard.

'Really?' said Mariner, feigning surprise. 'He's Sam Fleetwood, the man who's been giving your dad a hard time over possible illegal practices on your site. And now Mr Fleetwood has gone missing, and his car has miraculously appeared in your yard, with bloodstains in the boot, and the personalised plates were found in your caravan. Can you explain any of that?'

'I told you. I found it,' Danny insisted.

'Quite a coincidence though, isn't it?' Mariner observed. 'Have you ever been anywhere near Meadow Hall Rise?'

'Where's that?' Danny lifted his head from where he was still studying the photograph.

'It's where Sam Fleetwood's moving into with his new wife,' said Mariner. 'Did you ever follow Sam Fleetwood, when he left your site? We'll find out eventually, because you'll show up on Gatso cameras in the area, so it's probably best to come clean.' It would take hours of going through footage, and wasn't really worth the effort, but Carter didn't know that.

'I might have gone after him once,' Danny admitted finally.

'Why? What were you going to do?'

'I was trying to put the wind up him.'

'Is that all?' said Mariner. 'Are you sure you didn't want to do more than that? What were you doing on Saturday night, the week before last?'

'I got a lift in to the snooker hall down Redditch, with Kyle and Jordan.'

'Is that Jordan Wright?' asked Mariner.

'Yeah. We played a couple of frames, then went to the pub and sank a few pints then I went for a kebab.'

'What time was this?'

'I dunno, about half eleven.'

'And how did you get home?'

'Kyle dropped me off and then I walked the rest.' Carter's solicitor leaned across and said something. 'That's when I saw that car on fire – when I was letting myself into the van.'

'That was lucky, wasn't it?' said Mariner. 'That you just happened to see it.'

'Yeah, it was,' said Carter, his self-satisfied smile indicating that the sarcasm had gone over his head.

'Are you sure about that?' asked Mariner. 'Are you sure you weren't spying on Sam Fleetwood's house on Meadow Hall Rise that night? Perhaps you went to confront him about what had happened to your dad. Things got out of hand and you killed him, stuffed him in the boot of his car and drove it out here, where you set fire to it. Then, early the next morning, you came and winched it on to a low loader and brought it back to the compound, where you disposed of the body.'

'No, I never!' Danny protested.

'Maybe you didn't decide yourself to do it, Danny. Maybe someone put you up to it. Do you know this man, Clive Boswell?' Mariner slid a photograph across the table. It was one Bingley had printed off from Facebook, taken at Charlie's house a couple of weeks before. 'Or how about this one?' He added the photograph from Mike Figgis' personnel file.

There was a flicker of recognition at Boswell's picture, but Carter's lawyer chose that moment to lean in and whisper something to him. 'No comment,' Carter said, and sat back, his arms folded.

'And that was that,' Mariner told Bingley afterwards. 'Danny Carter's involvement would nicely explain how Sam Fleetwood's wallet turned up in Redditch. But if he's telling the truth then it confirms alibis for both him and Jordan Wright for that Saturday night, which clears them of any involvement in the fire too.'

'And if he's not?' said Bingley.

'Then they could both be in two different kinds of shit,' said Mariner.

'For the record, I haven't found anything yet on Clive Boswell's call history to show that he has direct links with the Carters,' Bingley said. 'But I haven't started on his company accounts yet.'

'That will keep you busy for a bit, won't it?' said Mariner.

When Jesson got to Rani's cash and carry, there was no sign of the silver Lexus, so she sat and waited on the forecourt, taking the opportunity to check through her phone messages. A tap on the car window made her jump, and she wound it down to show the security guard her warrant card. 'I'm waiting for Mr Rani,' she said.

The guard, a young Asian man, seemed satisfied with that. 'Are you here about that girl; the one who died?' he asked.

'That's right,' said Jesson.

He shook his head in disbelief. 'I can't get my head round it,' he said. 'She was only here a couple of hours before, alive and kicking. I mean literally kicking.'

'You were working that Saturday night?' said Jesson, getting out of the car.

'Yeah, I was down on the shop floor, doing the rounds, when she showed up. A minicab dropped her off. She'd been drinking; I could smell it on her and she looked rough; there was this rip in her dress.' He gestured across his chest. 'She was going on in some other language, but all I could get was "Mr Rani; talk to Mr Rani." It was mental. Then she kept saying sorry, but I didn't know what for.'

'What time was this?' Jesson asked.

'Must have been ten-ish,' the guard told her. 'I'd been on shift a couple of hours. I didn't know what to do with her. I took her up to the office and made her some coffee, then I tried to get hold of Mr Rani. He wasn't very happy. I had to get him out of some do he was at. As soon as he walked in, she was all over him.'

'How did Mr Rani seem?' asked Jesson.

'He was pretty mad, I could see that. He took her into his office, to calm her down, I suppose.' He looked awkward. 'I know I shouldn't have, but I stood outside the door for a bit, listening. I could hear her wailing, though I couldn't really get what she was saying. Then all of a sudden it went dead quiet. It was spooky.'

'Did you see Talayeh leave?'

'No. I had to get back on my rounds, or I'd get the sack. Mr Rani likes things done properly. By the time I got back here to the forecourt, Mr Rani's car had gone and there was no sign of him or the girl.'

'Did you know anything about Mr Rani's relationship with Talayeh?' Jesson asked.

'Was she the girl who turned him down? Everybody knows,

but we don't talk about it. For weeks he was making this thing about how he was getting married soon. There would be this big wedding and we were all invited.'

'How did you find out that it was off?'

'He told Mira in the office that he'd changed his mind, but it soon got round what had really happened. That was so *bad*.'

'Thanks,' said Jesson. 'That's been helpful.' The guard went off on his patrol, and she had to wait a further twenty minutes before Kaspa Rani arrived. From his demeanour, Jesson gathered that he had been warned. She approached the instant he got out of his car. 'Good morning, Mr Rani,' she said. 'I wonder if I could have a look at your satnav?'

For a second he was puzzled, but, working it out, he capitulated. 'You don't have to,' he said. 'You will see that I went to Wellington Road on the night of the fire.'

'So why did you lie about the last time you saw Talayeh?' asked Jesson.

'Because I knew how it would look,' said Rani. 'And it was of little consequence. I delivered her back to her cousin's house. You know that. It was where she was found. So clearly her death had nothing to do with me.'

'Except that we don't know what condition she was in when you took her back,' said Jesson. 'A witness reports hearing raised voices, followed by an abrupt silence. We know that Talayeh sustained a head injury sometime that day. Unfortunately, the condition of her body after the fire makes it impossible to ascertain whether it occurred before or after her death. It could have even been the cause. We also know that Talayeh had been drinking. She wasn't used to alcohol, so it wouldn't have taken much to knock her out completely, so that she wouldn't stir, even if the house was on fire. Talayeh had embarrassed you in front of your friends, and in front of the whole community. Everyone we've spoken to knows about it. How far would you go to avenge that humiliation? Where were you at one a.m. on that Sunday morning?'

'I told you,' said Rani. 'I admit that I saw the girl that night. She was intoxicated and raving about some man she claimed had tried to take advantage of her. All fantasy, of course. She would have thrown herself at him; it's the kind of woman she was.' His disgust was plain. 'I said I would talk to her when she was sober,' he went on. 'She was alive and fully conscious when I delivered her back to Wellington Road.'

'Then what did you do?'

'I drove to my house in Hall Green.'

'What do you think?' Mariner asked Jesson when she returned to Granville Lane.

'I don't know,' said Jesson. 'Rani admits taking Talayeh back to Wellington Road. But that doesn't mean he isn't responsible. He could have hit her. He could have plied her with more drink from that booze in his office, then waited until Talayeh went into the house and was out cold before setting the fire. He's Mustafa's friend; he'd probably been to Wellington Road before and knew that the office where she was sleeping was effectively an incendiary device.'

'But what about the risk to the others?'

'Maybe he wasn't thinking straight,' said Jesson. 'And he could be angry with the Shahs, too, for having put him in that position.'

'Yes, awkward for them too,' said Mariner. 'How close are Rani and Mustafa Shah? Could the two of them have conspired?'

'Oh crap, the money!' said Jesson suddenly. 'When Bingley was doing the initial checks on the Shahs, he started to tell me that Mustafa Shah withdrew ten thousand pounds in cash, shortly before he went to Sana'a.'

'Well, he couldn't have taken it with him,' said Mariner. 'He'd have had to declare a sum that large. Does this mean he paid someone to set the fire for him? Salwa could have been in on it too.'

'But she's seemed genuinely shocked and upset,' said Jesson. 'I don't think a woman would put her children at risk like that. There is another possibility,' she went on. 'Mai made it sound as if Talayeh was backed into a corner, with no way out. If Rani now refused *her*, how desperate would she be? She'd screwed up her chances with him and she couldn't go back to the Yemen. Would that be enough to cause her to take her own life? Could she have started the fire herself?'

There was only one person who could answer that question.

*   *   *

'It's possible,' said Gerry Docherty. 'There's accelerant splashed across the floor in that downstairs room.'

'But would she do that?' Mariner wasn't convinced. 'Talayeh's been raised a devout Muslim, and suicide is forbidden in the Islamic faith.'

'But we know she had also been drinking,' argued Jesson. 'It could have been an attempt to get back at the Shahs that went horribly wrong.'

But somehow neither of them wanted to believe that a young girl's life could have been ended in such a way.

'Let's knock it on the head,' said Mariner, rubbing a hand over his face. 'None of our possible suspects is going anywhere.'

'These weren't much use either,' said Jesson, picking up the folder Mustafa Shah had given her.

Mariner held out a hand for it. 'I've got a thing at Lloyd House tomorrow morning. I'll drop it back afterwards.'

On his way home that evening, Mariner phoned Suzy to check that she was all right. He found her working late. 'Don't start that,' he warned. 'It can get to be a habit.'

'You can talk,' she said. He could tell she was smiling. 'Don't worry, I don't plan on letting that happen. Just some things to finish off. The police have been in touch,' she told him. 'Gideon died from a lethal dose of morphine, almost twice what he should have been administered, so there's going to be a second post-mortem.'

'They'll bring in a Home Office pathologist,' said Mariner. 'That wouldn't be done lightly.' He knew that the additional cost was substantial – more than two thousand pounds the last time he'd looked. 'It means there will be a full investigation into the events of that evening.'

'Yes,' said Suzy. 'The police have asked me to provide a statement, so I'm planning to go to the station in Warwick when I leave here. They'll want to talk to you too, I expect.'

'I'm sure they will,' said Mariner. 'Are you all right?'

'Yes, I'm fine. I should have taken your advice. I'm sorry.'

'There's nothing to apologise for. We were both overwrought. It was a tough night.'

'Yes, it was.'

'And don't worry, we have nothing to hide. Just tell them exactly what happened. They just need to get a sense of how the events unfolded. Let me know how it goes.' He rang off.

When Mariner got home, he found a message on his answer machine from Warwickshire police, just as Suzy had predicted. He rang through, knowing that it might be acceptable for him to email them his written statement after getting it witnessed by someone at Granville Lane.

'You think it might have been the doctor?' he asked, once he'd been put through to a detective.

'Not necessarily,' said the detective. 'His records of what he was carrying that evening are entirely consistent with the surgery records, and we don't have any kind of motive. I don't think we're looking at another Harold Shipman.'

'So what then?' asked Mariner, already fairly sure of where this was going.

'Is there anything Mrs Wiley said to you, that might make you think she was planning to help her husband on his way?'

'I hardly know her,' said Mariner truthfully. 'If she's confided anything, it would be to my partner. But from what little I saw, she was devoted to her husband.'

'That's what I'm afraid of,' said the detective.

Having ended her call to Mariner, Suzy sat staring at the computer screen in front of her. Rosalind's computer. Sweet that Mariner thought she was worried about the police interview, and she wouldn't disabuse him just yet. It had been quite a day. From first thing this morning (was it really, only this morning?) when out of nowhere, life had thrown her a curve ball, that had the potential for further upheaval, before she'd even settled into the new job. She'd hardly known what to think at the time, and it had played on her mind all day; the temptation of something she'd wanted now for a long time, versus the safer option of letting life continue as it was. Timing is everything, she thought wryly. She should perhaps have shared it with Tom; he was as much a part of this as she was. But she wanted to make up her own mind about it first.

And now this. She'd been less than honest with Tom. There

wasn't really any urgent work to finish. Suzy had stayed late to make sure none of her colleagues would be around this time when she logged on to Rosalind's PC. It had taken her a little while to track back to the alert she had seen, just a little more than a week ago, and she had hoped above hope that she had been mistaken. But what was in front of her now was as plain as it could be: the information page of Journey's End, an organisation offering support to those considering assisted dying, for themselves or their loved one. Perhaps she should have told Mariner, but it might mean nothing at all. Looking at a website was no proof of anything. And she wanted to give Rosalind the opportunity to tell her that herself.

It was as she was driving home that Suzy realised that she had the perfect pretext for going round to Rosalind's. Developments earlier today had presented her with a weighty dilemma. And while she was reasonably confident of making a decision on her own, an objective opinion from someone outside the situation could only be helpful. And that might provide an opportunity to dispel the doubts Suzy had about her friend. But when she got to the Forge, Suzy found Rosalind wholly preoccupied. 'There's to be a second post-mortem on Gideon,' she said, before Suzy had even stepped across the threshold. 'The police don't think he died of natural causes.'

Suzy followed Rosalind into the kitchen, where they remained standing. She almost flinched at the intensity of Rosalind's gaze, but said nothing; it had to come from her. The air grew thicker with each second that passed, and Suzy was acutely aware of the ticking of the clock on the wall, the radio burbling in another room.

'I *had* to do it,' Rosalind blurted out at last. 'Please believe me.'

'What are you saying?' Suzy hardly dared breathe.

'I helped Gideon to die,' said Rosalind. 'But I was only doing what he wanted. He begged me to do it.'

'How . . .?' Suzy faltered.

'I waited until the doctor had delivered his evening injection, then I delivered another, as soon as the doctor had gone,' said Rosalind, examining her hands. 'There has often been a little left over from Gideon's prescribed amount, so I've been storing it up.'

'But surely suicide runs contrary to Gideon's beliefs?' Despite her suspicions, Suzy still didn't want to believe it.

'Since he has been ill and particularly during the last few months, Gideon has struggled with his faith,' said Rosalind. 'It has been one of the few things we've ever disagreed on. I hadn't told anyone that, but it's true.'

'I will have to tell the police,' said Suzy.

'I know.' And without another word, Rosalind handed her the phone.

After the police car came, and Rosalind was cautioned and taken to the police station, Suzy went back to Y Worry and called Mariner. 'Rosalind has been charged with Gideon's murder,' she said, still reeling from it.

Mariner exhaled. So it was more than conjecture. 'What do you think?' he asked Suzy.

'I know,' said Suzy. 'She did it; she told me. Gideon pleaded with her to do it. So now she's been arrested.'

'It's all right,' Mariner reassured her. 'They're following standard procedures. In practice, although they must follow due process, courts almost always take a lenient view. It's likely that Rosalind will get off with a suspended sentence at most. Anyway. Try not to worry, I'm sure it will be fine. Do you want me to come over?'

'No, I'll be fine,' said Suzy. 'It's just so awful for poor Rosalind.'

TWENTY-FOUR

The following morning Mariner attended his meeting at Lloyd House, and on his way back to Granville Lane, called in at the Yemeni Advice Centre to return the files given to Jesson by Mustafa Shah. They hadn't been much help and Mariner couldn't shake off the feeling that they were missing something; the fire had been about something personal. He wanted to ascertain the extent of Shah's friendship with Kaspa Rani. The nearest parking space he could find was on a side street some distance along the Ladypool Road, but he enjoyed the walk through this energetic neighbourhood, past a halal butcher, a draper, a sweet shop. Like most urban streets, it had its share of litter, and sidestepping a pushchair, Mariner's foot made contact with a plastic pop bottle that went scooting into the gutter. The sensation triggered a brief and inexplicable surge of adrenalin, which he was trying to fathom when he almost collided with a small child darting across the pavement. The mother, in colourful *al-masoon* was reading a printed notice pinned to the door of a shop whose window had been sprayed with graffiti. Mariner had come across the word *shaitan* before, in other contexts. He couldn't remember the exact translation but he knew that it wasn't flattering. What attracted his attention now was the name more formally stencilled across the glass underneath: Soltan Ahmed.

Mariner waited while the mother finished reading, and when she had stepped aside, he took a look at it. In both Arabic and English, it said that, due to unforeseen circumstances, the business was closed. The flyer had been posted just six weeks ago. A brass plate beside the door bore some Arabic script, and below that: *tabib at al 'asnan*. The woman and her child had remained nearby. 'Excuse me,' Mariner said. 'What does this mean?'

She smiled shyly and shook her head. She didn't speak English. But then, after thinking for a moment, she opened her mouth wide, exposing her teeth and miming a pulling motion. 'Thank you,' said Mariner. 'And this?' He indicated the graffiti, but this time she simply shook her head, moving her child away.

'Your father-in-law was a dentist?' Mariner said to Mustafa Shah, when he got to the advice centre.

'He was,' said Shah, who was completing some kind of application form.

'But the graffiti on the window; that word *shaitan*. What does it mean?'

Shah stopped what he was doing and let his pen drop onto the desk. 'Loosely translated it means "evil one".'

'I don't understand,' said Mariner. 'I thought your father-in-law was a respected member of the community?'

'He was,' Shah told him. 'But one of his patients, a teenage girl, developed hepatitis. Her parents got it into their heads that somehow it was Soltan's fault, related to the dental treatment she'd had. We didn't take it seriously. There are other ways in which the girl could have contracted the disease. The family didn't have clear evidence to sue for malpractice, but they were going to take their story to the press. And as your English expression has it: mud sticks. I had to persuade the family to think again.'

'You paid them off,' said Mariner. 'The ten thousand pounds you drew from your account was to buy their silence.'

'They were satisfied with that,' Shah insisted. 'Because there was no case to answer.'

'But your father-in-law closed his practice, nonetheless.'

'He had been thinking of retiring anyway,' said Shah, with a shrug.

'Is that when you took all his papers to Wellington Road?'

'The patient records had to be stored somewhere.'

'I will need details of this family,' said Mariner. 'And did your father-in-law have an assistant, a dental nurse?'

Shah was reluctant, but said eventually: 'It was Aisha, who helps me out here now. When Soltan's practice closed, we felt bad about making her redundant, so I offered her a few hours.'

'To guarantee her loyalty?' Mariner speculated.

'To help her out,' said Shah, evenly. 'I'll fetch her for you.'

Mustafa Shah had the grace to allow Mariner to speak to Aisha alone. 'The posters on the waiting room walls need to be updated,' he decided.

Aisha seemed nervous as she sat down across from Mariner.

'There's nothing to worry about,' he assured her. 'I just want to ask you about Mr Ahmed, particularly in the time leading up to his retirement.'

Her eyes flicked towards the waiting room.

'It's fine,' said Mariner. 'Mr Shah knows why I'm talking to you.'

'It was before that girl got sick,' Aisha said. 'I began to notice how forgetful he was becoming. Normally he was so careful about hygiene, but I began having to remind him to sterilise the instruments. A couple of times I came into the treatment room and found him about to use soiled ones. He mistakenly drilled a child's healthy tooth once too, though I don't think the mother realised. Mr Ahmed was a lovely man, and he used to get very cross with himself if he forgot anything, so I just tried to be vigilant and prompt him.' She shrugged. 'He was an old man. I mean, everyone gets forgetful as they get older, don't they?'

'I will need the name and address of the girl's family,' Mariner said, and before leaving he phoned through to Vicky Jesson to tell her what he had learned. 'I'm going there now,' he said. 'But ask Bingley to make some background checks on them, see if there's any history.'

Although she was recovering, the girl's parents were understandably emotional about what had happened to their daughter, but they seemed more than satisfied with the compensation they had received. To lay the matter to rest, when he was back in his car, Mariner contacted the family's GP, Dr Jill Wakefield.

'It would be impossible to prove a direct link with her dental treatment,' she told Mariner. 'The disease could have been contracted and lain dormant for years. In my view they were lucky that Mr Shah was so understanding.'

Bingley was undeniably efficient, thought Mariner. By the time he returned to Granville Lane at the end of the afternoon, the constable had already executed the search. 'Squeaky clean,' he said. 'Not a mark on the family or anyone at that address. Am I allowed to know who they are?'

'They were Soltan Ahmed's patients,' said Mariner. 'Up until six weeks ago, he was a practising dentist.'

'Ooh.' Bingley pulled a face. 'That wouldn't have been good.'

'Why?' asked Jesson. She was getting her things together, preparing to leave for the day.

'He was on Perantamine; that stuff you found in the medicine cabinet,' said Bingley. 'My dad was prescribed it for a while, before he really started to go downhill. It's a new and aggressive drug to treat early-onset Alzheimer's. According to those labels, Soltan Ahmed had been on it for ages.'

'But the family doctor believes that there can be no proven link between the girl's treatment and her illness,' said Mariner. 'So I think we can safely rule them out.'

'I'm off then, if that's OK?' said Jesson.

Mariner nodded. 'We'll start again in the morning.'

As she walked out, Jesson lobbed her empty water bottle towards the recycling bin, but missed it by a margin and it bounced off the floor.

'Go,' said Mariner, seeing her sigh. 'I'll get it.' He reached down to pick up the bottle, but as he dangled it over the bin, a thought occurred. 'You should get yourself off home, too,' he said to Bingley.

On the way down to his car, Mariner called the Yemeni Advice Centre, hoping that they hadn't closed for the day. He asked to speak to Aisha. 'Did you tell anyone else about Mr Ahmed's forgetfulness?'

'Only Mrs Shah,' said Aisha. 'She used to bring the children in for their check-ups. She asked me about how things were, how her father was. You know, it was just a chat.'

'How did she take it?' asked Mariner.

'Actually I made her cry. I didn't mean to. I told her I was keeping an eye on him, so everything was fine. Then that family made the complaint, and that was it. Mr Ahmed retired and closed the practice.'

It was the validation he had hoped for, and instead of driving home, Mariner took a detour via Wellington Road. Fire Investigation were still on site, but before talking to Docherty, Mariner went round to the back garden and clambered back on to the flat roof, revisiting the events of over two weeks ago. The window of the children's bedroom was still ajar, and climbing in, he was about to cross the room when there it was, in an instant flashback: the sound that toy had made as he kicked it across the floor. He felt sure it was the exact same sound he'd heard this afternoon, when his foot had struck that plastic bottle. Getting down on all fours he hunted under the children's beds, and there, right under Yousef's, he found it: a one-litre mineral water bottle. Putting on gloves, he reached under the bed and retrieved it, and when he opened the cap the smell hit him straight away. Petrol. He ran down the stairs to where Gerry Docherty was just finishing up. 'Yousef told us there was a funny smell that night, like the car,' said Mariner. 'I thought he was confusing the smoke with exhaust fumes, but he meant when they filled up with petrol. Have you done any forensics work in the children's room?'

'Not yet,' said Docherty. 'It hasn't been a priority.'

'Could you make it one, please?' said Mariner. 'As a matter of urgency.'

Gerry Docherty did as requested. By the following morning, with the aid of Dougal, he was able to confirm to Mariner the presence of accelerant on the stairs, and on the children's bedroom carpet. Fingerprint results would take longer, but Mariner didn't see any sense in waiting. 'I want to bring in Salwa Shah for formal questioning,' he said to Jesson. They were preparing to do just that when a call came through to Mariner from the desk sergeant. 'There's a Mrs Shah down here, with her solicitor. She wants to talk to you.'

This time Salwa Shah was interviewed under caution. She seemed calm and in control, as if this was something she had been expecting all along. Mariner thought she probably had. Vicky placed a glass of water on the table in front of her, but before they could even start with the questioning, Salwa produced a letter. 'Mrs Shah asks that you read this letter, and then she will give you her statement,' said her solicitor.

Once opened, Mariner held out the letter so that both he and Jesson could read it. Signed by Soltan Ahmed, the letter explained briefly but cogently, that, at his request and in accordance with his own wishes, his daughter had taken steps to end his life, and that she should not to be held to account after the event.

Mariner had seen this coming since yesterday evening, but it was stark nonetheless to see it set out so plainly. He wondered if Gideon Wiley had made the same provision. 'So why don't you tell us, from the beginning, what happened?' he said.

Salwa took a sip of water. 'My father was a dentist for many years, and he was a good one,' she began, her voice clear and steady. 'In his spare time, he set up the advice centre with his friends and had become a respected elder of the community. About a year ago, it became obvious to me at home that he was forgetting things and was sometimes confused and quick-tempered. But his work was important to him; part of what made him who he was. He didn't want to give it up, so I suppose I tried to ignore what was happening. His doctor prescribed some medication that we thought would help, and my father was advised to think about retirement. But he continued to work. It was what kept him going. Then a girl who he had treated contracted hepatitis. My husband paid her family compensation, but I knew that it might only be a matter of time before something else, perhaps more serious, happened. So I persuaded my father to retire.' She paused for more water. 'After that, he was lost. Although he continued to work a few hours at the advice centre, he made mistakes there too. He hated that his powers were failing and that he could no longer play a useful part in the community. He thought his life was over.' Her voice thickened. 'It's the first time I ever saw my father cry. He knew too that his condition would get worse, and he feared for himself but also for me, that I would have to look after him. He didn't want me to carry that burden, or his grandchildren to see him like that. He wanted to make a decision about his life before he was no longer able to. In our religion it is not an option to take your own life, so he begged me to help him, to make it look like an accident. It was the hardest thing—' Her voice broke and for several seconds she was silent. Then she gathered her resources. 'A fire was the best way we could think of. My father didn't want Mustafa to be implicated, so when he went to Sana'a, and after Talayeh had gone, it seemed like the right time.' Her tears fell, unstoppable. 'On that Saturday night my father took extra sedatives, we said our goodbyes, then in the early hours I crept downstairs and set the fire.'

'It's why you had your husband fit the new fire doors?' Mariner asked her. 'You were preparing, protecting yourselves?'

'Mustafa knew nothing about it!' she insisted, her eyes shining. 'We had planned to change the doors, and I persuaded him to do it sooner. I had to make sure that I could get out with the children.'

'And Talayeh?'

She looked up at Mariner, her face distorted with anguish. 'I thought she had *gone,*' she whispered.

'How did you burn your hand?' Mariner asked, genuinely curious. It seemed an enormous risk if it had happened as she'd described.

'For our dinner that night I had used some cans of tomatoes. After the children had gone to bed, I turned the oven very high, removed the label from one of the cans and placed it inside the oven. When I was sure that it would be hot enough to burn my skin, I put in my hand and took it out. I held it for as long as I could bear.' It was a remarkable indication of what she was prepared to suffer.

Mariner didn't prolong the interview. The letter set out clearly Salwa's father's wishes, and was signed by him. The signature had been witnessed, but the solicitor had been ignorant of the letter's contents until today. Mariner had no option but to charge Salwa Shah for the murder of her father, in an uncanny parallel with Rosalind Wiley. In the circumstances, it was likely that she would be granted unconditional bail, but her punishment would be a matter for the courts.

'So not an honour killing after all, but a mercy killing,' said Jesson afterwards. 'What a thing to do, to kill your own father.'

'She didn't want to see him unhappy and suffering,' said Mariner. It automatically channelled his thoughts towards Jamie.

As if by suggestion, shortly after Mariner returned to his office after the interview with Salwa Shah, he had a call from the medical officer at Manor Park.

'The good news is that there's nothing lurking inside Jamie that shouldn't be there. But he has got a urine infection, which would account for the blood. A course of antibiotics will sort that out.'

It was a huge relief. 'Does that explain the change in his behaviour too?' Mariner asked.

'To some extent, certainly,' said the doctor. 'But it may also be down to his age, and the significant changes to his life Jamie has experienced during the last few years. This could be his way of grieving, or showing us that he's depressed.'

'So what can be done?' Mariner asked. It seemed so unfair when Jamie's life was so limited, that he should be miserable too.

'In the short term I'll recommend that he stays on the Ritalin, and we'll monitor him to see if there's any improvement once the infection clears up. We could then explore options with anti-depressants. But obviously your continuing visits are important, as are keeping active and having as many varied experiences as he can. I don't know if you're aware that people with autism have a shorter life expectancy. It's something you need to be prepared for. But meanwhile it's all about Jamie's quality of life.'

Mariner rang Suzy to tell her. She was having her lunch.

'I'm so glad that he's OK,' she said.

'It's a wake-up call,' said Mariner. 'I've been complacent. I need to see Jamie more often and do more with him. Maybe we can take him out more?'

'Maybe,' she said. 'Actually, I've got something to tell you too.'

'Can't you tell me now?' asked Mariner, intrigued.

'No, I want to do it face-to-face.'

'Give me a clue,' Mariner pressed. 'Is it good or bad?'

'Well, I think it's exciting,' said Suzy. 'But I'm not sure if you'll feel the same way. It's something . . .' she paused, searching for the right words, '. . . life changing.'

'OK . . .' he said, uncertainly. He went on to tell her about Salwa Shah.

'How extraordinary,' she said, of the coincidence. 'But well done; you have a result.'

'Somehow it doesn't feel like that,' said Mariner. 'Just incredibly sad. Especially as it looks now as if Talayeh's death might just have been down to a terrible set of circumstances.'

'Do you want to come over tonight?' asked Suzy.

'Yes, I might do that.'

It was after dark when Suzy left work, and, driving into the village, she saw that there were lights on at the Forge. As Tom had predicted, Rosalind must have been released on bail. Suzy couldn't imagine her friend would feel much like cooking, and she wanted to be supportive, so she threw together some bits and pieces she had into a kind of picnic bag and took it round. There was no immediate reply when she knocked, but the door was unlocked so she slipped in, with the intention of leaving the food in the kitchen.

'Hello? Rosalind?' Everything was quiet. Rosalind must be having a nap. Not surprising; she must be exhausted. Suzy took the food into the kitchen, but as she was hunting round for a paper and pencil to leave a note, she became aware of sobbing, coming from upstairs. Going into the hall, Suzy called out softly again, but there was no answer, so she started to climb the stairs. It was as her eyes drew level with the landing that Suzy could see that most of the doors were closed. Only one was open and she saw Rosalind, lying back on the pillows. What Suzy couldn't at first fathom was the other head, belonging to a man, and that loomed over Rosalind's, eyes closed. Rosalind's sobbing had become rhythmic and was growing in intensity. Horrified, Suzy was about to retreat when Rosalind turned her head, and for two long seconds looked Suzy full in the face.

Suzy hurried back down the stairs, her heart pounding and her thoughts in a turmoil. What should she do? She couldn't un-see what she had just seen; besides, Rosalind had caught her. Retreating back to her cottage seemed like the coward's way out, but nor could she stay while that was happening up there. It felt as if she should apologise but that didn't seem quite right either. The sobbing she'd thought she had heard had stopped now, replaced by hushed and urgent voices, then Rosalind appeared, drifting serenely down the stairs, tying the belt of her robe. 'Well, this was unexpected,' she said, in a study of under-statement. 'Do you make it a habit to walk into other people's houses uninvited?'

'I was worried about you,' said Suzy, trying to remain calm and poised. 'I thought you were crying. I'm so sorry.'

'Well, now you know.' Rosalind went into the living room and sat down, so that Suzy was obliged to follow.

She heard further footsteps pounding down the stairs and saw a man flash by the doorway, before hearing the front door slam shut. She only glimpsed him for an instant, but it was long enough for her to see the collar. 'Father Peter?' said Suzy in disbelief.

'We've fallen in love,' said Rosalind. 'Don't look so shocked. It can happen to anyone; even Catholic priests. In fact, it's much more common than you might think. Did you know that in Ireland there's even a support group for women who have an affair with their priest? The notion of celibacy is so outdated these days, don't you think?' Decisively, she slapped her palms lightly on her thighs and stood up. 'Well, I'm going to have a cup of tea. Would you like one?'

It was surreal. Dazed, Suzy nodded, but sat rooted to the spot as Rosalind disappeared into the kitchen, returning minutes later with the tea tray, as if this was a routine social call.

'But what about Gideon?' Suzy said, automatically taking the mug from Rosalind.

'We haven't had that kind of relationship for years,' said Rosalind. 'Even before he became ill. But then he found out of, course, clever old sod. Peter came to see Gideon one afternoon, but he was too tired and needed to rest. It was an opportunity not to be wasted, but we had to be quick; no time to undress. I was careless. Gideon called it my "Monica Lewinsky" moment. I don't think he was as much offended by my infidelity, as he was by Peter breaking his vows. He wouldn't let it drop.'

Suzy was trying hard to focus on what Rosalind was saying, but the long day was catching up with her and she was beginning to feel drowsy.

'Contrary to what I told you, as Gideon approached the end, he became more devout than ever,' said Rosalind. 'Fanatical. He was outraged, and would have happily seen Peter and me disgraced. When you told me that Kirsten had visited, I knew Gideon was going to change his will and cut me out completely. He'd already talked about it. And that afternoon he asked me to make an appointment for his solicitor to come round.'

Rosalind's words were beginning to run into one another and Suzy was having difficulty deciphering them. Her head felt so heavy.

Rosalind must have noticed. 'God, Suzy, here am I prattling on, and you look all in,' she said. 'You've had a long week. Why don't you put your head down for a few minutes?' Coming over she took Suzy's empty mug from her and eased her down on to the sofa, tucking her legs up, and pulling a rug over her. Suzy felt sure there was something important she should do, but relaxing on to the soft cushions felt so good that she just had to give herself up to it . . .

Mariner was later setting off to Suzy's than he'd planned. On the drive over, his mind was racing. What could she have to tell him that would be potentially exciting and life-changing? She'd just moved jobs, so it couldn't be that. Finally, he had to concede the other possibility. Could it be that she was pregnant? Christ, they were at it like rabbits again at the moment. And if she was, what did he think about it? A baby. His baby; a son or a daughter. By the time he got to the cottage he was bursting with anticipation, but Suzy wasn't there. The cottage was dark and empty. She must be over at Rosalind's house. He rang the bell, but it was a while before Rosalind came to the door, in her dressing gown.

'I'm sorry,' said Mariner. 'I hope I haven't woken you? I thought Suzy might be here.'

'No,' said Rosalind. 'I haven't seen her today. Perhaps she's working late? There's always so much to do when you start a new job, isn't there?'

'Yes, that's probably it,' said Mariner. 'Sorry to have disturbed you,' he said absently, before remembering himself. 'How are you?' he added. 'Suzy told me about—'

Rosalind pulled a wan expression. 'Oh, you know.'

It was one of those rare occasions when Mariner wasn't really sure that he did. Heading back to the cottage, the first thing he saw as he rounded the corner was Suzy's car, parked on the drive. He realised then, that it had been there all along. Something was going on here. This time when Rosalind came to the door, Mariner pushed past her and into the house. 'Where is Suzy? What have you done?' Then he saw her, motionless on the sofa. He tried to wake her, but she was out cold. 'What have you given her?' he demanded, taking out his phone to call for an ambulance.

Mariner found the empty sedative packs in the kitchen bin

while the paramedics were tending to Suzy, though Rosalind denied having used them. Suzy was taken straight in to Warwick Hospital, where she could be monitored, though the paramedics had no concerns that she was in any immediate danger. Mariner stayed with her until she came round, but she was in a stupor. Whatever she had to tell him would have to wait.

TWENTY-FIVE

The following week was a strange one. The Wellington Road fire had been solved and Salwa Shah, as expected, was remanded on bail, for the manslaughter of her father and Talayeh Farzi. Rosalind Wiley had been charged with her husband's murder, following her confession to Suzy, and Father Peter had been relieved of his duties, pending an inquiry. But they still seemed no nearer to knowing what had happened to Sam Fleetwood.

'In the absence of a body, we may need to accept that we never will,' Mariner said, as he, Jesson and Bingley sat reviewing what evidence they had, yet again. Samples had been taken from the incinerator at Carter's to try and extract any DNA material, but the likelihood of successful identification was slim, meaning that there was insufficient evidence to bring a prosecution against either the Carters or Clive Boswell. Everything felt a little flat.

In certain circumstances, Mariner would have appreciated this hiatus. It was an opportunity to make a dent in the pile of material in his in tray. But he could only view it as a mixed blessing, when what was at the top of his 'to-do' list was the preparation of a statistical report on the department's activity for the last three months. It had been a mind-numbingly tedious task the first time, when there was at least some novelty value, but he'd been doing them for years now, since the Home Office had first demanded it, and it hadn't got any more compelling in that time. His attention was wandering. He looked up, suddenly aware that Vicky Jesson was addressing him from the doorway.

She raised an eyebrow. 'Are you all right?'

'Yes, why?'

'I just asked you three times if you want a coffee. Is it Suzy?'

'In a way, it is,' said Mariner. 'No, she's fine,' he added hastily, seeing Vicky's concern. 'But before all the excitement she said she'd got something important to tell me.'

'What do you think it is?' Jesson's curiosity was piqued now.

'The only thing I can think of is that she might be pregnant,' said Mariner. 'I mean, is that possible?'

'I'm sorry – you're asking me?'

'I mean, at her age, she's forty-four. How likely would that be?'

'That's nothing these days,' said Jesson. 'More and more women are having children at that age and way beyond. None of my beeswax, I know, but haven't you been taking any preventative measures?'

'I haven't,' said Mariner. 'Suzy's always said it wasn't necessary. I assumed that meant that she was taking care of it.'

'And if she is pregnant. What do you think?'

'That depends on what time of day you ask me.' The problem was that Mariner had been here before. Twice. And on both occasions the pregnancies had failed to go to full term. He'd often wondered if that was more than just coincidence; if he had a faulty gene or something. And now he was fearful that, because of him, Suzy might be about to go through that same trauma.

When he arrived at Suzy's on Friday evening, as he hugged her, she held him for that bit longer. Did she feel different, look different? Not to him. 'How are you?' he asked.

'I'm fine, apart from feeling a bit stupid,' she said. 'How did I not see that coming?'

'You liked her,' said Mariner, of Rosalind. 'You trusted her.'

'More fool me,' said Suzy. She got him a beer, and they settled down in front of the log burner. 'Anyway, thanks for coming over. I wanted you to know before I tell Mum and Dad. I'm being a bit of a coward, I suppose. I don't think they're going to like it very much, so I'd appreciate some moral support.'

Mariner's heart started thudding. It was now or never. 'Would they feel better about it if we were married?' he said.

'What?'

'Is it the being-a-bastard thing that's going to make them unhappy? I mean, we hadn't exactly planned this, but in the circumstances perhaps we *should* get married and give him or her that security. Sorry, I know this isn't the most romantic way of doing it, but—'

Suzy was staring at him wide-eyed. 'Oh my God. You think I'm pregnant.'

'Well, aren't you?'

It was some seconds before Suzy could control her laughter and by the time she did, her face was wet with tears. 'Sorry, sorry.' She wiped them away. 'I'm not pregnant,' she said. 'That really isn't it.'

'Well what then?' said Mariner.

'I've got the opportunity to go and do some work in China,' Suzy said. 'Another guy in the department had arranged a sabbatical, but, rather ironically, his wife *is* pregnant, so now he doesn't want to go.'

'Well,' said Mariner going from scared to relieved to actually quite irritated, in the space of just a few seconds. 'That's great.'

'It would be for a year in the first instance, maybe for longer. Trouble is, it's quite sudden. I'd leave at the beginning of next month.'

'That's two weeks away,' he pointed out.

'Yes.'

He had to ask. 'Does this have anything to do with . . .?'

'No, it really doesn't. And anyway, you seem to be over it. You could come too,' she said brightly.

'I couldn't,' said Mariner. 'Jamie.'

'Of course, Jamie. Sorry.'

'Wow,' said Mariner, short of any better response.

'I know,' said Suzy. 'You don't mind?'

Did he? He swallowed the lump that had suddenly developed in his throat. 'Of course not. It's a fantastic opportunity and you must take it.'

The following afternoon Suzy's parents arrived, though being introduced to them seemed somewhat irrelevant now. They were, as Mariner had expected, a charming couple, the kind of people who would have produced a charming daughter like Suzy. Their feelings about Suzy's news were mixed. Her father seemed delighted that she would be going back to his native country and returning to her Cantonese roots, while her mother, Mariner thought, looked more wistful and would have preferred it if Suzy's news had been closer to what he'd thought it was. Only when they had set off for Stratford did she begin to cheer up.

After dinner at the RSC theatre restaurant, overlooking the River Avon, they went in to the performance, where her parents' excitement was shared equally. And certainly the play was entertaining enough and the language no barrier. The actors seemed to play it for laughs and though Mariner was sure he missed many of the nuances, the main plot seemed to him much like a pantomime, jokes included. As far as he could tell, the whole tale was predicated on women pretending to be men and vice versa, even though it was pretty bloody obvious who was—

'Fuck . . .' He said it under his breath, but still Suzy turned to fix him with a disapproving glare.

Sometimes in an investigation a breakthrough presents itself as a tangible sensory experience; a chink of bright sunlight penetrating the darkness, the satisfying clunk of a cog dropping into place, or the emergent shape of a calcifying thought. It was part way through the first act, watching Viola disguised – to his mind pretty unconvincingly – as Cesario that Mariner suddenly knew for certain that Sam Fleetwood was dead, and understood why he had been killed and who had killed him. It was as much as he could do to resist leaping out of his seat, when what he wanted to do, right away, was get on the phone to Millie Khatoon. No chance of doing that right now. But the instant the stage darkened and the interval applause began, Mariner was on his feet. 'Sorry,' he said to Suzy. 'I've got to go.' He didn't wait around long enough to see how she felt about that. Outside, Mariner found he had three missed calls from Kevin Bingley's Granville Lane number. He rang back.

'I think I might know who killed Sam Fleetwood,' said Bingley. 'Though I don't really understand why.'

'I do,' said Mariner. 'Meet me at Clive Boswell's house.' He gave Bingley the address.

As he drove, Mariner put a call through to the McKinnons and asked to speak to Tanya. 'You told DC Khatoon that Sam came to your house to check the bridesmaids' dresses, but that wasn't quite true.'

'No,' she said quietly.

'What then?'

'He asked me to alter another dress. I assumed it was for Gaby.'

'But it wasn't, was it? You could have saved us a lot of time, Mrs McKinnon, if you'd been honest.'

'I promised Sam I wouldn't tell anyone, even Laurie.'

'Even though he's now dead?'

'Oh no . . .' she began, but he could hear, then, slow realisation dawning. 'Oh God.'

Mariner got to the Boswells' house to find Bingley waiting outside. Everything was in darkness and no amount of ringing the doorbell raised anyone. It was stretching the rules, but fortunately the next door neighbour had spare keys and the alarm code, and Mariner's warrant card was persuasive enough.

'We need to be quick,' said Mariner, disabling the alarm. 'And see what we can find before they come back. We'll start with Gaby's room.' He ran up the stairs, with Bingley following. 'What made you realise?' he asked, as they checked all the rooms, finally locating the one belonging to Gaby.

'I had to take Mum's car into the garage this morning,' said Bingley, opening wardrobe doors. 'She's smaller than me, so I had to move the driver's seat back. I don't know . . . that action . . . there was something about it that kind of nagged at me all day. Then it suddenly hit me. When I found Fleetwood's Astra in Carter's yard, I remember thinking that the driver's seat was way too close to the steering wheel, even for me. We knew Sam Fleetwood was tall from the position of the bike saddle in the garage. And Mike Figgis, Clive Boswell and Danny Carter are all quite tall. So I came in to check the forensic photographs that I wasn't mistaken. Hey, I've got something.'

From the bottom of the wardrobe, Bingley pulled out a leather holdall, like the one described as belonging to Sam Fleetwood. Mariner stopped what he was doing and watched as Bingley unzipped the bag and began to remove the contents: women's clothing and underwear. There was also a loyalty card for the Rookery Hotel, in the name of Hayley McQueen.

'Who the hell is she?' said Bingley.

'She doesn't exist,' said Mariner. They both jumped as the phone in the hall rang, puncturing the silence. Mariner started down the stairs, but before he could reach it, the answer machine cut in and bizarrely there was Charlie Glover, speaking as clearly as if he was standing right beside them, and sounding slightly drunk.

'Hi, Clive; hi, Gaby,' he said cheerfully. 'I'm afraid we've lost track a bit of what the time is over there, but Helen and I just wanted to wish you all the best for your big day. We're sorry we couldn't be . . .'

But Mariner didn't hear the rest of the message. 'What's the date today?' he asked Bingley.

'It's the twenty-third,' said Bingley. 'Saint George's Day.'

'Shit,' said Mariner. 'They're not coming back. Clive Boswell is taking his daughter on her honeymoon.'

TWENTY-SIX

While Bingley drove, Mariner called ahead to the Airport Police Unit, linked to Solihull OPU.

'But I don't get it,' said Bingley, squealing round a corner. 'Who's the other woman? Who's "Little Bear"?'

'There isn't one,' said Mariner. 'Your mum helped me with that too. You know the photograph on her mantelpiece of you and your teddy? Fiona Fleetwood has photographs on her wall too, of Sam, all with his faithful bear. I think that Valentine card was from her. It's probably something their mum started, and she's kept up the tradition.'

When they got to the airport, Clive and Gaby Boswell had been detained and were being kept in one of the holding cells, waiting to transfer to a PACE cell at Granville Lane. As the handover took place, Clive Boswell was livid. 'I don't know what's going on, but you need to understand that this has been a very stressful time for us. We deserve a break after all that has happened. It's the least that Gaby can have.'

'Whose idea was it, Mr Boswell, to go to Antigua after all?' asked Mariner, as they set off back to the station.

'What's the problem?' Indignation had set in. 'I've paid a lot of money for this holiday.'

'Was it Gaby's suggestion that you should go anyway?' asked Mariner.

'She's been under an enormous strain these last few weeks,' retorted Boswell. 'I don't think you can imagine—'

'Oh, I can, Mr Boswell, I really can,' said Mariner. 'But I wonder how far *your* imagination stretches. Do you have any idea why your daughter would want to leave the country, especially now?' He glanced in the rear-view mirror and saw Gaby Boswell calmly staring out of the car window. She said nothing on the drive back to Granville Lane, but once they'd got her in the interview room it was as if she had to offload the whole thing, and they couldn't stop her.

'I never meant it to happen. I don't expect you to believe that, but truly I didn't,' she said, all innocence. 'After the do at Helen and Charles', Sam said he was going over to the house to put up the shelves.' She looked at Mariner. 'What I told you was true; I really did have a headache after the party, so I planned a quiet night in. Then Dad went out and I thought, what am I doing here, on my own on a Saturday night? My headache had lifted, so I decided to go and surprise Sam, I mean really surprise him. So I packed my waterproof backpack, put on my wetsuit – in the dark it doesn't look that different from running clothes – and went over to the nature reserve. I ran through the woods on the opposite side of the lake, then swam across to our house.'

'Sam isn't the only triathlete,' said Mariner. 'The club where you met is a triathlon club.'

She smiled. 'We used to do events together. And this was so exciting. I felt like Tom Cruise in *Mission Impossible* or something. I knew Sam would love it. We'd talked about the idea of role play, and I knew he liked that kind of thing. But when I let myself into the house, I got the shock of my life.'

'He wasn't assembling the shelves?' said Mariner.

'Actually he was,' she said. 'It was what he was wearing to do it.' Whether for dramatic effect, or whether she really couldn't help it, she gagged. 'I hardly recognised him at first; couldn't work out what was going on. It was grotesque. He was wearing trousers and a top but they were skin tight, like a woman's. The top had a plunging neckline and he had – he had fake boobs! And he was wearing this awful wig, and make-up. It made my skin crawl.' She shuddered. 'I just screamed. Then he tried to *explain* it to me, as if it could be justified. Said it was something he'd always done, but that he hadn't told me because after we were married, he'd decided he would never do it again.'

'He was prepared to give it up for you,' Mariner pointed out.

'How could he?' She was defiant. 'I mean, if that's what someone is like, they don't just change overnight, do they? How could I possibly trust him? And now I'd *seen* it, I could never think of him in the same way. He told me to wait while he got changed; said we should talk about it, like adults; that he could help me to understand. So he went upstairs, and I was just left

there, my mind racing through it all. I couldn't bear it, the thought
of him—' Her face contorted with distaste. 'I couldn't marry
him now. The idea was repulsive. I knew I'd have to call off the
wedding, but then I imagined breaking the news to everyone.
*Hey, I'm not getting hitched after all, because the man I'm
marrying likes wearing women's clothes.*' She closed her eyes.
'Oh God, the shame!'

'Surely you could have worked something out together?' said
Mariner. 'You could have fabricated an affair, perhaps?'

'That would have been dishonest,' she said, the irony lost on
her. 'And Dad. Oh God, Dad,' Gaby went on. 'What would it do
to him?'

'So what happened?' prompted Mariner.

She took a breath. 'I was pacing around downstairs, not
knowing what to do, and then I saw it, the brand-new knife block,
and I thought how much easier it would be if something just
happened to Sam. It would be beyond my control. It wasn't a
serious idea, not to begin with. But the more I considered it, the
more it seemed like the only option. Those knives are razor sharp,
and I thought about how easy it would be to cut him and make
it look like suicide. People would feel sorry for me then, but in
a kind way. Then when it came to it, it all went wrong. Sam
came down into the living room and I tried to slash at his wrists.
But all I did was stab him and then the blood started pouring
out. Oh God, there was so much blood, and the wounds looked
nothing like suicide. And the look on his face; it was terrible.
And then he passed out. It all happened so fast. Suddenly I
realised he was dead.' She shivered. 'But amazingly that was
when I started to think really clearly, and everything seemed to
fall into place, as if it was meant to be.' Her eyes gleamed and
Mariner saw that this was what she really believed.

'Sam had fallen on the plastic covering the floor,' said Gaby.
'And I realised I could wrap him up in it, put him in his car and
drive him away. No one had seen me arrive, so they would just
think it was Sam leaving. The rest of it came to me bit by bit.
It was quite thrilling really.'

'So what did you do?'

'I managed to wrap him up and get him into the boot of his
car. It was tricky, but I'm strong. The hardest part was cleaning

up any traces of blood. Then I put down fresh polythene. The workmen were coming back on Monday and they make such a mess. I couldn't rely on them to cover the floors again before they started. My wetsuit was covered in blood by now, so once I'd made sure everything was clean, I had a shower and got changed into the clothes I'd brought with me. Then I put my bike in the car. It wouldn't go in on top of Sam, so I had to use more polythene and put it on the back seat. Dad's got a development just outside Redditch. I'd been there the week before and I knew that they were about to start filling in the utilities ditches. So I drove up and got as close as I could – there was no one around at all. I put Sam in the ditch and piled soil on top to cover him, knowing that on the Monday the ditch would be concreted over. I went into the site office to clean myself up again, before driving back to a spot near Carter's. Sam took me there once, when he was keeping them under surveillance. I got my bike out of the car then just threw in a lighted match and left it there. I rode back along the canal and came home.' She was delighted with her own ingenuity and Mariner had a sudden and uncharacteristic urge to slap her and wipe the self-satisfied smile from her face. 'Dad wasn't back yet,' she added. 'I know about him and his whore, by the way. I know he thinks I don't, but I followed him once in my car.'

'What about Sam's wallet?' asked Mariner. 'How did it find its way to Chantelle Brough?'

'That was down to you,' she said, with a knowing smile. 'When you asked about Sam's bank details, I realised that could be helpful. So, that weekend, I drove through Redditch and threw it out of the window. I put the pin number in to make sure his bank card would get used.'

When Mariner went to tell Clive Boswell his daughter had confessed to murder, Boswell was dazed and diminished. It was beyond his comprehension and Mariner guessed it would be a long time before he would be able to make sense of it. Right now, he simply didn't believe it. Neither, at first, did Charlie Glover, when he returned after his holiday, and for some weeks after he would suddenly stop what he was doing and stare into space, trying to rationalise it.

It was real enough when Sam Fleetwood's decomposing body

was recovered from the ditch Gaby had described, and there was nothing about his remains to contradict her version of events. It was Mariner's unhappy task to break the news to Fleetwood's sister, Fiona. She had a lot of questions, which he did his best to answer, but then he had one for her. 'Out of interest,' he said. 'Did you send Sam Valentine cards?'

'Yes,' she said. 'Mum used to send us both one from our favourite toys. It's a tradition that Sam and I continued. It got to be a daft joke between us.'

Following Gaby Boswell's indictment, as was the custom, Mariner and his team went out to celebrate in a Harborne pub, joined by Gerry Docherty and some of his crew. Mariner was standing at the bar, getting a round in, when he noticed the clock on the wall above the optics. Suzy would be in the air by now, two-thirds of the way through her flight to Beijing. They had said goodbye outside Y Worry, after the storage firm had been to collect all her things, and before Suzy set off to spend a few days with her parents, prior to flying out. She seemed to have forgiven him for deserting them at Stratford. 'Told you Shakespeare wasn't my thing,' he said.

'How are you holding up?' asked Sharp, coming up alongside him now. Having put in an appearance, she would soon tactfully retreat and leave them to it.

'Oh, I'm all right,' said Mariner.

'It's been a strange time,' said Sharp. 'A possible honour killing that turned out to be a mercy killing, a MisPer who was really the victim of honour killing, and for you and Suzy, a mercy killing that was murder.'

At that moment the door opened and an attractive young woman walked in, scanning the room, as she took off her coat. Having staked out the group in the corner, she went straight over to Kevin Bingley and gave him what was evidently rather more than a friendly kiss, to the accompaniment of cheers and wolf whistles that left Bingley red-faced.

'Who's that?' said Mariner.

Ralph Solomon was by his left shoulder. 'That's Sasha Petrovic from Forensics,' he said.

'So she's the one who's been fast-tracking the results for us,' said Mariner. 'Bloody hell, that's a turn up.'

'I know,' grinned Solomon. 'You wouldn't think he had it in him, would you? Pete Stone isn't impressed though.'

'What's it got to do with him?'

'Stone hit on her, but she went for Bingley.'

'Is that's what caused the animosity?' asked Sharp.

'Well, that and Bingley showing him up at a domestic,' said Solomon. 'Stone bottled it, so Bingley had to step up, and got whacked by a baseball bat. Bingley always plays it down, which gets Stone's goat even more.'

After a couple of hours, copious amounts of alcohol had been consumed and things were beginning to get loud. Mariner felt strangely detached, as he generally did in these situations. Vicky Jesson and Gerry Docherty seemed to be engaged in an intense conversation that required a lot of physical contact. Seeing them alongside Bingley with Bingley and Sasha draped all over each other, made Mariner think about what he was missing. Taking out his work phone he scrolled idly down through the contacts. Except he wasn't entirely without purpose. He was checking if one number was still there. Finding it, he escaped to the corridor. Once outside Mariner dialled Eleanor Kingsley's number. Apart from that day at the hospital, it had been about a year since he'd last seen her. He hadn't asked, but she could be married with a kid by now for all he knew.

'Hello?' She sounded sleepy.

'Hello, it's Tom Mariner.' He allowed her a couple of seconds to digest this. 'You may remember, I—'

'I know who you are.' The sleepiness evaporated. 'This is a surprise.'

He noted the absence of a positive qualifier.

'I said I'd let you know about Jamie,' Mariner said lamely.

'At ten fifteen on a random Saturday night?'

'Yeah, sorry. I shouldn't have—'

'No, it's fine.' She seemed amused. 'What was the outcome?' Mariner told her.

'That's good news,' she said. 'It sounds busy where you are.'

'I'm with work colleagues,' said Mariner. 'We're celebrating the end of a case, well, a couple of cases, but it's beginning to get a bit tiresome.'

'Probably beats watching box sets of *Homeland* for the third time around. Do you want to stop off here on your way home?'

'Yes.'

She came to the door wearing a sweater and checked pull-ons. Mariner wondered what she was wearing underneath. She made coffee and they sat in the lounge. But now he was here it felt awkward and suddenly Mariner realised that this wasn't fair on Eleanor and it wasn't fair on Suzy. They both deserved better. He said as much to Eleanor, and she didn't put up much resistance, so Mariner kissed her goodbye and headed for home.